THE BOY WHO LIVED WITH THE DEAD

It is 1920 and DI Albert Lincoln is still reeling from the disturbing events of the previous year. Before the War, he'd investigated the murder of a child in a Cheshire village, and now a woman has been murdered there and another child is missing. With the help of the village schoolmistress, Albert closes in on the original pre-war killer. He soon realises the only witness is in grave danger, possibly from somebody he call 'the Shadow Man'. And as he discovers more about the victims he finds information that might bring him a step closer to solving a mystery of his own — the whereabouts of his son.

KATE ELLIS

THE BOY WHO LIVED WITH THE DEAD

Complete and Unabridged

CHARNWOOD
Leicester

First published in Great Britain in 2018 by
Piatkus
an imprint of Little, Brown Book Group
London

First Charnwood Edition
published 2021
by arrangement with
Little, Brown Book Group
London

A catalogue record for this book is available
from the British Library.

ISBN 978–1–4448–4687–4

Published by
Ulverscroft Limited
Anstey, Leicestershire

Set by Words & Graphics Ltd.
Anstey, Leicestershire
Printed and bound in Great Britain by
TJ Books Ltd., Padstow, Cornwall

This book is printed on acid-free paper

In memory of Ruth Smith 1954–2017

1

Mabley Ridge, Cheshire –

September 1920

Patience Bailey looked down at the baby asleep in her arms and wondered why she'd ever agreed to meet there in that field of the dead where graves jutted from the ground like crooked teeth, stained with lichen and darkness. It was no place for a baby . . . or a woman alone.

The church bell in the distance tolled ten times and on the final chime a bat swooped from a nearby yew tree and flittered close to her face. She flinched at the unexpected movement. before wrapping the soft blanket tighter around the infant's body while she murmured a familiar and comforting prayer: deliver us from evil. Over the past few years evil had overwhelmed good; evil had sent men to be slaughtered like animals in the battlefields of France in trenches they'd shovelled out with their own hands. Now they were lost forever. The world was wicked and she would do her best to defend the little one from harm, especially now that harm was so close to home.

A white marble headstone a few yards away glowed in the dim moonlight like a deformed ghost burrowing its way out of the earth and the sight of it made her shudder. She took a deep

1

breath and carried on walking towards the agreed meeting place. She'd wanted to arrive first, to be in control, but now she feared this had been a mistake.

When the toe of her button boot met a raised patch of newly dug earth she almost tripped and she cupped the baby's head in her hand for protection, fearing she'd accidentally stepped on a fresh grave. But the tiny mound lacked any sort of marker so she convinced herself it was probably a molehill and continued walking, softly crooning his favourite lullaby.

The shadows shifted among the cold, still gravestones and she had an uncomfortable feeling that she was being watched by unseen eyes. When she turned her head she thought she could see a pale face at the upstairs window of the small lodge by the cemetery gates but when she looked again it was no longer there so she told herself she'd imagined it.

As she made her way along the cemetery path she noticed a gaping rectangle of darkness to her left; an open grave awaiting its occupant with a small hill of soil heaped up to one side. She paused, inhaling the damp stench of newly dug earth mingled with rotting vegetation. Then she heard an urgent whispering which might have been the wind in the surrounding trees — or it might have been a human voice. Although she wasn't sure, she gathered her courage and made for the source of the sound. She had no time for games.

'You're late,' she called to the darkness with a confidence she didn't feel.

The whispering stopped and everything was still for a few moments . . . until a dark shape rose slowly from behind a headstone.

'Come out. You're frightening me.' Her heart was beating fast, thumping against the baby's little body, but he didn't stir.

The shape emerged from its hiding place, unfolding itself until it loomed in front of her blocking out the sky.

'What are you doing here?' she said, backing away.

Then she heard another whisper, a hiss like a snake and the crack of a footstep behind her on the gravel path. As she turned she felt the child being tugged from her arms with a speed that left her too stunned to fight. She tried to snatch the infant back but in her confusion she flailed about and her blows hit air. Eventually she lost her balance and dropped to her knees but her every instinct was to save the child so she scrabbled blindly towards its whimpering cries. Then she heard the grinding of metal against earth and a moment later darkness descended and she felt nothing more.

She wasn't aware of toppling into the open grave; nor did she feel the earth falling on her, deeper and deeper, entering her nostrils and her throat.

After a short while she began to come round, struggling for breath beneath the veil of choking soil. Then, in one last desperate attempt to survive, she summoned what scant strength she had left to raise her right hand and push it upwards, feeling for the outside darkness before the heavy earth robbed her of life and her spirit drifted from her body.

2

Peter

I like to watch the graveyard while the others are asleep. Sometimes there are owls and bats but last night I only saw the Shadow Man.

If I'd looked out earlier I might have seen the old lady who always comes as soon as it's dark but Jack and Ernie told me to stay in bed and stop messing about or they'd tell Mam. By the time they were snoring it was late and only the Shadow Man was there which was funny 'cause he usually comes as soon as the old lady's gone.

He's big and tall and he doesn't have a face but our Ernie said everyone's got a face so I was having a bad dream — either that or I was making it up. But I never. The Shadow Man's real. One night I woke Jack and Ernie up to show them but by the time they looked out of the window he'd gone and they called me a liar. Everybody calls me a liar. But I'm not.

Ernie said it might have been my Shadow Man who took our Jimmy but I said the Shadow Man wasn't around back then. Anyway, our Jimmy wasn't taken, he was murdered.

I still talk to Jimmy. I still hear his voice in my head and I always will 'cause we're twins. When it happened I was only little but I'm nearly ten now and if I'd been as big as I am now I might have been able to save him. But I couldn't.

I don't think I'll tell anyone if I see the Shadow Man again 'cause nobody ever believes me. But I'm not lying. I have seen him. Just like I saw the lady in the grave when I went out this morning.

It was early when I went out 'cause I wanted to get there before the Body Snatcher. He looks for dead animals and birds just like I do but he just takes them away while I give them nice funerals with prayers and flowers and a little cross on the grave, all proper like. They're God's creatures so it's what they deserve — not to be taken away in the Body Snatcher's dirty old sack.

I didn't find any dead 'uns this morning but when I looked into the new grave Dad dug yesterday for old Mrs Potts I saw an arm sticking out and I knew it couldn't be Mrs Potts 'cause she hasn't been buried yet. Dad left his spade there so I lay down and scraped some of the soil off and the lady was just lying there — not even in a box. I touched her with the spade but she didn't move.

I might tell Miss Davies about the lady in the grave. She never calls me a liar.

3

Gwen Davies wouldn't have been there if it hadn't been for the war. If it hadn't been for the war she'd probably never have heard of Mabley Ridge — which might have been a good thing. Some might have called it fate but in her family there had never been time for such fanciful notions.

She stood in front of the children and they sat with their arms folded waiting for her signal, some fidgeting, others statue-still. She'd been teaching at the village school for six months and in the lonely evening hours when her marking was done she had a lot of time to think about the events that had brought her there; how she'd trained as a teacher in Liverpool where she was born and how, when war had broken out and her two brothers enlisted, she'd volunteered to do her bit for king and country by working on the land.

Fate had led her to the farm just outside Mabley Ridge where every night her bones and muscles had ached from the unaccustomed physical labour in the Cheshire fields, although she knew that was nothing compared to the sacrifices the men had had to make. Somehow she'd got through the days milking cows and harvesting hay; up before dawn and fast asleep when darkness fell. What little free time she'd had she spent in the village library and that was where she'd first met him. Fate again.

Her mother had insisted that she'd been quite wrong to return to Mabley Ridge when the war was over to face further temptation. But when she was offered the teaching post there she'd accepted eagerly, nursing hopes of picking up where she'd left off; of claiming the happiness that had been denied her that first time. Only when she'd returned to the village she'd found things had changed in her absence and cruel death had robbed her of the future she'd allowed herself to dream of.

She sometimes wondered why she stayed on in the village where her hopes had been shattered. According to her family, her loss was punishment that had to be endured; sometimes she hated her family.

She tore her thoughts back to the present and looked at the expectant faces in front of her. Twenty-three village children: boys and girls aged from seven to thirteen; good and bad; mischief-makers and dreamers.

'Hands together, eyes closed,' she said.

The children knew the routine and they obeyed, apart from a couple of the older boys who kept one eye open so it looked as though they were winking at her. She repeated the order and waited for total obedience.

'Lighten our darkness, we beseech Thee, oh Lord; and by Thy great mercy defend us from all perils and dangers of this night.'

The children joined in with a hearty 'Amen' and she wondered whether they knew what the perils and dangers of the night really were. She hoped they didn't because the reality behind the words was too terrible to contemplate. She dismissed the class to the thud of desk lids being lifted and closed and the hum of excited whispers. At this time of day the children reminded her of young cattle released into the fields after a winter in the barn and this memory of her days working on the farm brought on a pang of nostalgia.

'Quietly,' she said as they lined up to leave. The reminder was automatic; she said it every day before she watched her charges break into a trot as soon as they left the confines of the building and split up into groups. The girls skipped and chattered as she used to do at that age and the boys charged about fighting mock battles. Even after the horrors of the war years, little had changed on the surface. But underneath — where it really mattered — everything had.

'Miss.'

She turned to see a freckled face looking up at her, the wide eyes trusting. Peter Rudyard, with his fair curls and distant manner, was a strange boy and even his own siblings accused him of making things up. The other children called him a liar and Gwen hated their casual cruelty. Something about Peter made her want to protect him and she'd done her best to put a stop to the name-calling.

Not that she herself believed every word that came out of Peter's mouth. He was always full of tales of ghosts and monsters and, according to his elder brother Ernie, he loved playing amongst the gravestones near the cemetery lodge where they lived, as though he preferred the company of the dead to that of the living. Having said that, Peter wasn't a difficult child. Rather than getting up to mischief he spent half the school day staring out of the window, lost in his own world. His main talent lay in drawing pictures and making up stories — although a surfeit of imagination was probably a curse rather than a blessing for a child with his disadvantages in life.

Gwen gave him an encouraging smile, the sort she reserved for those who tried hard but couldn't quite manage the task. 'What is it, Peter? Isn't it time you went home?'

Peter looked her in the eye, his own eyes blue and unblinking. She'd seen that look before when he told his stories, as though he was able to see a different world, far beyond the humdrum life of the school and the village.

'I found a lady in a grave, Miss. I couldn't wake her up.'

'In a grave?'

'In Mrs Potts's grave — the one my dad dug yesterday. I saw her arm sticking up out of the ground so I got Dad's spade and scraped some soil off and there she was. Her eyes were open and she looked at me but she didn't move.'

'When was this, Peter?'

'Before school this morning. I told Mam but she said I was telling fibs again and told me off for getting dirty.'

'Did you tell your father?'

'He wouldn't believe me. He never does.' He looked at Gwen hopefully. 'But if you told me

Mam she'd believe you, Miss.'

Gwen knew she ought to tell him to go straight home and forget about it but she couldn't bring herself to be unkind. There was enough unkindness in the world. Millions had died because of it, and yet she knew it would be better in the long run to ignore Peter's fantasies rather than encourage them.

'Please, Miss, come and see.'

She hesitated. It might not be wise to indulge the boy but at least it would put off the moment she'd have to return to her lodgings and her landlady, Miss Fisher. 'Very well, Peter, I'll come. But I can't be long.'

After everything that had happened to her during the war years, after the love and bitter loss, she suspected she'd become too soft-hearted for her own good.

To her surprise Peter grabbed her hand. He was almost ten and most boys of his age thought themselves too old to hold hands even with their mothers, let alone their teachers. Peter, though, had always been different.

Gwen allowed herself to be led down the road, past the small streets of terraced houses built to house the staff who worked in the big houses. The rich had come to Mabley Ridge when the railway was built; cotton barons from Manchester fifteen miles away. The people in the village called them the Cottontots and every day these masters of industry caught the train to their work amidst the smoke and grime of Manchester and returned each night to their leafy mansions and their silk-clad wives. Even the war hadn't

11

changed all that; perhaps nothing ever would.

The cemetery lay at the very edge of the village, the land of the dead slightly apart from that of the living. The entrance was guarded by the small red-brick lodge that was home to the Rudyard family: mother, father and four children, although Gwen wasn't sure whether the latest addition was a boy or girl.

It was common knowledge in the village that in 1914, shortly before the outbreak of war, Peter Rudyard's twin brother had died in tragic circumstances and that a detective from Scotland Yard had been called in but hadn't been able to find the culprit. When she'd asked Miss Fisher about it she'd said it was something best forgotten.

Peter's grip on Gwen's hand tightened as they neared the cemetery lodge, as though he wanted to make sure she wouldn't escape.

'This way, Miss.'

When they reached the house Gwen wondered how she'd explain herself to Mrs Rudyard if she emerged from the front door to see her son leading his teacher by the hand. Peter's mother was a large woman with a round, pasty face and a snub nose and Gwen had always found her rather fearsome. Her husband was a stocky, taciturn man with a reputation for being handy with his fists after taking too much drink. Word had it that he'd suffered some unspecified injury during the war which had left him morose and short-tempered. Whatever the truth, it didn't prevent him digging graves for the people of the village, rich and poor alike, an occupation he combined with working as a gardener at one of the big houses. On leaving school his eldest son, Jack, had joined him in his work, whereas Ernie, his second son, still in her class for one more year, had ambitions to work in the garage that had once served as the local smithy. The Cotton-tots had now, without exception, exchanged their grand carriages for the latest motor cars; shiny, noisy things that chugged down the High Street terrifying dogs and children.

'She's over here, Miss.'

Peter led the way down the central path towards the back of the cemetery and came to a sudden halt near the boundary wall.

'She's still here, Miss. I told you, didn't I?'

Gwen could see a newly dug grave, yawning to receive its occupant, and she stepped forward to peer into the shadowy hole, trying not to think of death. A spade lay on the heap of soil beside the grave and she hesitated before picking it up and kneeling at the edge. Then she lay flat on her stomach, no longer caring about the state of her clothes, because she'd seen a hand protruding from the earth, pointing at the air accusingly, and a partially uncovered face veiled with soil. She began work, leaning over to scrape the earth away with the spade, and eventually her efforts revealed a woman in a black dress with what would once have been a crisp white collar. Gwen could see she was wearing lisle stockings but she couldn't make out the colour of the hair beneath the small black hat still pinned in place on her head. A shoe lay at the side of the grave but the other had tumbled in with her, probably lost while she'd been struggling for her life.

Gwen hauled herself to her knees and brushed the soil from her dress.

'Do you know who she is, Miss?'

She saw the excited anticipation on Peter's face, as though the horror of a woman being buried alive was a great adventure he might read about in a comic.

Gwen knew the boy should be home with his parents and yet she was reluctant to let him go because that would mean being alone with the body. But this was selfish because a child shouldn't have to stay within sight of something so horrible, and, when she was growing up, selfishness had been considered the deadliest of sins.

Before she could stop him Peter rushed to the edge of the gaping grave and stared into its depths, studying the body as though he was examining an interesting item on the class nature table. 'I saw him last night. I wonder if he killed her.'

'Who are you talking about, Peter?'

'The Shadow Man, Miss.'

'Who's the Shadow Man?'

'I don't know. He doesn't have a face.'

Gwen placed her hands on his shoulders and steered him firmly away from the grave.

'Run to the police station and fetch the sergeant please, Peter,' she said, trying to sound as though she was in control. She knew it was no use calling Dr Michaels because the woman was well and truly dead and, as corpses don't bury themselves, somebody in Mabley Ridge had killed her.

4

Mallory Ghent took his gold watch from his waistcoat pocket and examined it as the train chugged into Mabley Ridge station under a cloud of sooty steam. The watch had been his father's, acquired when the mill was in its heyday, and the weight of the gold felt reassuring in his fingers.

Ghent recognised many of his fellow passengers and doled out businesslike nods as they alighted on to the platform. He felt grimy after a day in Manchester where the air itself was grey but at least it hadn't rained that day, which was a rare blessing.

He no longer had a chauffeur to meet him — after the war the last occupant of the position had chosen to open his own garage selling motor cars in nearby Wilmslow — so Mallory walked the length of the High Street, self-consciously swinging his cane and politely raising his hat to a lady who was emerging from the milliner's; the wife of a cotton trader he was hoping to do further business with. After turning the corner by the post office his pace slowed as the road became steeper until at last he reached the grand wrought-iron gates of Gramercy House. As he marched up the drive he was surprised to see his wife standing at the open front door, as though she was waiting to greet him, though when he drew closer he could tell by her expression that something was wrong.

Jane Ghent was standing quite still, a thin figure in grey, her fair hair gathered in a bun at the back of her head. Not for her the bobbed haircut of the fashionable; her skirt was longer than was now in vogue and the collar of her frilly blouse sat high on her neck as though she was anxious to avoid any unnecessary display of flesh. Ghent's heart sank. It was only since the war ended that she'd become so dowdy; since the telegram had arrived to tell them their son, Monty, had been killed in France a few weeks before peace was declared. Until she'd received that terrible news Jane had taken pride in her appearance and she'd enjoyed parties more than her husband had. Yet even before the telegram arrived the couple hadn't been close and they hadn't shared a bedroom since the birth of their daughter. When Mallory had married Jane for her father's factory he had expected other benefits to follow but these had never materialised as he had hoped.

'Patience is missing,' she said anxiously as soon as he was within earshot.

Ghent saw that she was fidgeting with her cuff. Since her paid companion Patience Bailey had come into their lives four months ago Jane had become dependent on her. Too dependent perhaps.

'What do you mean, missing?'

'She went out last night and she hasn't come back.' The words came out in a whine, like a child who'd been deprived of its favourite toy.

Ghent, who'd spent the previous night at his

16

club — or so he told his wife — did his best to look sympathetic. 'What about the child?'

'He's gone too. How could she leave me like this?'

'Some people are just ungrateful, my dear. You'd think after all we've done for her — taking her and her child in because we considered it our duty to help a war widow . . .'

Ghent had never liked Patience Bailey, let alone had any idea what was going on in her mind, but he could see his wife was on the verge of tears.

'Have you looked in her room? Has she taken her things?'

Jane Ghent looked affronted. 'It wouldn't be right to pry.'

'But if something's wrong . . . She might have had an accident.'

Jane hesitated. 'She takes the little one out walking a lot . . . sometimes in the evening to get him off to sleep. If she went up to the Ridge she might have . . .'

'Why on earth would she go there?'

'She said she sometimes walks up that way and I told her to be careful. But perhaps you're right. Maybe we should find out whether anything's missing.'

Jane turned away from her husband and headed for the stairs while he hovered in the doorway, unsure how to react. When he saw the maid emerge from the kitchen at the back he called out to her.

'Daisy, have you seen Mrs Bailey?'

Daisy straightened her cap and smoothed her

hair in a swift, automatic movement before walking towards him. 'No, sir. Not since yesterday.'

'She didn't say anything to you? Or to Cook?'

'No, sir. Nothing.' She looked at her employer through lowered lashes. 'The mistress asked me earlier and I told her the same.'

A secretive smile appeared on Daisy's lips, as though she was gratified that the lady's companion had put a foot wrong. Before the war, servants had known their place but recently things had changed — and Daisy knew it.

'Is Miss Esme at home?' he said, his eyes meeting Daisy's in a brief moment of intimacy.

'No, sir. She went out this morning.'

Ghent glanced up at his wife who'd just reached the top of the stairs. Neither of them liked the set their daughter was mixing with. Fast motor cars, jazz and champagne .... and, he suspected, other things besides.

Slowly Mallory Ghent followed his wife upstairs. His knees ached and he suddenly felt old; too old, perhaps, for the life he was leading. As soon as he reached the landing he saw Jane making for the narrow corridor leading to what had been the nursery wing in days gone by; the wing of smaller, humbler rooms where the children of the house, along with their nannies, had been banished until they were old enough and sufficiently civilised to join the adult world. His heart often ached for those simpler days when Monty and Esme had occupied those rooms; the days before war had destroyed everything.

He watched as Jane entered Patience Bailey's room and as he waited his gaze was drawn to the side window that overlooked the stable yard. From there he could see the door leading to the place that was his and his alone. He'd seen Patience Bailey trying that door once, but he'd soon put a stop to that.

After a few seconds his wife called out, her voice quivering with panic.

He'd always feared that Patience Bailey and her brat would bring trouble.

5

Grace Rudyard ignored the crying baby and stared out of the window. She could see Peter standing with his teacher near the grave her husband had dug the previous day for old Mrs Potts who'd passed away at the age of ninety-three. The teacher was young — not much more than a girl — and she seemed to believe every word that came from her son's lying mouth. Grace cursed her naivety. Paying heed to his nonsense like that would only encourage him and bring no end of trouble.

There were times she feared for Peter and times when his words frightened her. He'd been one of twins but his brother, Jimmy, was dead, although Peter often spoke as though he was still there. He claimed that he still talked to Jimmy, having no notion of the pain this caused her, and no amount of good hidings from his father would make the nightmare stop.

When Peter had come rushing into the house, breathless and excited, he'd told her he'd been to fetch Sergeant Stark and as Grace watched him run outside again she began to doubt her assumptions. Perhaps this time he'd been telling the truth.

A while later the sergeant had arrived on his bicycle and the sight of him revived memories so vivid that Grace felt the breath being knocked out of her. It had been Sergeant Stark who'd found Jimmy on the Ridge and carried him back home to those who loved him. When the man from London — the Inspector Lincoln she remembered so well — had arrived to investigate Jimmy's murder, he'd scolded Stark for moving Jimmy's body; destroying evidence he'd called it. But Grace had understood that Stark had done it because he hadn't wanted to leave the child alone out there in that desolate place. The sergeant was a good man who gave young scallywags a solemn talking-to rather than a blow. And now he was here again at her door.

Stark was a big man with black hair and a face that looked as though it had been chiselled from rock, and as he stood on the doorstep towering over her, she saw the concern in his eyes.

He cleared his throat as though he was about to make a long and challenging speech. 'Your lad says he's found a body. A lady, he said.'

Grace nodded.

'It's not one of his . . . stories?'

Grace didn't answer.

'How are you, Grace?' The question brought back memories of that dreadful day. Her husband had always done his best to ignore the tragedy of her son's death as though it had never happened; as though Jimmy had never been born. 'Least said, soonest mended' someone had once said to her. She'd felt like screaming at the stupid woman and grabbing her by the hair until she said she was sorry.

'You have to get on with it, don't you? The little 'uns keep me busy.' As if on cue, the baby began to cry and Grace gave Stark a thin-lipped

21

smile before shutting the door on him.

But instead of attending to the infant she climbed the stairs and made for the back bedroom, to the window with the best view over the cemetery. From there she watched Peter and his teacher standing a few yards from the open grave, waiting as Stark walked towards them with a lack of urgency that suggested Peter's story hadn't been believed.

But a few moments after the sergeant reached them Grace saw him drop to his knees and bow his head — just as she supposed he must have done when he found the body of her Jimmy all those years ago.

6

It was raining and the rain blended with the soot from several thousand London chimneys so that the once-pure water that fell from the sky had turned grey with grime by the time it reached the pavements.

Detective Inspector Albert Lincoln raised the collar of his coat against the damp as he trudged through the Bermondsey streets between the tram stop and his home, the respectable red-brick terraced house in the treelined street that had once echoed with a child's laughter.

He was home earlier than usual. These days he tried to spend as much time as possible at work in Scotland Yard because the home that had once given him such joy had become a source of pain and misery. He knew it must be harder for his wife, Mary, because she'd lost Freddy too and she didn't even have the consolation of work to distract her. All she had these days was her widowed mother Vera who lived nearby and called in each day, encouraging her daughter's quest to find little Frederick's lost soul somewhere out there on the astral plane.

Mary was spending a fortune on spiritualists, all, in Albert's opinion, charlatans. She'd joined a spurious church — the League of Departed Spirits — run by an unctuous man who called himself the Reverend Gillit. Gillit, according to Mary, brought comfort to his little flock, made up of women — and more rarely men — who'd lost loved ones in the war. At their meetings contact was invariably made with the 'other side' and on each occasion Mary returned home elated and bursting with news. Freddy was so happy with the angels, she said, her eyes shining as though she'd been granted a divine vision. He was playing with other children; hide-and-seek in the most beautiful wood you could imagine, carpeted with bluebells and dappled with eternal sunshine.

Albert knew Gillit was a fraud, although he feared there was little he could do about it. Attempting to persuade Mary that the comfort she found at her meetings was an illusion seemed pointless at best and cruel at worst so he said nothing. Since Frederick's death all communication between them had been superficial and functional, but that wasn't the only thing that broke Albert's heart.

He was still haunted by the events of the previous year. He'd travelled up North to investigate a series of strange murders in a Derbyshire village and the scars left by that investigation had caused him more pain than the wounds he'd sustained in the war, although it was damage nobody could see. In Wenfield he'd met a woman, a doctor's daughter who'd worked as a volunteer nurse during the war, and she'd seemed to him like the angel of mercy he'd been longing for ever since his life had been shattered by the loss of Frederick.

With the exception of his trusted second in command, Sergeant Sam Poltimore, he'd never revealed the truth about his relationship with Flora Winsmore to his London colleagues. As far as they were concerned he'd wrapped up the case in the village of Wenfield successfully and brought the perpetrator to justice. How were they to know that there had been far more to the story than those stark, unemotional facts?

In spite of his maimed leg, a souvenir from the trenches that had left him with a limp, he managed to dodge out of the path of a horse-drawn delivery van as he crossed the street, In contrast to the hustle and bustle of crowded London, Wenfield had been a haven of rural peace — but the village had held horrors he had never encountered in the capital.

His footsteps slowed as he turned into his street. Once upon a time his spirits used to lift when he crossed his threshold at the end of the working day. But since Frederick's death the only greeting he received from his wife, if he received one at all, was cold indifference. She no longer cared about her appearance, wearing the same faded overall for days on end and pinning her mousy hair back in an untidy bun. The cuffs of her coat were fraying and although he'd given her money to buy a new one she'd never bothered. He knew the money was still in the battered tea caddy on the mantelpiece, no doubt destined for the pocket of the Reverend Gillit.

Before taking his key from his coat pocket he hesitated, wondering how much longer he could bear the situation. Whenever he closed his eyes he saw Flora's face smiling that innocent, caring smile of hers. But he had to carry on because he had no choice.

When he called out a greeting there was no reply, but he could detect a faint odour of cooking cabbage which he hoped at least meant there'd be something to eat. When she went to one of the Reverend Gillit's meetings he usually had to shift for himself.

He found Mary standing by the range, stirring a pan containing some grey and unappetising-looking meat. Albert could almost taste the gristle as he forced himself to smile.

'What have you been doing today?' he asked, shedding his hat and coat and placing them near the range. As they began to steam the scent of warm wool battled for supremacy with the stench of cabbage being boiled to a pulp.

When Mary didn't acknowledge his question he knew the answer. She'd spent the day brooding again.

'What's for supper?' He tried to inject some enthusiasm into the words.

'Stew. And cabbage.'

'Lovely. I'm starving. Been working on that brewery robbery today. We think we've got the right men — it's just a question of persuading Tommy Helston to give evidence against his mates.'

He always tried his best to interest her in his day and always made a point of asking her about her own. But it was like talking to a statue. He turned away, fighting the frustration welling up inside.

The silence of the house was shattered by the

26

sound of hammering on the front door. They had a visitor and he hoped it wasn't Vera because he didn't feel up to being polite to his mother-in-law just at that moment.

He rushed to answer and was relieved when he found Sam Poltimore standing on the doorstep. Sam was a wiry man nearing retirement, a full six inches smaller than Albert. He had been too old to serve in the war and he'd witnessed those of his younger colleagues who had survived returning with horrific scars, mental and physical. Albert sensed the sadness he'd felt at the sight of so much damaged young flesh but Sam had rarely spoken on the matter, except to observe that it was better than them not returning at all.

'What is it, Sam?' Albert tried to sound annoyed about this interruption to his evening of 'domestic bliss' but he failed because the truth was he was glad of the distraction, and curious to find out what was so urgent that it had brought Sam Poltimore to his door so soon after the working day had ended.

Poltimore looked sheepish. 'Sorry to disturb you, sir. But there's been a telephone call. From up North.' He said it as if 'up North' was some distant exotic land. 'Do you remember that case in 'fourteen? That little lad who was murdered up in Cheshire?'

Albert remembered the case all right. His rare failure had eaten away at him for years.

A few weeks before his fifth birthday little Jimmy Rudyard had last been seen playing with his twin, Peter, and their two elder brothers one sunny Thursday evening in early July 1914; a dream time of heat and sunshine just before the clouds of war gathered on the horizon. Jimmy's mother had told the older boys, Jack and Ernie, to bring the young twins home in time for bed but they'd been distracted by some school friends playing nearby and the twins had wandered off. Eventually the older boys found Peter but Jimmy had vanished, and all Peter would say was that a knight on horseback had taken him. According to a well-known local legend, King Arthur's knights were asleep in a hidden cavern up on the Ridge where the twins had been playing, ready to reawaken and come to England's aid in her hour of need, so Ernie and Jack had assumed Peter had made up a story as he so often did.

Unwisely, the boys had left, trusting Jimmy would find his way back home. But when they arrived at the cemetery lodge there was no sign of him and when the boys' irate father alerted the village, a search was conducted and Jimmy was found dead, lying in the centre of a stone circle, near the place he'd last been seen. At first it was assumed he'd met an unfortunate accident — until the local doctor broke the news the following day that the boy had been murdered. Somebody had smothered him; held their hand over his mouth until he stopped breathing.

It soon became clear it wasn't a case the local police were capable of dealing with alone so the call was made to Scotland Yard and it fell to Albert to take charge of the investigation.

When Peter Rudyard had been questioned

about that day he'd said nothing so Albert had no way of knowing whether that boy hadn't seen what happened . . . or whether the shock of witnessing his twin's death had buried the memory deep in his mind. Jimmy had been just a year older than Albert's own son Freddy had been at the time, and the man from Scotland Yard had wondered whether he'd failed because he'd been unable to look at the case dispassionately; whether he'd tried too hard.

'I remember. What about it?'

'There's been a report of another murder in the same village. Mabley Ridge.'

Albert didn't have to be told the name. The location was forever imprinted on his memory.

Back in 1914 it hadn't taken Albert long to discover that Mabley Ridge wasn't a typical Cheshire village. It had been his first time up North and he'd been pleasantly surprised by the gentle green landscape of cattle-filled fields and, as he neared Manchester, the conspicuous wealth generated by the textile trade. The owners of the mills and those who traded in their products had built their fine houses in Mabley Ridge and made their own little community, as select as any Albert had encountered in the wealthy squares of London.

'Remember the dead lad's family lived in the cemetery lodge?' Poltimore continued. 'Well, a body's been found not far from his house . . . in a newly dug grave.'

Albert knew that if they'd been in the office, some wag would be unable to resist joking about a body being found in a cemetery but he wasn't tempted to make light of it. Little Jimmy Rudyard's death had been no laughing matter.

'Not another child?' Albert asked, praying the answer would be no.

To his relief Sam shook his head. 'No. A woman.' He paused. 'According to the local sergeant who rang us, the murdered kiddy's twin brother found the body and told his teacher. There are no obvious suspects so he felt obliged to call in Scotland Yard and the superintendent thought with your connection to the Rudyard murder . . . and as you know the area so to speak . . . '

Albert understood. Rural forces didn't have the expertise to conduct complex murder investigations and he was used to being called to all corners of the country. These days he was sometimes glad of it, although the thought of returning to Mabley Ridge filled him with dread.

'Do we know who the victim is?' he said.

'She's been provisionally identified as a Mrs Patience Bailey, a war widow with a young baby. She was working as a paid companion to a Mrs Ghent whose husband owns a cotton mill in Manchester. Mrs Bailey went missing on Tuesday night and was found yesterday after-noon.'

'Cause of death?'

'The sergeant I spoke to — ' Sam took his notebook from his pocket and examined it — 'name of Stark, says it looks as though she was rendered unconscious with a blow to the head then pushed into the grave and buried alive. The local doctor'll conduct the post-mortem when you get there.'

Albert remembered Sergeant Stark as a big man of few words; he might have been lacking in imagination but was hard-working and always ready to share local knowledge. He'd shown none of the resentment some local officers displayed when a man from Scotland Yard intruded on their patch; not that their combined efforts had done much good in the case of Jimmy Rudyard.

'Did you say the victim had a child?'

Poltimore paused for a few moments before answering. 'Er . . . yes, sir. A baby boy about six months old.'

Albert made a swift calculation. 'I thought you said she was a war widow.'

'That's what I was told, sir. I don't know any more. Only that the baby's missing.'

'Missing?'

'That's right. They found his pram in the cemetery but it was empty. The superintendent suggested you go up there as soon as possible, sir.'

'Telephone Sergeant Stark and tell him I'll set off first thing tomorrow morning.' As soon as the words had left his lips he wondered whether he should have asked for the case to be given to somebody else. But it was too late now.

Albert returned to the cabbage-scented kitchen, dreading the return to Mabley Ridge with its bitter memories of failure.

He sat down at the table and closed his eyes. Once again his mind conjured Flora's face, and this time she was laughing at him.

7

Mary said nothing when Albert told her he was going up North and wasn't sure when he'd be back. Sometimes he suspected that she had no more need of him; that her mother, her mediums and the ghostly company of their dead son were enough for her.

First thing the next morning he packed a suitcase and left the house for the station, giving his wife a tentative kiss on the cheek. He saw her wipe the cheek with her hand as though she couldn't bear for any trace of him to remain on her flesh. He noted the gesture and felt a jolt of anguish.

He sat in the smoky second-class compartment of the Manchester train and once it reached Cheshire he gazed out of the window at the passing countryside with its hedged fields and magpie half-timbered villages, all too aware that during the long hot summer of 1914 that green paradise had harboured something evil, something he'd failed to root out.

Lulled by the rhythm of the train, his mind kept wandering back to the last time he'd journeyed in the same direction in the spring of the previous year; to Flora Winsmore and those terrible events in Wenfield. She'd given birth to his son in prison before her execution and now the child was out there somewhere, as distant and inaccessible to him as dead Frederick. He'd asked himself so often how it was that he hadn't been able to see her true nature. When he lay in his lonely, narrow bed at night listening to Mary breathing through the paper-thin wall between him and the adjoining bedroom, the hurt he felt was almost physical as he realised he could no longer trust his own judgement.

This latest murder had taken place in the same village that had seen little Jimmy Rudyard's murder six years before and he clung on to the hope that, even after all this time, he would find some new clue that would lead him to the child's killer. Perhaps this new case would allow him to redeem himself and he hoped with all his heart he wouldn't fail again.

On his last visit he'd thought Mabley Ridge was a peculiar place. Originally a small settlement, its nature had altered drastically with the coming of the railway when wealthy cotton manufacturers and traders from Manchester migrated there to escape the filth and chaos of the town. Many of their mansions stood on the road leading to the Ridge itself, a dramatic wooded sandstone escarpment half a mile outside the village which afforded a magnificent view over the surrounding countryside with the chimneys and grime of Manchester safely in the distance.

The centre of the village with its shops and streets of terraced houses was home to those who worked for the big houses roundabout but although the classes rarely mixed, in his experience the people of the village knew more about the inhabitants of the big houses than their so-called betters ever suspected.

And it was in the village that he planned to start asking questions.

8

Mallory Ghent saw no reason to break his routine just because his wife's paid companion had got herself murdered. Someone had to run the mill; someone had to restore prosperity and normality after those four lost years of conflict.

Besides, earlier that morning Sergeant Stark had asked him to call in at the Cottage Hospital on his way to catch the train to make a formal identification of the dead woman. He'd kept this from his wife because he hadn't wanted to upset her, although he'd confided in Daisy as he so often did these days. The maid always seemed to understand.

Mallory's daughter, Esme, had overheard her father's hushed conversation with Daisy and she suspected the police request wasn't the only thing he was keeping from her mother. Esme had eyes and ears and she knew more about her father's secrets than he imagined.

As soon as Mallory left the house Esme emerged from her room. She never breakfasted with her father if she could help it. They'd had little to say to each other since the telegram had arrived at the end of October 1918 informing them that her brother, Monty, had been killed in action. To her disgust her father had carried on as normal, acting as though he didn't care. Her aunt, his sister, had assured her this was his way of hiding his grief but Esme hadn't believed this for one moment. She was sure he had another woman and she'd even seen Daisy making eyes at him, although as yet she'd never caught them together.

Esme found her mother annoying too. Throughout her childhood Jane Ghent had been the life and soul of every party thrown by the Ridge's prosperous residents. But since Monty's death she had retreated into mourning and now seemed so distant that Esme was convinced that she no longer cared what her daughter felt or did.

But what did that matter? The war had proved that life was all too short and, now it was over, pleasure was the only thing worth living for and it was there for the taking. As she descended the stairs she caught sight of herself in a mirror and smiled. She'd bobbed her straight dark hair, bound her small breasts until they were fashionably flat and her dress was as short as she could get away with. She was nineteen years old and the future held the promise of excitement — especially now she'd met Sydney.

She pushed open the heavy mahogany door between the hall and the dining room, sending up a silent prayer that her mother would be taking her breakfast in bed so she could eat undisturbed, but when the door swung open she saw Jane seated at the head of the table, picking at the food in front of her. She looked up as Esme walked in but there was no smile of greeting.

'Have you heard about Mrs Bailey?' she asked as Esme helped herself to the devilled kidneys on the sideboard. Her voice was unsteady as though she was on the verge of tears.

'What about her?' Esme chose a seat at right angles to her mother's so she wouldn't have to look her in the face.

'She's been found . . . dead.'

'Dead? How?'

'Sergeant Stark said the circumstances were suspicious, whatever that means.'

'It means she was murdered.' Esme's eyes shone. At last Patience Bailey had done something interesting.

Jane shook her head. 'That can't be right. Who would want to kill Patience? I can't help wondering whether . . . ' She lowered her voice, as though she was about to voice the unspeakable. 'She took her own life.'

'Why should you think that?'

Jane looked flustered. 'I don't know.'

'What about the brat?'

'He has a name,' Jane snapped.

Esme snorted. 'Lancelot. What kind of a name is that?'

Her mother looked away for a few moments. Then she turned to face her daughter. 'She must have taken him with her when she went out. She often takes him walking in the evenings to get him off to sleep but the police say there's no sign of him.'

'Have you looked in her room?'

Jane hesitated. 'Yes, I looked in before I heard she'd been found, just to check if her things were still there. Your father thought she might have decided to go away for a few days but I couldn't believe she'd leave without letting me know. She's always been so reliable.'

'She didn't leave a note?'

'Not that I could see. Your father said we should try to contact her family but I don't know anything about them. Whenever I asked her about them she always changed the subject.' She rose from her seat, folding the white linen napkin in her hand absent-mindedly and placing it back in its monogrammed silver ring. 'I'm sure Sergeant Stark will know what to do.'

'I expect we're going to have a load of coppers with their size twelve boots tramping all over the house and asking all sorts of questions.'

All of a sudden Jane's timidity vanished. 'I'm well aware of that, Esme, but it's our duty to help the police. We have to do the right thing.' She rushed from the room, almost colliding with Daisy who was entering with a tray.

Esme stayed where she was, helping herself to tea from the pot in front of her. It was stewed but she couldn't be bothered asking Daisy for fresh because her mind was on Patience Bailey. She'd been surprised when her father had suggested that her mother should employ a companion. He had even placed the advertisement in the *Lady* himself, as though Jane was incapable of making her own decision on the matter. After that she'd been vaguely aware of a procession of shabby women in rusty black traipsing through the house to be interviewed and in the end, when Patience Bailey took up residence, she'd avoided her whenever possible. Patience was a war widow with a young baby and Esme convinced herself that she'd have nothing in common with her — although she did wonder how a woman whose husband had died in the last months of the war could have given birth to a baby sixteen months later. But everybody has their secrets; Esme had quite a few herself.

She hadn't allowed Patience to touch her life because she represented a world of sadness and loss. Now, in death, the woman had suddenly become more interesting. If she had taken her own life, what was the reason? And what had become of the child? If someone had killed her, it meant the dull, quiet companion had aroused the sort of violent passions Esme had only read about in cheap novels, unless there was a madman on the loose in Mabley Ridge. She'd heard it said that the war had had a disturbing effect on some men.

Sergeant Stark would soon be there and she didn't want to be around when he arrived. After pushing her half-finished breakfast away she walked into the large square hall where the telephone sat on a side table and spoke to the operator, asking for a local number. If Sydney answered then her problem would be solved.

9

Esme arranged to meet Sydney Rich at the end of the drive, just out of sight of Gramercy House because the last thing she wanted was to be seen, either by her mother or by nosy Daisy. In her opinion Daisy was becoming too cocky by half and Esme wondered if this had something to do with her father. But as soon as she saw Sydney leaning against his car waiting for her, all thoughts of the maid vanished from her mind.

She watched as he lit a cigarette and inhaled the smoke, enjoying the hit of nicotine.

When she'd told him about Patience Bailey during their brief telephone conversation he'd muttered sympathetic platitudes. 'How beastly it must be for you, darling,' he'd said. 'Such a bore having all those bobbies trampling around the house like a herd of elephants.' Then, to her delight, he'd invited her over to the house he'd been renting since his arrival in the village a few weeks before.

Ridgeside Lodge reminded her of a doll's house she'd once owned, long banished to the attics of Gramercy House. It stood down a small lane near the path leading to the Ridge and although it was a pretty place, an overgrown cottage with climbing roses growing round the door, the furnishings — the fussy chintz and heavy furniture from the previous century

40

— were definitely not to her taste. According to Sydney the furniture had come with the house and he said he planned to replace it with something more up to date as soon as he could. She imagined herself in some swish Manchester shop helping him choose some sleek modern pieces. Perhaps one day, she thought hopefully, they might even make a home together.

Sitting in the passenger seat of the Alvis, she imagined how jealous her friends would be of her new-found sophistication if they saw her driving by. To her disappointment she saw nobody she knew but when they arrived at Ridgeside Lodge and she watched him pour the champagne, she experienced an excitement verging on joy. She had only ever drunk champagne during the day once before and that was at a cousin's wedding so she'd been impressed when Sydney had a bottle standing ready in a silver ice bucket.

As he poured expertly to prevent the erupting bubbles spilling over the edge of the glass, she compared him to her male contemporaries and found them wanting; those clean-cut boys who were so polite and eager to please.

Sydney possessed an aura of excitement — even danger — and as he handed her the champagne glass his fingers touched hers and she felt an unfamiliar thrill passing through her body.

'Come on, darling, relax. I'm not going to bite you.'

Esme took a long sip of champagne, wrinkling her nose when the bubbles hit, before stretching out on the velvet sofa.

'Do your parents know you're here with me?'

This was a question she hadn't expected. 'Where I go and who I see is none of their business. I'm a big girl now.' She knew her last words held promise and they were meant to. She looked Sydney in the eye, challenging him to make a move.

He was a good fifteen years older than her with a worldliness that added to his attraction. His body was lean and muscular and his black hair was slicked back to reveal a high forehead — an intelligent forehead, she told herself. His eyes were a piercing green and he had a habit of looking at her, direct and unblinking, that made her feel she was the sole focus of his attention . . . and that he could read her every thought. His only physical flaw was his injured foot which he dragged on the ground when he walked. He had been caught by a ricocheting bullet from the rifle of an enemy sniper, he told her, but he'd been lucky because two of his comrades had bought it.

'You haven't told your mother about us, have you?'

'Why should I?' She leaned forward, feigning indifference. 'You don't want me to take you home and introduce you to my parents do you? I wouldn't have thought that was your style.'

'You're quite right,' he said quickly. 'The last thing I want is to have to sit through afternoon tea with your boring parents.' There was a short silence before he asked his next question, this time lowering his gaze to her legs. 'At least I assume they're boring. Tell me about them. Start with your mother.'

'Why do you keep asking about her? I told you before — she's not very interesting.'

He put his glass down and leaned forward to kiss her on the lips, a kiss she returned. 'Because I want to know everything about you. What's she like? How does she fill her day?' He hesitated. 'Has she got a lover?'

Esme was shocked by the final question but she was determined not to show it. 'Of course not. She's old.'

'Not that old, surely.'

For a long time Esme hadn't given her mother much thought but Sydney's questions focused her mind. 'Mummy used to be fun — she liked pretty clothes and parties, that sort of thing — but since my brother was killed . . . It's as if she died inside as well. I feel sorry for her in a way.' She suddenly realised what she'd said. It wouldn't do at all. 'She's turned into a frightful bore. Honestly.'

'I'd like to meet her.'

'Why?'

'Any woman who has such a gorgeous daughter can't be all bad.'

She hesitated before replying. 'If you really want to meet her why don't you come to the house tomorrow. My father won't be there. He spends all day at the mill. And whenever he's home in the evenings he disappears into his room by the stables. But nobody else is allowed to go in.'

'Why not?'

She shrugged. 'He says there are dangerous chemicals in there.'

'What sort of chemicals?'

'How should I know?'

'Does your mother go out much?'

'Hardly ever. And now she won't have Patience around things will probably get worse.'

'Do the police know what happened to her?'

'I've heard they're going to send someone up from Scotland Yard but I don't know when he'll arrive.' She looked straight at him, a challenge in her eyes. 'Will you come tomorrow? Are you brave enough to face my fearsome mama?'

'It's probably best if we leave it for another time,' Sydney said quickly. 'More champagne?'

'Why not?' She held out her glass and he poured with a steady hand.

10

Sergeant Stark had arranged to meet Albert at the small railway station that served the village and as the train laboured away and the cloud of smoke from the engine cleared Albert saw him standing there, stiff in his high-collared serge uniform. As soon as Stark spotted him a businesslike smile of greeting appeared on his face as though he was pleased the man from Scotland Yard had arrived to lift the burden from his shoulders, even though their last encounter hadn't ended in success.

Albert hurried forward, his right hand outstretched, and he noticed Stark staring at his other hand which was hanging by his side. War had left the hand a reddened stump with only the thumb and forefinger remaining. His face too bore red, shiny scars, although his disfigurement was trivial compared to the terrible injuries suffered by many of his comrades. Stark had last seen him before conflict left its marks on his flesh and Albert saw a brief look of shock pass across his heavy features.

'I've taken a room for you at the Station Hotel,' Stark said, averting his gaze from Albert's face. 'It's where you stayed before and you said it was comfortable. It has electric light now, I believe.'

'I'm sure it'll be satisfactory.'

'We've had electric light put in at the police station too . . . very modern,' he added as though

45

he hoped Albert would be impressed by this evidence of Northern sophistication.

When Albert didn't reply Stark picked up his suitcase; whether this was out of politeness or because the sergeant assumed he needed help because of his injured hand, Albert wasn't sure. But he said nothing and allowed Stark to lead the way to the hotel which stood near to the station. Albert had been cooped up in a train compartment for hours and all he wanted was to unpack, wash and have something to eat.

'My missus says would you like to come round for your dinner on Sunday,' Stark said as though he'd read Albert's mind.

'That's very kind of her.'

'Half past twelve, after church if that's all right with you.'

Albert thanked him. The results of Mary's recent halfhearted efforts at cooking had hardly been appetising and Albert recalled that Mrs Stark — Hetty — was a good, if unimaginative, cook. When he had been there in 1914 she had taken pity on the detective from London so far away from home and he'd often been invited to eat at the police house where her talkative nature had compensated for her husband's frequent silences. He had enjoyed those hearty meals but then in those days he'd had a wife and a son and the world hadn't been scarred by war. A lot had changed in the intervening years.

When they reached the hotel Albert took his case to his room while Stark waited for him downstairs because they needed to talk about the investigation.

To avoid being overheard by curious ears Albert knew it would be wise to conduct their conversation at the police station but he couldn't resist asking questions on the way.

'Tell me about the victim.'

'She's been identified by her employer's husband as Patience Bailey.'

'Employer?'

'She was a war widow — lost her husband in France near the end of the war — and she was working as a paid companion to Mrs Ghent at Gramercy House; big place in its own grounds off the Ridge Road. The dead woman had a young baby but, according to Mr Ghent, she never talked about any other relatives.'

'No relatives at all?'

'None she ever mentioned to the Ghents.'

'Any followers?'

'No sign of any men. That's what her employers say anyway.'

'Enemies?'

'According to everyone we've spoken to she was a quiet woman and a devoted mother. Mr and Mrs Ghent say she didn't know anybody in the village apart from to pass the time of day, although my missus took pity on her and chatted to her if she ever saw her on her own in the tearoom. Said she seemed like a nice woman. Lonely life being a paid companion. You're neither fish nor fowl.'

'What about her background?'

'She came from Manchester but the Ghents say she had no visitors and never mentioned anyone, although she sometimes left the village on her days off — caught the train but she never said where to. My missus asked her about her late husband and her family but she wasn't very forthcoming. Seems she was a bit of an enigma.' He paused and looked round, as though to make sure nobody was listening. 'Between you and me, the sums don't add up . . . with the baby. It's only about seven months old and she told the Ghents her husband died at the end of the war — November nineteen eighteen. It's September nineteen twenty now which means the little one was born in February, so he must have been conceived around April or May nineteen nineteen when her husband had already been dead six months.'

Stark's words hit Albert like a punch. But he couldn't allow Stark to know the mention of the baby's date of birth disturbed him so he fixed his eyes ahead and carried on walking. He had to put all thoughts of Flora and their child out of his mind.

'So who was the father of Patience Bailey's child?' Albert forced himself to ask after a minute of silence.

'That's what we need to find out. That and where the little 'un is.'

'Have you organised a search?'

Stark nodded. 'I've had men looking for him in the village and in farm outbuildings.'

'What about the Ridge?'

Stark's face clouded. 'If he's up there I don't hold out much hope. There's all sorts of hidden mineworkings and quarries and caves and . . . '

He didn't need to say more. The landscape of

48

the Ridge contained all manner of perils. If somebody had taken the child up there its chances of survival were slim, although Albert couldn't understand why someone would kill a mother and take her child if they didn't intend to care for it, unless the killer intended to use it as a hostage, assuming the wealthy Ghents would pay up to ensure its safe return. Or was the child's father — whoever he was — involved in some way? Had he killed his former lover and taken his son? It was a puzzle — as was the mother's past life.

11

Sergeant Stark had warned Gwen Davies that the man from Scotland Yard would be arriving that day and that he'd want to speak to her at some point. She'd found the body after all, or rather, Peter Rudyard had.

Peter hadn't been in school that day because, according to his sister Maud, he wasn't well. But Maud wasn't a good liar. Unlike her brother, Peter, she was an unimaginative child and Gwen knew she was holding something back.

All sorts of possibilities ran through Gwen's mind. What if Maud was trying to cover up the fact that Peter was missing? What if whoever had killed the woman imagined he was a witness who needed to be silenced? She felt uneasy about the boy's absence so she made plans to call at the cemetery lodge on her way back to her lodgings. Surely nobody could criticise her for making sure her pupil was safe.

At the end of the school day she was wiping the blackboard when she heard a man's voice behind her. His accent was unfamiliar and he sounded almost apologetic.

'Miss Davies?'

Gwen spun round, the board duster still in her hand. The man standing in the classroom doorway was tall with dark hair and a rugged face that would have been handsome were it not for the angry scarring running down one cheek from the edge of his eye to his jaw. He held his hat in his right hand but her eyes were drawn to his damaged left hand. She guessed that he'd sustained his wounds in the service of his country and if those were his only injuries he'd been luckier than many.

'I'm Gwen Davies,' she said. 'How can I help you?'

'Inspector Lincoln — Albert Lincoln. Scotland Yard. I'm investigating the death of Patience Bailey and I understand you found her body.'

She extended her hand and for a second or so he looked confused. Then he gathered his thoughts and deposited his hat on a nearby bookcase so that he was able to shake her hand and their eyes met for a brief moment.

'Sergeant Stark told me you'd want to speak to me about . . . what we found in the cemetery.'

'We?'

'One of my pupils, Peter Rudyard, was with me. He lives in the cemetery lodge and he found the body in the morning but he didn't tell me about it until school was over for the day.'

'Why you and not his parents?'

She smiled. 'Peter's — how shall I put it? — an imaginative child. He makes up stories. I'm not saying he tells lies as such because I'm sure he believes that most of what he says is the truth but other people tend to take what he says with a pinch of salt. It's like that old story of the Boy who Cried Wolf. He tells so many tall tales that nobody takes what he says seriously, only one day it turns out he's right.'

'What made you believe Peter this time?'

51

'There was something about the way he said it, as if he was genuinely frightened. Did you know that Peter's twin brother was murdered before the war? I wasn't here at the time but Mabley Ridge is a small community and people talk.'

'Yes, I know about it,' he said and Gwen saw a shadow pass across his face, as though the death of Peter's brother had affected him personally. 'Did you recognise the dead woman?'

'I've seen her around in the village with her baby but I never spoke to her.'

'She worked for a family called Ghent who live up on Ridge Lane. Are you acquainted with them at all?'

'Dear me, no. The Cottontots, as they're known round here, have nothing to do with the village school. My pupils come from the village proper; the little streets. The wealthy make other arrangements for their own children's education.'

She excused herself and disappeared through a small door beside the blackboard and when she emerged she was wearing her hat and carrying the battered leather briefcase her parents had given her when she first went to college to train as a teacher; a time before she became such a disappointment to them.

'Would you mind if we talk while we walk?'

'Of course. I'll carry your bag if you'd like?'

When she passed him her bag he looked surprised at its weight.

'It's full of books,' she said. 'I have a lot of arithmetic to mark this evening.'

'I want to speak to Peter and it might help if you're there as well. Would you mind very much?'

He looked at her hopefully and she realised this could be the solution to her problem.

'I don't mind at all. In fact he hasn't been in school today so I was planning to call in before I went back to my lodgings . . . just to make sure everything's all right.'

They walked out of the village towards the cemetery in silence, side by side. When they were halfway there Gwen asked the question that had been on her mind all day. 'I've heard that Mrs Bailey's baby's missing. Do you think . . . do you think someone might have killed her for the child?'

'Why would they do that?'

'If someone was desperate for a child . . . if they'd lost their own . . .'

She knew she'd said too much because the inspector stared at her as though some dreadful curse had come upon him. Something about her words had hurt him and she wished she knew what she'd said that had been so wrong. She wondered whether she should tell him that the thought of the baby caused her pain too. But some things are best left unsaid.

12

The schoolmistress couldn't have known that Albert had lost Frederick and then he'd gone on to lose the child Flora had given birth to. She wasn't to know that the thought of his two losses caused a pain that was almost physical — as though some small, vicious creature was gnawing at his heart. She'd spoken in ignorance, that was all.

When they reached the cemetery lodge he saw that the house hadn't changed one iota since he'd last been there in 1914. It was built of red brick with Gothic architectural flourishes and stood beside a pair of impressive ornamental gates that remained open during daylight hours.

Beyond the gates Albert could see the cemetery where the rich and poor of Mabley Ridge ended their earthly existence, kept pristine by the efforts of John Rudyard who also worked as a gardener in one of the big houses. Staring at the lodge, he felt the urge to run away. He'd failed the Rudyards all those years ago and the thought of having to face them again paralysed him with a mixture of embarrassment and fear.

He wondered how the family would react when they saw him. Would Grace Rudyard spit in his face like she had before when he'd been forced to tell her that her son Jimmy's killer had left no clue to his identity and that he had to return to London, his task left unfinished?

54

He stood back as Gwen Davies knocked on the front door, imagining his embarrassment if she were to witness Grace Rudyard's fury. But it was too late to change things now.

When Grace answered the door Albert stayed in the background and allowed Gwen to do the talking. It took a special kind of courage to face a bereaved parent you've failed and Albert wasn't sure whether he could summon that kind of bravery any more. There were times it was easier to face the aggression of an enemy in war than the pain of grief.

'Mrs Rudyard. I'm sorry to bother you. I wonder if I might have a word with Peter. Maud said he was unwell. I do hope he's feeling better.'

In spite of Gwen's cheerful confidence Albert suspected that she felt as nervous about facing Grace Rudyard as he was.

Grace hesitated for a moment before answering. 'He's been poorly today, Miss — tummy ache.' The woman's eyes wandered from her children's teacher to Albert, who was hovering behind her.

As soon as she saw him her face hardened. 'What's he doing here?'

Albert stepped forward and fixed an apologetic smile to his face which he feared had turned into a grimace of agony, betraying how he felt.

'How do you do, Mrs Rudyard. I need to ask Peter some questions and I thought he'd feel more comfortable if Miss Davies was present too.' He spoke softly, trying to ignore the hatred in her eyes.

'Whoever killed that woman, you'll never find him . . . or the little one. You're useless. A waste of God's good air.'

She spat the words with such hatred that he felt the blood rushing to his face.

'I'm sorry, Mrs Rudyard, but I really need to speak to Peter . . . and the rest of the family.'

She stared at him. Her eyes were bulbous with dark bags beneath. For years those eyes had haunted his dreams — until worse things had replaced them in his nightmares.

Gwen had bowed her head and he could tell that the news of his connection with Jimmy's death had come as a shock to her.

To his relief Mrs Rudyard gave a curt nod. 'You'd better come through. Peter's in the kitchen.'

Albert followed Gwen inside, feeling like a naughty schoolboy.

The large black range was lit and the heat in the small room, mingled with the smell of cooking vegetables, was oppressive. Near the range washing hung from a rack fixed to the ceiling: towelling nappies beside vests, long johns and shirts, all drooping grey and damp like mourning flags at half-mast in the rain. Peter was sitting at the scrubbed kitchen table peeling potatoes and dropping them into a large pan of starchy water. When he saw Gwen his face lit up.

'Miss,' he said, rising from his seat, an old wooden chair spattered with paint.

'Hello, Peter,' Gwen said with forced cheeriness. 'Maud told me you haven't been well. I've brought you some work to do. Are you feeling up to doing some sums?'

When Peter nodded enthusiastically Gwen produced an exercise book from her bag and sat down next to the boy. For a minute or so Albert stood as she explained what she wanted the boy to do, their heads together in a tableau of concentration. Albert was aware of Grace Rudyard standing in the doorway, watching the scene in silence, but he didn't turn his head to look at her.

Once Gwen had finished she gave him a small nod, a signal that it was his turn.

He sat down opposite Peter and the boy gave him a nervous half-smile. 'Hello, Peter. We've met before . . . a long time ago.'

'I remember,' the boy said, staring at the exercise book in front of him.

Albert was glad when Gwen spoke.

'I know you've already spoken to Sergeant Stark but Inspector Lincoln's come all the way from London.' She paused to let the name of the capital sink in. 'He'd like to talk to you about the lady in the cemetery. Is that all right, Peter?'

Peter nodded, fidgeting with the pencil he was holding.

'Had you ever seen the lady before?'

'Only once in the village.'

'Did she have a baby with her?'

Another nod. 'She was pushing a pram. Left it outside the post office while she went in.'

'Did you take a peep at the baby?'

'That's something girls do,' he said dismiss-ively.

'Of course,' said Albert, giving him a 'we're all

men of the world' smile.

'Where's your bedroom, Peter?'

'What's that got to do with you?' There was no mistaking the aggression in Grace Rudyard's voice.

Albert twisted round to face her. 'If his room overlooks the cemetery he might have seen something if he looked out of his window.'

To his surprise Gwen interrupted. 'You often look out of your window at night, don't you, Peter. You write stories about what you see.'

'What did you see that night, Peter?' said Albert, suddenly hopeful. Something in the way Gwen asked her question had suggested to him that he had seen more than wildlife during his nocturnal vigils.

The boy shot a nervous look at his mother, who was still glowering from the doorway.

'Don't you dare tell any of your lies, now,' she snapped. 'You don't want to believe a word he says. Always fibbing, he is.'

'I'll remember that, Mrs Rudyard,' said Albert, wondering whether her animosity towards her son was a result of him surviving when his twin was dead.

The woman folded her plump arms and stood her ground as Albert caught Gwen's eye.

'I've seen the old lady . . . Mrs Pearce,' said Peter. 'She comes every night and leaves food.'

Albert gave Grace a questioning look.

'She's a batty old biddy,' she said by way of explanation. 'Her son went missing in the war and she leaves food for him by the grave where his sister and father are buried. My husband told her to stop but she swears it's always gone by morning. She says that proves her son's alive but if you ask me animals have had it.'

A smug look appeared on Peter's face, as though he was privy to a secret nobody else knew about.

'What time does Mrs Pearce usually come, Peter?' Albert asked gently.

Peter looked confused. 'When it's just got dark. I didn't see her that night but she's sometimes a bit late so she might have come while I was in bed.' He hesitated. 'But I got up later once Jack and Ernie were asleep. That's when he came.'

'Who are you talking about, Peter? Mrs Pearce's son?'

'Might be. He wears a soldier's coat.'

'You call him the Shadow Man in your stories,' said Gwen.

Peter nodded. 'That's 'cause he's like a shadow.'

'Did you see him with the dead lady, Peter?'

The boy shook his head. 'No, I never saw her till the next morning when I found her in Mrs Potts's grave.'

'Do you know who the Shadow Man is?' Albert held his breath, waiting for an answer.

'Mr Nobody, that's who he is,' Grace Rudyard interrupted harshly before the boy could reply. 'There ain't no such person as this Shadow Man he goes on about.'

'You've seen him in the cemetery before?' Albert asked, ignoring the mother.

'He always comes after Mrs Pearce has gone.

I've seen him take the food she leaves.'

'What does he look like?'

'He's big and tall and he hasn't got a face.'

'Everybody's got a face,' Mrs Rudyard muttered. 'Either he's had a bad dream or he's making it up.'

'I drew a picture of him, didn't I, Miss?'

'Yes, Peter, you did.'

'I've done another.' He rummaged among the papers on the table and produced a picture which he handed to Albert. It showed a figure in a big coat with long lank hair and a blank space where the face should have been. Albert handed it back.

'You can keep it. It's a present.'

'Thank you, Peter. Have your brothers or Maud ever seen him?'

'No, just me,' the boy said quickly.

'He shares with our Jack and Ernie and they've never said anything about no Shadow Man,' said Mrs Rudyard. 'It's all in his head.'

'They're always asleep when he comes, that's why,' said Peter with a hint of defiance. 'They don't see nothing.'

'Next time you see the Shadow Man you should wake Jack or Ernie so they can tell us what they saw.'

'Jack and Ernie need their sleep,' Mrs Rudyard snapped. 'I don't want them woken up in the middle of the night with some cock and bull story.'

One glance at his mother's face was enough to crush Peter's enthusiasm for detective work. He bowed his head and Albert knew he'd lost the fight. Even so he decided to have one last try.

'Think hard, Peter. Tell me exactly what you saw on the night before you found the lady. Were you looking out of the window?'

Peter's eyes slid towards his mother before he replied. 'Yes.'

'What time was this?'

'Don't know. Just before dark. I was looking out waiting for Mrs Pearce to come but Jack and Ernie told me to get into bed 'cause they couldn't get to sleep with the curtain open.'

'And you did as they said?'

He nodded. 'But I woke up later when it was dark 'cause Jack was snoring. That's when I saw the Shadow Man near the place where she leaves the food. I think she must have come while I'd been asleep 'cause the Shadow Man was carrying something.'

'You saw him clearly? It was night-time and he must have been some way away.'

Peter thought for a moment. 'There was a full moon.'

'How did he get into the cemetery? Surely your father locks the gates at sunset.'

'That's only the main gates. There's a wooden gate at the side which doesn't lock. He must use that.'

Albert stood up. 'Why don't we go outside and you can show me where you saw the Shadow Man. Is that all right, Mrs Rudyard?'

Grace Rudyard shrugged, as though she was washing her hands of the whole affair. If this fool of a detective wanted to believe the boy's lies, that was up to him.

Albert was relieved when the noise of a baby crying in the next room made the woman hurry out, leaving them alone with Peter. Five minutes later they were outside following the boy down the path to the back of the cemetery where tall yew trees fringed the boundary between the territory of the dead and the fields beyond.

One grave in particular stood out in Albert's memory: a small headstone lovingly tended with a vase of fresh flowers placed in front of it. He didn't need to read the name. He knew it: *Jimmy Rudyard. Taken from us July 1914 aged 4. With the angels*. Jimmy and Peter had been identical twins so the boy by his side was a constant reminder of the one who lay there beneath the earth. He wondered how Grace Rudyard could bear the sight of him.

Albert walked beside Gwen in silence, longing to ask her what she was thinking. As Peter's teacher she knew the child better than anybody outside his immediate family and he valued her opinion.

Peter stopped suddenly beside a well-tended grave. On it was a single late rose, fading now, its red petals limp and turning rusty-brown. 'I can see this grave from my window. It glows when the moon's out. Like a ghost.' He pointed to the sad single rose. 'Someone's left a flower. Do you think it was the dead lady?'

Albert bent forward to read the words on the headstone, a neat white marble slab matching the marble strips that outlined the shape of the grave. The centre was filled with grey chippings, neat and weed-free. The grave looked fairly new.

'It belongs to a George Sedding.' He looked at Peter. 'Know who he is?'

'One of the Cottontots. Owned a big mill in Stockport. Died last year.'

'Did he fight in the war?' Albert asked. He glanced at Gwen and saw that her pale cheeks were red as though something had upset her.

'Nah. He never went to war,' Peter said dismissively. 'He had a lovely funeral. Six black horses with fancy plumes pulling his hearse. I watched it from my bedroom. Me mam said it was better than a show.'

'I expect you see a lot of funerals.'

Peter's face lit up. 'I like funerals. If I find a dead bird or animal I always give it a nice funeral — a proper box and flowers. That's if the Body Snatcher hasn't found it first.'

'Who's the Body Snatcher?'

Peter looked away. 'That's a secret.'

'Are you sure you've never seen the dead lady in the graveyard before?'

Peter shook his head again.

'Did you see the Shadow Man leave that night?'

A look of disappointment passed across Peter's open face. 'No. Me dad came in from the pub and told me he'd take his belt to me if I didn't get back into bed.'

'And you did as you were told?'

'Didn't want to get a belt, did I?'

'Have you seen the Shadow Man since that night?'

He shook his head.

Albert squatted down so his face was level

with the boy's. 'If you see him again will you tell me or Miss Davies?'

Peter gave him a solemn nod. 'I promise,' he said. Before Albert could say anything else he heard Grace Rudyard's voice, calling her son home.

13

On his return from the cemetery Albert Lincoln installed himself in the back office at the village police station at a desk allocated to him by Sergeant Stark for the duration of his visit. It was Stark's own desk and he'd removed all his things. Albert found the neatness disconcerting. His desk at Scotland Yard was notoriously cluttered with reports, stationery and his favourite photograph: the silver-framed image of Frederick taken in a studio at great expense on the boy's fifth birthday. In the picture Frederick sat in his sailor suit staring at the camera; to Albert it wasn't a particularly good likeness because it lacked any suggestion of his son's cheerful nature, but it was the only one he possessed and he kept it with him always, placing it at the top of his suitcase on every trip away. The only occasion he'd forgotten and left it behind on his London desk, had been when he'd travelled to Wenfield to conduct the investigation which had ended in so much personal tragedy. Ever since then he'd made sure he had it with him, like a talisman against future misfortune.

The photograph sat at the back of the desk now and as Albert looked at it he couldn't help wondering whether his other son, his and Flora's, bore any resemblance to Frederick. But he had to face the possibility he might never find out. For all he knew the boy — the only thing he knew about the baby was its sex — could be anywhere. He might even be dead; the influenza epidemic had claimed so many young and otherwise healthy lives in the year following the war, just as it had claimed Frederick.

Albert was almost relieved when Stark poked his head round the door of the little office, the best the village station had to offer. He needed a distraction to take his mind off his losses.

'I've telephoned Gramercy House, sir. Mr and Mrs Ghent are home if you want to speak to them. Mr Ghent says his wife's still upset about her companion so . . . '

'Mrs Ghent presumably knew the dead woman best so I need to speak to her.' He saw Stark frown. 'Don't worry, Sergeant, I'll mind my p's and q's. I take it the search for the child is still going on.'

'Yes, sir, but there's still no sign.'

'There are a lot of big houses around here. Have they all been visited?'

Stark hesitated, shuffling his feet. Albert recognised embarrassment when he saw it. 'Er . . . I didn't think there was any point visiting the big houses. It's hard to hide a baby in servants' quarters — there's always some cook or housekeeper around to bring any silly young girl into line and the servants who live out have homes in the village so they've been spoken to already.'

'What about the families who own the houses?' He tilted his head to one side and awaited the answer.

'Oh we don't need to bother them, sir. They

66

won't know anything.'

Albert raised his eyebrows.

'I don't give a damn if a man owns ten cotton mills — he's as capable of murder as anybody else. Someone out there knows something and I don't care if their majesties King George and Queen Mary themselves are in residence. I want every house in the area visited, and that's an order.'

There was a look of horror on Stark's face, as though he thought Albert had just uttered a blasphemy. The sergeant had spent his professional career deferring to the inhabitants of the big houses and no doubt he regarded keeping them and their property safe as the main purpose of his job, but if Albert had any say in the matter the wealthy would come under suspicion just like anybody else. Back in London this was something he'd been used to since the beginning of his police career; here however things were different and it was time Stark learned a few vital lessons.

Albert took his watch from his waistcoat pocket and checked the time. 'If the Ghents are expecting me I won't waste any more time,' he said, taking his hat from the coat-stand in the corner of the room. It was a pleasant September day and the rain that had threatened earlier hadn't arrived. From his previous experiences of this part of England he knew that this was a blessing.

'Would you like me to come with you, sir?'

Albert shook his head. He would do things his own way and make his own judgements.

Fifteen minutes later he was tugging at the bell pull beside the Ghents' grand front door. There was a time before the war when police officers had been expected to use the tradesman's entrance near the kitchens but, as far as Albert was concerned, those rules no longer applied, especially to a Scotland Yard inspector.

The door was opened by a plump, pretty girl with a pale face and sharp eyes. Her hair too was pale and her eyebrows so light that they were barely visible. She wore a clean white apron over a pale-blue dress which didn't suit her complexion.

'Inspector Lincoln. Mr and Mrs Ghent are expecting me. Daisy is it?'

'Yes, sir,' she said even as Albert saw a challenge in her eyes. The initial impression of meekness had suddenly vanished.

'I'll need to speak to you later if that's all right?'

She nodded warily and as Albert followed her through the entrance hall he heard the faint sound of music drifting down from upstairs, jazz from a gramophone. He remembered Stark saying that the Ghents' son had been killed in action but that they also had a daughter who was, presumably, the unseen jazz enthusiast. She would be another person to ask about the life of Patience Bailey.

Daisy showed Albert into an elegant drawing room, announcing him like a butler in a play, and the two people sitting facing each other on the twin sofas at right angles to the fireplace turned their heads as one to look at him. He had the vague impression that the tableau was contrived but he wasn't sure why.

The man stood while the woman remained seated. He paused for a moment as though he wasn't quite sure of the etiquette when a detective from Scotland Yard came to call. Then he thrust out his hand. Albert took it, suppressing a wince at the strength of Ghent's grip. Perhaps the man was used to using a handshake as a demonstration of power to underlings and business rivals; almost as a weapon.

Ghent wasn't particularly tall but he gave the impression of bulk and his waistcoat stretched tightly over his prosperous stomach. His well-cut suit was in the very best fabric, tailored in Savile Row, Albert guessed, and well beyond a policeman's pocket. Albert felt shabby in comparison, although perhaps this was the intention. Ghent sported a small dark beard and his dark hair had turned grey at the temples. His eyes too were grey, piercing and intelligent and Albert suspected that not much would get past him.

In contrast Mrs Ghent was thin and colourless, although her fawn dress was silk and her shoes expensive. The grand piano in the large bay window was home to a hoard of silver-framed photographs, mainly of a fairhaired boy at various stages of childhood. There were very few of the daughter Albert had heard mentioned.

'We've already spoken to Sergeant Stark,' said Ghent as though he considered Albert's visit an impertinent intrusion. 'I was even obliged to identify Mrs Bailey's body and that wasn't pleasant, I can tell you. But I knew it was my public duty,' he added self-righteously.

'I'm sure it was a great help, sir.'

Ghent made a point of examining the gold watch hanging on a thick chain tucked into his waistcoat. 'I really don't see the point of your visit, Inspector, and I'll say as much to the chief constable when I see him. I'm a busy man; I hope you realise that.' Albert noticed the man's accent was local, Manchester probably. Somehow he'd expected something more refined.

'Of course, sir, but you and your wife employed Mrs Bailey and were, presumably, the people who knew her best around here so I really do need a word.' He looked at Mrs Ghent and gave her a hopeful smile which she didn't return. The woman looked terrified and Albert wondered why.

He took his notebook from his pocket. Ghent's attitude had made him all the more determined to ask this couple some searching questions.

'Can you tell me how you came to employ Mrs Bailey?'

'My husband placed an advertisement in the *Lady* and I received a letter from Mrs Bailey,' said Mrs Ghent with a nervous glance at her husband. 'From her letter she sounded most suitable so we interviewed her.'

'Both of you?'

Mrs Ghent nodded. 'I haven't been well since . . .'

'I'll say it, my dear. Since our son was killed in

70

action. Monty was the apple of our eye, Inspector. He worked with me at the mill but he would insist on signing up. Doing his bit.'

It was an all-too-familiar story and for the first time Albert found himself feeling sympathy for the Ghents. They'd suffered badly for their loss as had many others.

'How long had Mrs Bailey worked for you?'

'Just four months. The baby, little Lancelot — Lance she called him — was only tiny when she came.'

'I'm surprised you employed a woman with such a young child.'

'She was a war widow so it was a way of doing our bit.' There was a note of defiance in Mrs Ghent's voice.

'The woman was no trouble. Neither was the kiddie,' said Ghent. 'Her room was in the nursery wing so the baby didn't disturb us. This is a big house,' he added proudly.

'What do you know about Mrs Bailey's background? Where was she before she came to you?'

It was Mrs Ghent who spoke. 'She lived in Didsbury near Manchester with her husband until he was . . . ' She paused, as though she was reluctant to utter the words. Albert knew that, having lost her own son, the very thought of another soldier's death caused her pain. 'After his death she was left in straitened circumstances so she became a companion to an elderly lady in Didsbury who was sympathetic to her . . . plight. However, since the house was too small to accommodate her and the baby Mrs Bailey

71

thought it best to apply for another post, somewhere with more space for the child. She came with an excellent reference from her former employer and she was a pleasant woman who went about her duties with quiet diligence. I really can't think who would want to kill her in that dreadful way.' She looked at Albert, her eyes brimming with unshed tears. 'Is it true? Was she . . . buried alive?'

Albert gave a reluctant nod. 'You don't know what she was doing in the cemetery that night?'

'Of course I don't.'

'She took the baby with her.'

'Sometimes she took him walking in the evenings — she said it was to get him off to sleep. But even so, the cemetery's hardly a suitable place for a woman on her own with . . . Lancelot's such a sweet baby.' There was a sob in her voice. 'Is there any sign of him? I'd be happy to offer him a home if no relatives can be found.'

'That's very kind of you, Mrs Ghent.' Albert noticed that her husband was frowning in disapproval as though he didn't share his wife's generous instincts. Or perhaps he saw her offer as a gesture of desperation; a yearning for someone to love; perhaps a child to replace the boy taken from her by the war. 'Do you know whether Mrs Bailey had any relatives? We really would like to speak to them.'

'I understand she had a brother in Manchester with a family of his own but as far as I know she never saw him while she was here and I don't think they corresponded.'

Albert knew he'd have to get used to the mention of Manchester. For a long time he'd flinched at the very name because Manchester was where Flora had been incarcerated following her trial. He'd tried his best to banish all thoughts of the place from his mind but now it was something he couldn't avoid. 'Is there anything else you can tell me?'

'I'm afraid not. Whenever I enquired about her family she changed the subject so I presumed they weren't close.' She gave her husband a sideways look. 'Some families aren't.'

'My next question is rather delicate,' said Albert quietly, trying to gauge the couple's mood. 'If Mrs Bailey's husband died in the war, it means that he can't have been Lancelot's father.'

He waited for a reaction but none came. The Ghents didn't even look at each other.

'I didn't feel it was my place to pry,' said Mrs Ghent eventually. 'As you say, Inspector, the subject was delicate. It was easier to ignore the obvious discrepancy in the dates and accept the child was her late husband's as she said. She told me he'd died a hero defending his comrades so to enquire too deeply would have seemed like a slur on his memory.'

'Of course.' Albert suspected he wouldn't discover any more about Patience Bailey from her employers; but there was somebody in the household who might be more forthcoming. 'May I speak to Daisy? And anyone else in your household who knew Mrs Bailey?'

Mallory Ghent strode to the fireplace and

pressed the bell push. Albert imagined a bell jangling in some distant scullery and the maid scurrying out, straightening her apron.

'It might be best if I speak to her alone,' Albert said and he saw the Ghents exchange an uneasy look. However, Mallory could hardly refuse his request and when Daisy arrived he assumed an avuncular manner. 'The inspector would like a word with you, Daisy. Don't be nervous. There's nothing to worry about.'

Albert caught a note of warning behind his bland words. Don't say anything about the family. Don't give away our secrets or there might be consequences.

Mallory allowed them to use the breakfast room at the back of the house and Daisy followed Albert, her head bowed meekly like a frightened schoolgirl, although there was something about her, an alertness as though she was on her guard, which made Albert suspect she wasn't the timid creature she wanted him to think she was.

'Please, Daisy, sit down. I promise you I don't bite.' He smiled but he saw that his small joke had made no difference. Something was worrying her and he was sure it wasn't himself. 'What can you tell me about Patience Bailey? Did you talk to her much?'

'No, sir. She was companion to Mrs Ghent so we didn't have much to do with each other.'

Albert understood the hierarchy but he'd harboured a hope that the two women, isolated in the same house, had made some connection, possibly through the baby.

'Did she ever talk about her husband?'

'She said he was a corporal. Died near the end of the war.'

'In France?'

'I think so.'

'What did she do in the war?'

'She told me she worked in a hospital — giving out medicines and that. But she never spoke about it much.'

'Did she ever mention that she'd found herself another sweetheart after her husband died?'

A knowing look passed across Daisy's face. 'You're thinking the sums don't add up. If the little one was only seven months old then . . .'

'Did you see her with any men while she was here?'

'No. But she used to go out alone on her days off and I sometimes minded the baby for her. When I asked her where she was going she told me she was catching the train to see a friend . . . someone she knew from when she worked at the hospital.'

'Did you believe her?' He'd seen the sceptical look on Daisy's face.

'Can't rightly say I did. She might have been telling the truth though. Who's to say?' Her eyes suddenly lit up. 'I've heard she was buried alive. Is it true?'

'Who told you that?'

'Cook. She heard it in the village. One of the Rudyard lads told someone and word gets round fast in a place like this. Is it true?' she repeated anxiously.

Albert knew she was bright enough to see

through any lies so he told her the truth.

'Who'd do a thing like that?' she said with a shudder of horrified delight.

'That's why I need your help, Daisy.'

'I've told you everything I know. Honest. Do you think you'll find the little one? Do you think someone's got him safe?'

'I hope so, Daisy. I really do.'

As soon as Daisy returned to her duties he had a brief word with the cook, who came in from the village each day. Cook claimed to have had a happy working relationship with the mistress's paid companion even though she wasn't on gossiping terms with the woman. Mrs Bailey seemed a nice woman but she kept herself to herself, Cook said, adding that she thought she might have been a little shy.

After he'd finished with the servants, Albert returned to the drawing room and asked the Ghents for the name and address of Patience Bailey's former employer in Didsbury. It was a Mrs Esther Schuman of Belfield Road, and she was suddenly top of Albert's list of people he needed to speak to.

When he asked to speak to the Ghents' daughter, Mallory Ghent made a great show of climbing the stairs to knock on her bedroom door while his wife watched nervously from the drawing-room doorway. But there was no answer and the jazz music could no longer be heard.

'I'm sorry, Inspector, she must have gone out without telling us while you were speaking to Daisy. She's young. Comes and goes as she pleases.' He gave a shrug, his palms facing

76

upwards, as though he wanted to convince the detective he wasn't lying.

Albert left the house wondering whether his arrival was the reason for the daughter's absence. And, if so, why had she wanted to avoid him?

14

Esme Ghent had made her escape through the servants' entrance while the inspector from London was talking to Daisy in the breakfast room. The door had been left slightly ajar so she'd stood outside the room for a few moments straining to hear what they were saying, listening for her own name . . . or Sydney's. Even though Daisy was a sly girl and a lot sharper than she appeared she didn't know the truth about her and Sydney. How could she? Besides, Esme didn't care what the silly girl thought as long as everyone left her and Sydney alone. There were far too many ready to disapprove of people like Sydney in Mabley Ridge; far too many who didn't realise how the world outside had changed since the end of the war.

Sydney had introduced her to a new world of jazz, champagne and the white powder he'd persuaded her to sniff that made her feel invincible. He drove his motor car too fast; he climbed up the rocks on the Ridge without fear in spite of his wounded foot. He said it was 'just a scratch' and that others had fared a lot worse which meant he was a hero as well as being the most exciting man she'd ever met.

Her friend Betty had advised caution. 'Just be careful,' she'd said with an intense look that put years on her.

'The war's proved you have to live for the day

and squeeze every drop of pleasure from life,' Esme had replied defensively, echoing something Sydney had told her. 'I'll keep on seeing Sydney for as long as I want and I don't care about the consequences. I'm having fun for the first time in my bloody life.'

Betty had always been a bore and a killjoy and she'd shaken her head sadly like a headmistress telling parents that regrettably their child, having committed a major misdemeanour, had let the school and themselves down. Esme hadn't seen Betty since that day even though they'd known each other since early childhood.

The edges of the drive were thick with overhanging rhododendrons, their glossy dark-green foliage making the approach to the front door gloomier than necessary in Esme's opinion. If she had her way she'd dig the whole lot up, which would make the whole place look brighter and more up to date. But her parents didn't seem to care about things like that — not since Monty died.

Sydney had promised to wait for her at the gate but when she reached the meeting place there was no sign of him. However, Esme was undeterred because his house wasn't that far away so she could walk. Sydney had been adamant that she shouldn't tell her parents about their relationship but there were times when she longed to blurt it out, if only to enjoy their reaction — because she knew they'd disapprove.

She began to walk up the road, wishing her fashionable shoes were more comfortable, but when she reached Ridgeside Lodge there was no sign of his car so she assumed they'd somehow missed each other. Even so, she knocked at his door, just in case; when there was no reply she began to retrace her steps with a heavy heart, kicking at the gravel in the drive and creating a white cloud of dust that landed on the soft leather of her shoes, making them instantly shabby. It didn't matter — Daisy would clean them.

Then, just as she reached the road, Sydney's Alvis swung into the drive, missing her by inches.

As he opened the car door she pouted like a disappointed child. 'We arranged to meet by my gate. Where were you?'

'Sorry, darling. Had things to see to.' He hesitated and then his thin lips turned upwards in a smile that didn't spread to his eyes. 'Er . . . I saw that detective from London leaving your house. What did he want?'

Esme was surprised by the urgency behind his question, although she was careful not to show it.

'He came about the Bailey woman but I got away before he could collar me. I didn't want to have to suffer hours of questions. Too boring. He spoke to Ma and Pa and the maid and the cook but if he wanted me he was in for a disappointment. I couldn't tell him anything anyway. I hardly had anything to do with Ma's dreary companion and her brat.'

'The kid's not been found?'

Esme shook her head.

'Maybe we should look for it.'

'Why?'

'It'll be like a treasure hunt ... up on the Ridge. There's a few more hours of daylight left and it's a nice evening for it. I'll bring some champers. What do you say?'

Esme sighed. A walk on the Ridge wasn't how she'd planned to spend the evening but it might have its compensations.

15

Mallory Ghent's spirits lifted as he stood at the drawing-room window and watched the inspector walk off down the drive. He'd noticed Albert Lincoln's limp and when they'd been speaking he hadn't been able to take his eyes off the man's maimed left hand and the scarring on his face. He'd clearly suffered in the recent conflict and Ghent guessed from the look in his eyes that he was suffering still. He'd seen that same look on the men at the mill who'd made it back alive.

Before the inspector's arrival he'd told Jane to advertise for another companion but she'd looked at him as though he'd made an obscene suggestion. It was far too soon to think of replacing Patience, she said. It would seem disrespectful. Mallory couldn't see her logic. In his opinion there was no room for sentimentality in business or anywhere else but women, he thought, were like that, or at any rate some of them were.

The one he'd arranged to meet was quite different — so different that he felt a thrill of desire whenever he thought of her. From the first time he'd seen Dora Devereaux performing on stage in Manchester he'd been enchanted. Blonde and beautiful, she had the face and voice of an angel and he hadn't been able to resist accepting the invitation of his business acquaintance, Leonard Parms, to go with him to the stage door to meet her. Leonard owned a hat factory in Stockport and he'd boasted that he'd set Dora up in a little cottage at the other end of Mabley Ridge, handy for clandestine trysts away from his wife's watchful gaze. He'd introduced Mallory to his beautiful mistress because he'd wanted to show her off like a prized possession — a new house or a motor car.

It was a few days after this first encounter that a chance meeting in the village had sparked a change in the situation. Mallory had been driving to the station in the rain that morning when he'd spotted Dora walking down the street, her dainty umbrella held aloft. He'd pulled over and she'd accepted his offer of a lift with a flirtatious smile. They'd travelled to the station together and although they'd sat in separate carriages on the train they'd met up again on the station platform at the end of the journey and walked together in the direction of the theatre, sharing the shelter of his large black umbrella. The detour had taken Mallory out of his way but he hadn't cared because by the time they'd parted they'd arranged to meet for a meal after she'd finished her rehearsal. Mallory had arrived late at the mill that morning, feeling twenty years younger and irresistible. He'd never felt like that with Jane, not even in the first days of their courtship, which had been a plodding affair.

In Dora's company he felt like a romantic hero who could conquer the world and he longed to shout his love for her from the well-heeled rooftops of Mabley Ridge. And once Patience

Bailey had been installed in his household things had taken a turn for the better. With a paid companion his wife had become less dependent on his company, which meant he could see Dora whenever he liked with a clear conscience. He tried to convince himself that although Patience had gone his wife still had Esme around, ignoring the fact that Esme wasn't the sort of girl who'd enjoy sitting with a mother who'd never recovered from the loss of her son. He hadn't recovered from Monty's death either but that was a secret he kept well hidden from the world.

Without telling anybody where he was going, Mallory left the house and, after walking through the centre of the village, he made his way down the main road towards the open countryside. When he reached Dora's cottage near the cemetery he smoothed his hair and adjusted his tie. He'd bought some pomade from a chemist's shop in King Street and he could smell it as he walked. He wondered whether he'd applied the pomade a little too liberally and whether the scent would arouse Jane's suspicions on his return. Whenever he saw Dora he was in the habit of telling Jane he was at his club in Manchester, but as she'd been upset by the inspector's visit earlier he felt obliged to be home at a reasonable time that evening. With only a couple of hours to spend with Dora, he was determined to make the most of it.

He rang her doorbell, feeling like a teenage suitor as his heart raced and his palms sweated. He held his stomach in and raised his head slightly in an attempt to hide the roll of fat that had accumulated round his chin, the result of too many business lunches.

It was a while before the door opened. She always kept him waiting a little and he couldn't help wondering whether she did the same with Leonard Parms. There were times when the thought of sharing her was almost unbearable — although she always assured him he was the only one and she kept her liaison with Leonard going because she felt she owed him something for paying her rent. Besides, according to Dora, she said it didn't matter because she had enough love for two. He suspected she said exactly the same to Leonard on the nights she saw him but it was easier to believe her.

She stood in the doorway, the light behind her creating a halo around her blonde curls. Her generous lips formed a slow smile and her wide eyes held an invitation that made Mallory's heart leap.

'Mally, don't stand there on the doorstep,' she said, dragging him into the hall. 'I've got some champers in the front room.' She gave him a coquettish smile. 'To tell the truth I could do with some. The matinee audience was an absolute nightmare. I'm glad Dolores is doing my spot this evening.'

'So am I,' said Mallory, his voice thick with desire. He took her in his arms and her body seemed to melt into his as he kissed her.

'Lenny gave me a lovely present yesterday,' she said, breaking away to dangle a diamond bracelet in front of his face. He caught her meaning immediately.

'Meet me in St Ann's Square tomorrow lunchtime. We'll go shopping.'

If she'd been a cat she would have purred.

* * *

Sydney had used the search for the child as an excuse. The Ridge had a bad reputation and the locals tended to stay away, so they had the wild place all to themselves . . . which Sydney said was perfect.

He and Esme had walked to Oak Tree Edge where they'd sat on a rug drinking champagne and enjoying the spectacular view over the countryside to the distant chimneys of Manchester. Esme had giggled as she neared the precipitous drop, standing on the boulders and daring herself to look down before retreating to safety. Then they'd called out the child's name a few times, shouting 'Lancelot!' as though a seven-month-old baby could answer back, before making love on the car rug and opening a second bottle.

By the time Sydney drove her back home it was dark and when he dropped her off he watched as she stumbled down the drive in the moonlight, her feet crunching on the gravel as loud as a platoon on the march. In spite of the amount of champagne she'd consumed she moved fast, making for the light of the windows like a moth to a street light, and Sydney wondered whether the murder of Patience Bailey had made her nervous.

He sat in the driver's seat of the Alvis and lit a

86

cigarette. Then when that was finished he lit another to allow her time to get safely indoors because he couldn't risk her seeing him hanging around. She asked far too many questions as it was — just like her mother once had.

Ten minutes passed before he climbed out of the motor car, shutting the door quietly behind him. Then he began to walk towards the house, keeping to the sparse grass at the edge of the drive that struggled to grow in the shadow of the rhododendrons, avoiding the gravel because the last thing he wanted was to announce his arrival.

He crept nearer the house, his eyes fixed on the bay window which was lit like a stage set. The light, he noted, was electric. Only the best would do for the Ghents. He stood there like a hungry orphan gazing at the opulent interior, confident that the darkness rendered him invisible. He could see Esme's mother Jane sitting on a brocade sofa near the unlit fire, perched on the edge as if poised for flight.

He watched her for a while, wishing he was close enough to see her face, although that would have been too risky. Then he saw her shoulders shaking slightly. She was either laughing or crying but he would have put money on the latter.

And if she ever discovered the identity of her daughter's lover, she'd have even more to cry about.

16

The Station Hotel was more comfortable than Albert Lincoln was used to. He knew from his last visit in 1914 that it catered for businessmen visiting the homes of the local cotton barons, men who had high expectations and a low tolerance of bad service. As he sat at breakfast the next day he felt a little out of place as he noted the expensive tailoring and conspicuous gold watches of his fellow guests.

It was Saturday, a working day in industrial Manchester where time was money. Sunday was the sole day of leisure for most — that was after a morning in church and a heavy roast dinner. Stark had invited him to Sunday dinner and, although on reflection he would have preferred to spend the day alone with his own thoughts, manners dictated that the sergeant's invitation had been accepted gratefully.

The previous day a constable had called at the home of Mrs Pearce, the woman who, according to the Rudyards, left offerings of food at her family grave each night in the hope that her missing son would one day return, visit his dead relatives' last resting place and find sustenance waiting for him there. Grief, Albert knew, came in many forms and this denial was Mrs Pearce's way of dealing with it. The fact that the food was usually gone in the morning intrigued him. Perhaps it was taken by wild animals as Grace Rudyard suggested, but Peter Rudyard's sighting of the so-called Shadow Man opened up other possibilities if the boy was to be believed.

Mrs Pearce lived in a close of small terraced houses just off the main village street. There had been no answer when the constable called and her neighbours hadn't seen her, although one said she sometimes visited her sister in Northwich.

'Poor soul,' the neighbour had said. 'She hardly says a word to anyone now — nothing that makes sense any road. Her lass passed away before the war then her son went missing in action, then some months back her husband passed on too. Some people attract bad luck, don't they? Goes out shopping once a day, she does, and then she's off out again once it's dark carrying that old basket of hers. She's never been the same since she got the telegram saying her Harry was missing in France. Talks as though she's expecting him back any time. Such a shame.'

Albert had asked Stark to check the cemetery to see if any food parcels had been left since the night of Patience Bailey's murder but the answer had been no. Stark suggested that the police presence had frightened her off, or maybe what had happened to Patience Bailey had terrified her into seeking refuge with the sister whose name they didn't yet know.

Whatever the truth was Albert needed to speak to Mrs Pearce because there was a chance she'd witnessed something on the night of

Patience Bailey's murder. He'd asked for her sister in Northwich to be traced as a matter of urgency.

A letter with a London postmark had been waiting for him at reception when he'd come down first thing that morning, the address written in Mary's neat, almost childlike hand. She was in the habit of writing to him whenever he was away but he was never sure how to reply. She'd written to him when he'd been in Wenfield and back then the very sight of her letters had brought on pangs of guilt. Thanks to his infatuation with Flora Winsmore, he'd chosen to ignore those small paper reminders that he had a wife back in London. When Flora betrayed him in the most horrifying way it had seemed like a judgement on him for his disloyalty.

He opened Mary's letter at the breakfast table and spread it out in front of him, dropping a globule of marmalade on it in the process.

All is well here and Mother is feeling a lot better. We went to see the Reverend Gillit last night but he said Freddy was only coming through faintly. He said he was busy playing with some little friends and had become engrossed in his game. It sometimes happens with children, he said. I'm going back on Sunday and I have high hopes of making contact with our little one then. It's so wonderful when I hear his voice. I wish you would share it with me. The house is empty without you, Albert.
Yours, Mary

90

He'd often thought it strange that she always managed to say more in a letter than she ever said to his face, as though she found it easier to put her thoughts on to paper than into words.

He stared at the letter for a while, then wiped the marmalade off with his napkin before folding it and stuffing it into the inside pocket of his jacket.

His thoughts were interrupted by the sound of somebody clearing their throat politely. Albert looked up and saw Sergeant Stark standing there in his uniform looking slightly embarrassed. When he glanced round at his fellow guests Albert noticed some curious stares. Others studied their newspapers intently; perhaps those with guilty consciences, Albert thought.

'The post-mortem's been arranged for this morning,' Stark said in a discreet whisper. 'If you remember I promised to pick you up and . . . '

'Of course, Stark. Thank you.'

Albert followed Stark out of the hotel and allowed him to lead the way to the Cottage Hospital.

'Any developments overnight?' Albert asked, knowing the answer would be no. If Stark had had news he would have shared it by now.

'Sorry, sir. No. But I've arranged for some lads to come over from Macclesfield on Monday to extend the search for the little mite.'

Albert pressed his lips together. 'That should have been done as soon as you found out the child was missing.'

If Stark had been one of his underlings at Scotland Yard his words might have been harsher but he knew it was wise to keep the local officers on his side when he was working in an unfamiliar location. He saw Stark's face redden, as though he imagined the criticism was personal.

'What about the Ridge?'

'When we found the mother we'd no reason to suppose the little one was anywhere but the village. There was certainly no suggestion that the Ridge . . . '

Albert knew he was right. The murder of Patience Bailey bore no resemblance to that of Jimmy Rudyard, who'd been found on the Ridge lying like a broken doll on the bare earth in the centre of the ring of tall stones. He took a deep breath and forced himself to continue.

'If the child was taken by anyone with a motor car he could be miles away from Mabley Ridge by now.'

'Surely it wouldn't be anybody with a motor car, sir.' Stark sounded shocked at the suggestion that someone of a higher social standing might be responsible.

'Any news of Mrs Pearce?'

The sergeant looked crestfallen as he shook his head. 'Nothing and we've not been able to get an address for the sister yet. Neighbours say she's hardly said a word to anyone since her lad went. Keeps herself to herself.'

'We need to find her. She could be a vital witness.'

They walked the rest of the way to the hospital in silence and when they were about to pass the gates of Gramercy House Albert came to an abrupt halt. A mass of rhododendrons formed a tunnel over the drive, framing a view of the house at the end, white stucco like an Italianate mansion. He was about to carry on walking when he looked down at his feet and saw the stubs of several cigarettes. Somebody had stood there for a considerable amount of time; watching the house maybe. When he pointed this out to Stark the sergeant shrugged his shoulders and said it was probably the postman or the gardener — or perhaps a delivery boy. Albert couldn't share his certainty and as Stark began to walk on he picked up one of the stubs and studied it. No delivery boy, in his experience, had ever smoked such an expensive brand.

He took Mary's letter from his pocket and placed the stub carefully inside the envelope before catching up with Stark.

The Cottage Hospital stood down a side road, about two hundred yards away from Gramercy House, looking very much like a large villa, with an expanse of lawn to the front and large bay windows which gave the place a light and airy look. The mortuary was hidden tactfully around the back of the building and it was the local doctor who greeted them at the door. Dr Michaels was a well-built, hairy man in his forties who reminded Albert of a benevolent gorilla. But the doctor's hands, in contrast to the rest of him, were small with long, sensitive fingers that worked deftly as he made his incisions into Patience Bailey's naked body.

Albert focused his gaze on the woman's face. She had now been washed clean of the soil that had covered her and he saw that her hair was dark, almost black, and cut into a neat bob, the height of fashion. Her mouth was wide and there was a trio of small brown moles on her face: one on her chin, one on her cheek and the largest on her forehead. But these blemishes wouldn't have marred her attractiveness in life. She was a pretty woman, small and slim, and it was Albert's job to find out who was responsible for her death.

When the post-mortem was over Dr Michaels announced that he'd found nothing to contradict his initial conclusion. Patience Bailey had been rendered unconscious by a blow, probably from the spade which was later used to bury her; the spade that had been left there by John Rudyard who'd dug the grave earlier that day. As well as the head injury, there was bruising sustained around the time of death, probably from her tumble into the open grave. The doctor supposed that she'd been unconscious when her killer began to shovel the earth on top of her, although she'd managed to push one arm through the soil before she lost her fight for life so that it had protruded from the earth at the bottom of the grave. She must have suffered as she fought for breath but if she hadn't come round for that short time and the intended funeral of Mrs Potts had gone ahead as planned, her body would never have been found, which had probably been the killer's intention. Dr Michaels concluded that there was no evidence she'd been interfered with — which, he said, was a mercy.

'There is one unusual thing.' The doctor

paused like a magician preparing to stun his audience with the culmination of his most spectacular trick. 'I keep being told she had a baby. Well she didn't. This woman -' he gestured towards the corpse — 'has never given birth.'

Albert frowned. 'Are you certain of that?'

'I wouldn't have said it if I wasn't,' Michaels replied with a hint of irritation.

Albert exchanged a look with Stark who was standing open-mouthed; as lost for words as he was.

'So the baby she had with her wasn't hers,' Albert said, trying to make sense of the doctor's revelation.

'Perhaps she'd adopted it,' Stark suggested. 'Or she was looking after it for a friend.'

Albert gave the sergeant a nod of appreciation. His suggestion had opened up several new possibilities.

However there was one possibility Stark hadn't mentioned and it wasn't until they were almost back at the police station that Albert decided to share the theory that was bubbling through his head.

'What if Patience Bailey stole the baby for some reason? Perhaps she thought it wasn't being cared for properly and she could give it a better home. The real mother tracks her down and they arrange to meet in the cemetery. When Patience refuses to hand the child back, the mother kills her and takes the child.'

Now he'd put his new theory into words Albert felt rather pleased with himself. 'What we need to do now,' he continued, 'is to ask the station master whether he noticed a woman travelling to and from the station on the night in question — particularly one who came without a baby and left with one. And I need to speak to Patience Bailey's former employer in Didsbury — Mrs Esther Schuman. If anybody knows the truth about the baby, it's bound to be her.'

17

Peter

I'm fed up of that baby crying all night. Me mam said we were all the same at that age but I don't believe her. I'm sure I didn't make that racket and neither did our Jimmy.

Jack went out with Dad first thing to do the garden at that big house on Ridge Lane. It's the house where the dead lady used to live, he says. The cook there says our Jack needs fattening up so she gives him cake. I said why didn't he bring some cake back for me and he told me to get lost.

There's no school today 'cause it's Saturday and I'm going up to the Ridge. Our Ernie said I'll get into trouble if Dad finds out 'cause he says it's dangerous with all the old mines and that but I don't care 'cause I like the trees and the magic well and the ghosts and there's even a chance I'll see the knight like our Jimmy told me about in my dream. He was rescuing a lady 'cause she was ill and making funny noises but I've never told no one 'cause they wouldn't believe me. They never do. I like to go to the stone circle 'cause I hear Jimmy's voice in the trees there. He tells me things, magic things nobody else knows. Secrets.

Mam doesn't see me leave the house 'cause she's busy with the baby and when I get to the

Ridge I can hear the big black crows sitting in the trees laughing at me. I don't like the way they watch me with their mean little eyes and even if I wave my arms to chase them off they still stay there watching. There aren't as many trees as there used to be before the war 'cause some were cut down. Dad says they were taken to France to make trenches but I thought trenches were something you dug — like graves.

I want to get to the place where I saw the Shadow Man that time. I told that policeman about him — the one who talks funny 'cause he's from London — but I don't think he believed me. Everyone calls me a liar but I'm not.

I haven't seen the Shadow Man since I found the dead lady but if it was him who killed her he'll be on the run from the police. That's what murderers do. I read it in a comic once.

I'll be at Oak Tree Edge soon and you can see the whole world from there. You can look across at the mill chimneys far away and see the cloud of dirty smoke over Manchester and when you stand there it's like you're a bird flying above the fields and houses. Sometimes I'd like to be a bird so I wouldn't have to go to school. I like Miss Davies but I don't like the way the others laugh at my stories.

Some of the boys at school say the Devil's Grave's near the Edge and they're scared of coming here now 'cause the Devil might get them like he got our Jimmy. I said if the Devil's got a grave that means he's dead. I don't think the vicar knows and I think someone should tell him the Devil's dead which means he can't drag anyone down to hell any more. The boys say people have heard music coming from the Devil's Grave. I heard Dad telling Mam that people in the big houses listen to jazz and that's the Devil's music. I don't know what jazz sounds like but it must be horrid if the Devil likes it.

I can see Oak Tree Edge now and if I walk along the path for a bit I'll reach the stone circle where they found our Jimmy. They kept asking me what happened that day and I told them the rock opened up and a knight came out to take him away. But Dad said I was lying again and gave me a belt 'cause Mam kept crying as though she'd never stop.

When I get to Oak Tree Edge I cross the rocks till I reach the very edge and when I look down I get a funny feeling in my tummy 'cause it's a long way down so I step back and look at Manchester in the distance. Dad says thousands of people live there and the Cottontots have big mills where they all work. I like watching ants marching to and fro and I wonder if the people in Manchester are small like that. I might go there one day.

I get fed up with the view so I walk through the trees towards the Magic Well. I was scared when I went there first because of the face in the rock but then I drank the water and it was nice.

Miss Davies says I should write my stories down but my mam says I'll be leaving school in three years so there's no point in reading or writing.

As soon as I get near the Magic Well I can smell smoke, very faint like someone's burning leaves, but it's the wrong time of year for that. I think I'm on the wrong path 'cause there's big rocks either side like walls and I don't remember coming this way before. At the end of the path there's a big round place with bushes and high rocks all around like a huge castle and I creep forward like a soldier, making sure I'm hidden by the bushes. I can see a big dark hole in the rock about the size of one of the graves my dad digs and I think it must be a cave.

There's a puff of smoke coming from the hole so I creep away 'cause I'm getting scared but the bushes start grabbing my clothes like they don't want me to escape. I try harder to get away but they won't let me. Then he comes out of the cave and looks straight at me.

I recognise the big soldier's coat he wears. And this time the Shadow Man's got a face.

18

Gwen Davies was trying her best to read but it was difficult to concentrate. Out of the corner of her eye she could see Miss Fisher at her little writing desk, head down over a letter she was writing, a picture of concentration. Her mousy hair had escaped from its pins and Gwen saw her push back a tendril that had flopped on to her face.

Apart from the scratching of Miss Fisher's pen against the paper the only sound Gwen could hear was the ticking of the grandfather clock in the corner of the room and she felt a sudden urge to liven things up with conversation, although Miss Fisher wasn't the easiest person to talk to.

Gwen presumed that the rent she paid for her room was the woman's only income. There were many ladies in Miss Fisher's situation, spinsters who existed in genteel poverty; a sad sisterhood whose ranks had been swelled since the war because so many eligible men had been lost. Gwen could tell that the woman resented the fact that she had to let out a room to a stranger, although she was always polite enough to conceal her feelings.

There were times when Gwen felt that returning to her parents in Liverpool might be preferable to lodging with Miss Fisher. She couldn't bring herself to like the woman whose thoughts were so hard to read and whose moods were so unpredictable, but, even so, she experienced an urge to break the silence.

'Have you heard any more about that poor woman in the cemetery, Miss Fisher?'

Miss Fisher twisted round in her seat. 'I haven't, Miss Davies. And I don't think it's a suitable subject for gossip.' She made a tutting noise with her tongue to emphasise her disgust at recent events, yet Gwen noticed that her eyes were shining with interest.

'I've met the policeman who's come up from Scotland Yard to investigate. He was injured in the war, you know.'

'Indeed?' Miss Fisher turned her face away, a signal that the subject was closed, before returning to her letter.

Gwen watched her landlady for a while. It was hard to tell her age but Gwen wondered whether she was younger than she first appeared. Her skin was clear and her hair untouched by grey and Gwen had seen her studying herself in the mirror when she thought no one was watching so she suspected there was a streak of vanity somewhere in her nature. Her figure was good but her old-fashioned clothes, probably chosen by her mother who'd passed away just after the war ended, did her no favours. Miss Fisher had once told Gwen that the room she rented used to be the mother's and Gwen often wondered whether the old lady had actually breathed her last in the bed she slept in. Sometimes when she lay awake at night she imagined old Mrs Fisher lying exactly where she was lying, dead and cold. But she'd never asked Miss Fisher whether there was any truth in her morbid imaginings, partly out of politeness — and partly through desperation because digs were so hard to come by in Mabley Ridge.

Gwen had the impression that Miss Fisher's mother had been the domineering sort and perhaps that was why her daughter had never married. But who knew what went on in other people's lives? Nobody outside Gwen's immediate family knew her own secret — although there'd been times when she'd longed to shout it from the rooftops.

She looked down at her book again — a copy of *Prufrock and Other Observations* by T S Eliot that he'd given her during the war soon after they'd first met. She treasured the slim volume and often turned to the dedication he'd inscribed at the front for comfort — *Will you still talk to me of Michelangelo when we both grow old?* It had been a private joke between them because there had been a lot of laughter in their secret world. The dedication ended with *I give you all my love and more. Forever. G.*

She'd left Mabley Ridge that first time because she'd had no choice, and by the time she managed to return, hoping to be with him forever, she found it was too late.

Miss Fisher closed her writing desk and locked it, dropping the key into her pocket before standing up and leaving the room without a word. Gwen had often been intrigued about the contents of the desk and why she considered it necessary to lock them away. Perhaps it was just Miss Fisher's way of asserting her privacy.

She wondered whether there had ever been a man in Miss Fisher's life — a sweetheart killed in the war, perhaps — but the woman's reserve, verging on the secretive, had prevented her raising the subject, even in a general way.

Miss Fisher had seemed nervous since the death of Patience Bailey and as Gwen looked up from her book she had an uneasy feeling that if the murder had been a random act of violence then any lone women, such as herself and Miss Fisher, were under threat. Miss Fisher was in the habit of walking out alone in the evenings to various meetings and church events and Gwen herself had never considered Mabley Ridge a dangerous place until now.

She tried to banish this uncomfortable thought from her mind and returned her attention to her book. But after a couple of minutes the peaceful silence was broken abruptly by a knocking on the door; the sort of urgent rapping that often heralds bad news.

She heard Miss Fisher open the front door and muffled voices in the little hallway. Then the parlour door burst open to reveal Jack Rudyard standing there, twisting his cap in his hands.

'It seems this young man would like a word with you, Miss Davies,' Miss Fisher said disapprovingly as though she suspected Jack had come to rob her.

'Have you seen our Peter, Miss? He went off first thing and didn't come back for his dinner. Mam said not to bother you, Miss, but Peter likes you ... and he likes books and things so ... '

'I'm sorry, Jack, I haven't seen him today. Did he say where he was going?'

Jack hesitated. 'No, but someone saw him walking towards the Ridge. Dad told him never to go there. Not after . . . what happened to our Jimmy.'

'Perhaps we should tell the police.' She glanced at Miss Fisher, who was staring at the empty fireplace as though she was determined to ignore any potential unpleasantness. 'I'll come with you to the police station if you like.'

Since it was a warm evening Gwen left the house without a coat, placing her hat on her head and making a swift adjustment in the hall mirror on the way out.

As she walked to the police station she quickened her pace to keep up with Jack, and when they arrived the inspector from London was talking to a young constable behind the station's mahogany front desk. He looked round and smiled at her, apparently unaware that Jack was there too.

'Miss Davies. How can I help you?'

Gwen turned to the boy by her side. 'Jack, tell the inspector what you told me.'

Jack took his cap off again before reciting his story nervously, as though he feared the police more than his brother's schoolmistress.

The inspector hesitated then looked at his watch. 'Perhaps we should go up to the Ridge — see if there's any sign of the lad.'

To Gwen's surprise she realised she was looking forward to spending time in Inspector Lincoln's company. Then she felt a tiny pang of guilt. Was she being disloyal to the memory of the man to whom she'd pledged her devotion in the wartime years? But he'd broken his promises to her. He'd never left his wife. And besides, he was dead.

They walked up to the Ridge in silence, Jack hanging back a few steps behind. When they arrived at the little white tearoom next to the gate that barred the footpath, the inspector asked Jack to show the way, saying he hadn't been there for years and had forgotten the route. Gwen noticed he was careful not to mention the reason for his last visit in Jack's presence. She knew it was six years since Jimmy Rudyard was found dead up there but for the Rudyard family the pain had never gone away and she appreciated the inspector's thoughtfulness.

Gwen had never been to the Ridge before. She'd avoided the place when she lived in the village during the war and she'd had no reason to go there since.

'They say there are all sorts of hidden places up here that nobody knows about,' the inspector said to her quietly.

'So I've heard. The children at school talk about quarries and ancient mines, although I've never been here before myself.'

The inspector whispered a few words to Jack, who walked on ahead calling out Peter's name. Gwen, feeling she should be doing something useful, decided to follow him, calling out, hoping her voice would carry on the air. But only the crows answered, mocking her from the canopy of trees above.

When she glanced back she was shocked to see the expression on the inspector's face. He looked haunted, as though being in that place had reawakened unpleasant memories.

She waited until he'd drawn level with her. 'Is something the matter?'

After a long silence he pointed to the stones shaped, to the fanciful eye, like twisted figures condemned to perform some eternal round dance to unheard music. 'That's where Jimmy Rudyard was found, Peter's twin brother,' he said quietly. 'In the centre of the circle . . . just there.'

'Was it . . . was it some sort of sacrifice or . . . '

'The stones aren't ancient — they're a folly put here by the person who owned the land in the last century. But who knows what goes on in a killer's mind?'

She suspected he could be right. In spite of the circle's humdrum origins, the clearing did have an otherworldly atmosphere, as though countless generations had worshipped the ancient gods of the landscape there.

He started to walk away, as though he could no longer bear to be there within sight of the stones, and she began to follow. Jack had chosen another direction and she could hear his voice calling Peter's name, fading slowly as he moved away.

For a while the inspector seemed unaware that she was following a few paces behind him, then he stopped suddenly and waited for her to catch up.

'Where are we going?' she asked.

'It's a place called the Devil's Grave. Children used to play there.'

'Not any more. At school they say they're too scared to come up here since Jimmy died. Where did Jack go?'

'He didn't say. But I think he might have been heading for the great quarry. It's somewhere else they used to play before the war.'

A sudden breeze snatched at her hat and as she clamped her hand against her head to keep it in place she heard a whispering, there for a moment then gone.

'Did you hear that?'

'I heard something. What was it?'

'It sounded like voices. Children's voices.'

They both stood quite still, straining to listen, but all they could hear was bird song and the wind rustling the surrounding branches.

'I must have imagined it,' she said. Then suddenly the sound came again. A muffled giggle, as though someone was watching them, concealed from view.

She could see the inspector poised, like a hound who'd caught the scent of its quarry. The sound could have been coming from anywhere. Or nowhere.

After a while he walked on, ignoring Gwen as though he'd forgotten she was there. She followed him because the prospect of being alone in that strange, echoing place frightened her; a primal fear she knew made no sense but which at that moment seemed all too real.

'Where are we?' she asked.

'I think we're near the quarry now. Yes, I'm

sure this is the way in,' he said as he walked ahead between towering rocks that formed a sandstone passage slimy with moss where the sun never reached. He stopped to sniff the air. She could smell it too, a faint whiff of cigarette smoke drifting in the air.

Then she heard another sound, nearer this time, echoing as if it was coming from inside the rocks that towered either side. 'Shh,' it seemed to hiss. 'Quiet.'

The children in her class told tales of people vanishing up there; being swallowed by an evil creature that dwelled in the caves, hungry for human blood. She'd always dismissed the stories as ridiculous but now a glimmer of doubt was entering her mind. What if there were hidden mine workings and passages inside those rocks? Rather than meeting a blood-hungry creature, what if Peter was trapped inside, consumed by the earth itself and imprisoned in a living tomb?

She hurried after the inspector, careful not to break into a run.

19

They found Jack Rudyard standing in the centre of the quarry smoking a cigarette, taking a break in his search for his brother. Jack was insistent that he hadn't heard any voices so Albert concluded that either he'd imagined them or it had been the wind whispering between the rocks and vegetation.

As there was no sign of Peter up on the Ridge he walked back into the village with Miss Davies, leaving Jack behind searching for his younger brother with a promise he'd send a constable up to help him if necessary. For the moment there seemed to be nothing else either of them could do.

He could tell Miss Davies was upset about Peter. He'd seen her face when she stood on the rocks at Oak Tree Edge, looking down, expecting to see the child's broken, lifeless corpse stretched out below.

She'd talked of little else but the boy on the way back, telling Albert about his fanciful stories. Albert listened. Others might dismiss Peter's stories as the product of an overactive imagination but he knew only too well that there was often a kernel of truth in even the most outlandish fantasies.

He escorted Miss Davies back to her lodgings, wondering how she got along with her landlady. He remembered Miss Fisher from his last time there. She'd lived with her elderly mother and as a matter of routine he'd interviewed them about Jimmy Rudyard's death, along with everyone else in Mabley Ridge. During the interview the mother had done all the talking while the daughter listened, her eyes lowered modestly, inscrutable as the Sphinx. She was a young woman he'd barely noticed; grey and pale as a ghost, someone whose personality had been subsumed by a stronger will. But when he'd eventually managed to study her he'd seen that her mousy hair framed a pretty face with even features.

He'd felt sorry for Miss Fisher. In his opinion, her mother had been a poisonous woman who'd kept her daughter at her beck and call. He wondered whether Miss Fisher had managed to build a life of her own now the old woman was dead. Somehow he doubted it; the captive bird often clings to the security of its prison even when the cage door is opened.

When they reached Miss Fisher's front door he was tempted for a moment to ask Gwen if she'd like to eat with him at the hotel but he knew the suggestion was inappropriate. He was a married man, she was a single lady and this was a small village with eyes everywhere.

He walked away without issuing the invitation, guiltily aware of the attraction he felt. Gwen Davies reminded him a little of Flora, although her hair was darker and her features sharper; she even reminded him somewhat of Mary in the days of their courtship, before their world collapsed. He plunged his hand into his jacket pocket and felt Mary's letter there; a reminder of his duty. Last time he'd forgotten his duty he had paid a heavy price.

On his return to the police station he found Sergeant Stark at his post behind the polished front desk. As soon as he saw Albert he stood to attention.

'I need a couple of men up at the Ridge.'

'We're a bit short-handed, I'm afraid, sir.'

Constable Mitchell emerged from a back office. 'I'm happy to go up there, sir,' he said. 'Although they say there are caves up there so well hidden that nobody's ever found them.'

Mitchell was a tall young man with a shock of ginger hair. He looked as if he was barely out of school and Albert found himself wondering whether he'd managed to escape being sent to war. There was an innocence in the boy's eyes which suggested to Albert that he hadn't experienced the horrors of conflict. Perhaps the whole dreadful thing had been over before he could be sent to France.

'I've just been up there with Peter Rudyard's brother and his teacher and I'm sure that he would have called out if he'd heard us. But there's always a chance he might have fallen.' Albert did his best to keep the emotion he felt out of his voice. He needed to find the boy for his mother's sake but he wasn't sure where to start. Suddenly he felt helpless.

'He might be trapped somewhere up there or . . . 'The young constable didn't have to finish his sentence. It was what they were all thinking. Peter could have taken a tumble and be lying

112

lifeless at the bottom of some concealed pothole or ancient quarry, disused and hidden since the days of the Romans. There was a chance he would never be found.

Albert retreated into his temporary office. Needing to think, he sat at the desk and closed his eyes as the memories of all his past failures flooded back unbidden. When he opened his eyes again he took his notebook from his pocket. He couldn't wallow in self-pity if he was to catch Patience Bailey's killer and find Peter Rudyard alive.

He stared at his notebook, focusing on one name. Before she'd come to Mabley Ridge to work for Jane Ghent Patience Bailey had been companion to a lady in Didsbury: a Mrs Esther Schuman. It was a German name and Albert was surprised she hadn't changed it when war broke out as so many others had done — including the Royal Family themselves.

He returned to the front desk and asked Mitchell to telephone Didsbury Police Station and ask them what, if anything, they knew about Mrs Schuman. The answer came back sooner than expected. Mrs Esther Schuman was the widow of a respected cotton trader and she lived in a well-appointed villa in Belfield Road. Like many people in the area she was Jewish, he added, which meant that it would be best to call on her on Sunday rather than Saturday, the Jewish Sabbath. He promised to break the news to her and inform her of the inspector's impending visit, for which Albert was grateful.

Just as Albert ended the telephone call a boy entered the station and sidled up to the front desk. Albert recognised him at once as Peter Rudyard's brother Ernest. A couple of years older than Peter, Ernest was tall for his age and gangling as a young colt. However he was considerably smaller than Sergeant Stark and he gazed up at the man who towered on the other side of the counter.

'Me mam sent me. She says to tell you our Peter's back. Our Jack found him walking back from the Ridge.'

The station suddenly fell silent.

'What was he doing up there? Didn't he hear us calling him?' It was Albert who asked the question and Ernest turned to look at him. There was wariness in his eyes which made Albert wonder whether the boy remembered him from his last time there six years before. After a quick calculation he concluded that Ernest would have been six back then; he remembered him as a lively, happy child who'd seemed unaware of the tragic events unfolding around him. But now he'd changed to suit his name, subdued and serious as though the truth had dawned on him in the intervening years.

'He wouldn't say, even when me dad said he'd take his belt to him.'

'I'll have a word with him if you like,' Albert said quickly.

He saw scepticism on the boy's face. This was the man who'd failed the family six years ago so anything he had to say was bound to be useless. Ernest turned and marched out of the front door. He'd delivered his message. His job was done.

But Albert still wanted to know what Peter Rudyard had been up to during those lost hours spent on the Ridge.

20

Peter

I told the Shadow Man I had to be back before dark or they'd come looking for me. I thought he'd be cross but he wasn't.

When I asked him what his real name was he said it didn't matter. He said he was a ghost but I don't think he is. Ghosts don't smell like he does — not that I've ever met a ghost before. I told him I'd seen him in the cemetery and he made me promise not to tell anyone 'cause some very bad people are after him. I asked him who they were but he said it was better if I didn't know because they'd shoot him if they found him — or hang him, which was worse. I promised not to tell. Cross my heart and hope to die.

The Shadow Man said King Arthur's knights are hiding on the Ridge. I told him I'd seen one of them once but he said that couldn't be right because they were fast asleep in a cave with their white horses and they wouldn't wake up until their country needed them. I asked him where the cave was but he said it was a big secret and he'd found it by accident. I asked him to show me and he promised he would one day.

I thought I'd be scared of the Shadow Man but I'm not, although I did get a bit scared when he started crying and rushed into the cave to hide from the bad people. I said they weren't there but I don't think he heard me. He sat in the corner shaking all over with his arms over his head and I didn't know what to do.

Then he seemed to get better and he asked me to get him some food but I said I didn't know whether I can because me mam'll notice if food goes missing. Then he said there are a lot of farms round about so he can steal food if he needs it. But my dad says stealing's wrong so I said I'll try my best to bring him something 'cause if the police catch you stealing they put you in prison.

When I got home I kept my promise and never mentioned the Shadow Man but I told Mam about the sleeping knights and I said I'd spoken to our Jimmy's ghost. But she started crying and Dad took his belt to me again.

21

The previous evening Albert had toyed with the idea of visiting the cemetery lodge to make sure Peter Rudyard was all right and to ask him if he had anything more to say about the Shadow Man he claimed to have seen. In the end he decided against another encounter with the Rudyards. Peter had returned safe and well so for now he'd leave things be.

He slept badly that night, tossing and turning in his bed, throwing off the eiderdown and blankets then scrabbling for them on the floor when he began to feel a chill in the northern air. He wondered how Mary was faring back in London and he hoped the Reverend Gillit hadn't decided to take advantage of his absence to call more often. They managed on Albert's wages but he hated the idea of wasting precious money on what he saw as Gillit's fraudulent activities.

A while ago he'd asked one of his colleagues to make discreet enquiries about the reverend. He'd come up with nothing — as well as being a charlatan the man was clever. He would have liked to put a stop to Gillit but he knew this would leave Mary with no source of comfort. Besides, he had no actual proof of any wrongdoing. The problem went round in his head half the night until he fell into a fitful slumber in the early hours.

On Sunday morning he woke exhausted and at

breakfast he gulped down a strong cup of tea to wake himself up before tackling his bacon and fried egg.

Most of the businessmen who occupied the Station Hotel during the week had returned to their families so there was a dignified hush over the hotel's dining room. Albert tried not to feel self-conscious as he ate in the reverent silence, under the gaze of a team of watchful waiters. Once he'd finished breakfast he took out his watch and saw that it was almost ten o'clock. He intended to go to church that morning, not from a desire for spiritual comfort but to take a good look at the assembled village because, in his experience, you could learn a lot about a community by observing how people interacted with their neighbours.

He wondered whether Mrs Pearce would reappear at the service. Her absence was nagging away at the back of Albert's mind. Why would a woman who left food for a son she believed was still alive suddenly stop and disappear? Unless that son had turned up, on the run from the authorities, and she'd gone away with him; somewhere neither of them were known.

He put on his work suit and brushed his hair so that he looked presentable. Mabley Ridge was the sort of place where the wealthier ladies regarded a visit to church as a chance to show off their latest fashions, the fruits of their husbands' business acumen, rather than an opportunity for prayer.

He knew he'd see Abraham Stark in church. He remembered Stark from his last visit wearing

119

his Sunday best and singing heartily with his wife by his side.

As Albert walked down the street he passed a crowd of villagers on their way to church; the men in suits, the women wearing their best hats. A parade of cars, some driven by chauffeurs, purred down the road to park outside the parish church. Albert paused at the church gate, watching the passengers alight; the self-satisfied, prosperous couples eyeing their business rivals and doling out purse-lipped smiles: the Cottontots at prayer.

The Ghents were among the last to arrive. Their car pulled up at five to eleven, driven by Mallory Ghent himself with his wife and daughter in the rear seat. As they made their way into the church their social inferiors stood aside to let them go ahead while Albert held back, watching with interest. Mrs Ghent, he noticed, didn't look well. There was a distant, haunted look in her bloodshot eyes while the daughter, Esme, looked bored and restless as if she'd rather be somewhere else.

Once inside the church Albert took a seat at the back, glad that there was no room next to the Starks a few rows in front or he'd have felt obliged to join them. From where he sat he had a good view of the congregation and the divide between the wealthy and their servants couldn't have been more blatant if they'd been in the chapel of a great house. The Cottontots had their own pews at the front and from where he sat Albert had a good view of the Ghents, who were ignoring each other as though they were strangers, seated together by chance. He wondered whether Patience Bailey had attended church with them — or whether she'd sat in the back section of the nave with the servants and the villagers.

It surprised him that the vicar made no mention of her murder and no prayers were offered for her or her family. It was as though Patience Bailey was somebody the village would rather forget.

During the sermon, which was lengthy and tedious, he took the opportunity to observe his fellow worshippers, scanning each face and wondering whether one of them was a murderer. He'd done exactly the same when Jimmy Rudyard had been killed, studying each face and wondering whether the pious façade concealed a killer's soul. Sitting there now brought that memory back, sharp and painful.

There was no sign of Mrs Pearce who, so he'd heard, was a regular. Neither was there any sign of the Rudyards. Then he remembered from his last stay that they patronised the Methodist chapel down the road. However, he spotted Gwen Davies in the centre of the church sitting next to her landlady, although the two women hardly looked at each other. Miss Fisher wore an elegant hat and a pair of pristine pale-blue gloves which she fidgeted with while casting looks at the Starks in the pew opposite as though she was longing to remonstrate with the sergeant about the police intrusion the previous evening. Eventually she settled down, paying close attention to her prayer book.

121

Albert tried to catch Gwen's eye but she was looking ahead, deep in thought as though something was troubling her, so instead he watched Mallory Ghent and noticed how uncomfortable he looked when the vicar mentioned the words 'sin' and 'adultery'. Albert saw Ghent's wife give him a sideways glance which seemed more guilty than accusatory while their daughter, Esme, studied her well-polished nails as the vicar spoke, making no attempt to hide the fact that she was there under sufferance and she had better things to do. The maid, Daisy, sat near the back, wearing an inscrutable expression and a smart hat which must have cost most of her wages.

Sitting near the west door, Albert was able to be first out after the service and he was tempted to wait around to speak to Gwen, but the Starks had just emerged from the church porch, shaking hands with the vicar and exchanging pleasantries.

As Albert stood outside the church waiting for them he was conscious of being an outsider; an alien observer of a foreign race. When the Starks eventually joined him the sergeant shook his hand firmly and Mrs Stark announced that 'Sunday dinner will be ready presently.'

When they arrived at the police house that was home to the Starks, Abraham Stark discarded his suit jacket, a concession to the warmth of the day and Mrs Stark busied herself basting the roast potatoes she'd prepared before church in anticipation of having company for dinner. A small, plump woman with a round face, she wore a shapeless blue dress beneath a crossover apron. She smiled a lot and seemed full of nervous energy, as though she feared inactivity.

Albert couldn't help noticing that, although she chattered away, she barely looked at her husband, but he'd long ago learned not to dig too deeply into other people's marriages.

Mrs Stark was still speaking and Albert wondered whether her husband found it easier to let her do the talking for both of them. Albert smiled and made noises of agreement from time to time because he guessed it was expected of him. It was only when she began to ask what they were doing to find the missing baby that his brain began to register what she was saying.

'Is there still no sign of the little mite?'

'I'm afraid not. Everyone in the village has been spoken to and the search is being widened tomorrow.'

'Let's just pray nothing's happened to him.' She paused. 'I must admit I felt sorry for Mrs Bailey.'

'Your husband said you'd spoken to her once or twice.'

'That's right. I saw her in the tearooms all on her own and I invited her here with the little one for a cup of tea. I'd just made some scones and she looked as if she could do with a bit of feeding up, if you know what I mean. Nice woman, she was. I told you, didn't I, Abraham?'

Stark nodded meekly.

'What did you talk about?'

'The baby mostly. She was friendly enough but reserved. I thought she might be shy and if we got to know each other better she might be more forthcoming. But she never got the chance, did she, poor lass,' she said with a loud sniff. 'There are some wicked people in the world.'

'There are indeed,' her husband said.

'I saw her walking towards the Ridge with that poor little mite, you know. Pushing the pram she was.'

'When was this?' Albert asked.

'A couple of weeks ago — that's why I didn't think it was important.' There was a nervousness in her words. Albert had always assumed that she was the one who ruled the household but now he wasn't so sure.

'Where did you see her?'

'In Ridge Lane, between Gramercy House and the Ridge. I was on my way back from Jenner's farm — I'd just bought some eggs from Mrs Jenner and I'd stayed for a cup of tea. Anyway, I would have stopped to chat but I don't think she saw me. If you ask me, she had something on her mind and she wouldn't have noticed if a military band had marched past.'

'You think something was troubling her?' Stark asked.

His wife didn't answer, but her words had given Albert something to think about.

The dinner was good and by the time he'd finished, accepting second helpings out of politeness, he felt full and a little drowsy. However there was no time to relax after dinner because he'd arranged, through the police station in Didsbury, to pay Esther Schuman a visit to talk to her about her former companion.

The constable at Didsbury had told him Mrs Schuman was looking forward to his visit — which seemed like a good omen. And he didn't want to be late.

He levered himself out of the comfortable armchair and thanked Mrs Stark profusely for the meal. The praise made her cheeks glow and she looked positively coy as she shook his hand, making him promise to come again.

He looked into her eyes and saw anxiety there. Perhaps like Mary she too suffered from having a husband whose work deprived her of his companionship. Or perhaps she was blaming herself for not having been a better friend to Patience Bailey.

22

As soon as Albert arrived in Didsbury he asked directions of a smartly dressed middle-aged couple who told him that Mrs Schuman's address was close to the station. Finding Belfield Road was straightforward enough and when he reached the house he was surprised to see that it was a spacious detached villa, rather large for one woman. And yet, according to Mrs Ghent, Patience Bailey had left Mrs Schuman's employ because the house was too small to accommodate herself and the new baby comfortably. This had obviously been a lie, which suggested that Patience wanted to get away from Mrs Schuman for some other reason. Perhaps she was a strict and demanding employer and Patience hadn't been happy there. He was about to meet the woman so he'd be able to judge for himself.

A neat dark-haired maid opened the front door, looking Albert up and down with curiosity, as though a visiting Scotland Yard detective was a rare and unpredictable animal, the sort she would gawp at during a visit to a zoo.

She told him her mistress was expecting him and led the way to a bright drawing room lit by a tall bay window which overlooked the front garden.

Mrs Schuman had been sitting on a chaise longue near the fireplace but she rose as soon as he entered. She was a small, birdlike woman with a wizened face but there was a liveliness about her which belied her years and she looked positively excited at the prospect of a police interview.

'Mrs Schuman. Thank you for seeing me.'

'Tea?'

'That's very kind. Thank you.'

When the woman gave her maid a nod she left the room, closing the door carefully behind her.

Mrs Schuman sat down again and leaned forward as though she was about to share a confidence.

'I was so upset to hear about Patience. She was such a nice girl. It's a dreadful shame she was widowed like that but that's war for you.' She gave a sad little shrug. Although her accent was European, German perhaps, her English was impeccable. She examined his face as though she was an artist studying him with a view to painting his portrait. 'You were injured yourself I see,' she said, pointing at his disfigured hand.

'I got away lightly compared to many.'

'You're so right, Inspector. War's a dreadful business.'

'You lost someone yourself?'

'Fortunately not, thank God. My grandson David came back unscathed but a lot of his friends weren't so lucky.' She bowed her head, as if in respect for the fallen. Then she raised her eyes to meet his. 'Patience's late husband was one of David's comrades. That's why I took her in.'

'And the baby?'

127

'There was no baby when she first came to me.' Esther Schuman tapped the side of her nose. 'I have eyes and ears and I pride myself on being an observant woman but on this occasion . . .'

'What did you observe, Mrs Schuman?'

As she opened her mouth to answer the maid entered with a tray. Albert curbed his impatience as she poured the tea and handed it to him, asking whether he took sugar. He waited until she'd gone before repeating his question.

Mrs Schuman thought for a few moments. 'I must confess it never occurred to me that she was . . . in the family way. Of course she used to go out a lot — used to tell me she was visiting her friend in Cheadle not far away. Come to think of it she was rather quiet during those last few months she spent here, as though something was worrying her, but when I asked her if anything was wrong she said everything was fine. Then a short time later she told me she had to go away for a few weeks. She said her friend was ill and she needed to stay with her.'

'What happened?'

Esther hesitated. 'I didn't hear from her for a couple of weeks but I didn't worry because she'd told me about her friend's illness. Then one day she turned up with the baby, saying it was her friend's but she was ill so she couldn't look after it. She asked if it could live here with her. Now I'm a sympathetic woman, Inspector, and of course I asked her if she had something to tell me — hoping she'd admit that it was hers. Patience had always struck me as a very

128

. . . moral girl. But even the most upright of us have our moments, don't we?' she said with a knowing smile.

'What did she say to that?'

'She denied absolutely that the child was hers; in fact she seemed rather offended by my question. However she still wouldn't tell me the name of the friend or the man responsible for her alleged plight.'

'Did you believe her?'

She thought for a moment. 'I'm really not sure. I wasn't aware of her being sick or showing the usual symptoms of pregnancy but this is a large house and with this modern fashion for loose dresses with low waists it was possible she could have concealed her pregnancy until she went away to have the baby. Anyway I pretended to believe her story because that seemed the kindest thing to do.' She gave Albert a wistful smile. 'I told her that it was perfectly fine for her to bring the baby to live here. I miss having children about the place and . . .'

'Not many employers would be so under-standing.'

'Maybe not but . . .'

'Why did she leave you?'

'To tell you the truth, Inspector, I have no idea because I would have given her and the baby a home for as long as she wanted it.' The woman sounded hurt. She'd showed Patience Bailey kindness and it had been thrown back in her face; or perhaps that wasn't the whole story.

'Did she offer any sort of explanation?'

'She said she wanted to move to the country.

129

She found a job in Mabley Ridge and gave me a week's notice.'

'What about her friend, the one she claimed was the baby's real mother?'

'All I know about her is that she lived in Cheadle and that she'd worked with Patience during the war. Patience worked in a hospital dispensary and she told me her friend had been a nurse. I asked my grandson David if he knew anything more about the friend and he said he'd met her. He said she was a very nice girl.'

'What was David's relationship with Patience?'

'She was the widow of one of his men. I think he felt responsible for her welfare.'

Albert was reluctant to ask the next question but it had to be done. 'Is it possible the baby was David's?'

She shook her head. 'No. I could tell by the way he talked about her . . . interested but not involved, if you know what I mean. No, I'm quite certain my grandson wasn't the father. By the time you get to my age, Inspector, you can tell these things.'

'So what was Patience Bailey like?'

'She was a kind girl; the sort of girl who would take on other people's problems. If the baby was hers, as I suspect it was, she would have done her best for it. I'm sure of that.'

Albert wondered whether to share what Dr Michaels had told him; that Patience Bailey had never given birth, then decided against it.

Esther sighed. 'The constable who broke the news told me how she . . . Poor Patience didn't deserve such a dreadful end. She'd had a lot of

130

tragedy in her life, you know.'

'I don't know anything about her background.'

'Her parents owned a chemist's shop in Withington not far from here,' she said, making herself comfortable on the chaise longue. 'And she married a man called Victor Bailey who was a corporal serving under David. When Victor was killed in action David asked me to take his widow in as my companion because her parents had both passed away by then. I'm perfectly capable of looking after myself, Inspector, but I was glad to give the girl a home in exchange for some company.'

'Had she any other family?'

'She had a brother in Manchester and I think there was a sister too. I remember David saying she lived in London but Patience never mentioned her, which I thought rather odd. I believe there was another brother as well,who died in an accident when he was a child. As I said, what with that and her parents and her husband, poor Patience had experienced a lot of tragedy in her life.' She paused for a moment, as if something had just occurred to her. 'It's strange . . .'

'What is?'

'The family she went to work for in Mabley Ridge — the Ghents — their son Monty who was killed in France used to be a close friend of David's. They were at Manchester Grammar School together.'

Albert had often been told it was a small world but, after all his years in the police, he was always sceptical about coincidences. 'Do you think the Ghents employed her because of the connection?'

'That's possible, I suppose. Poor Monty was such a clever boy. He was at the university studying . . . ' She frowned, trying to remember. 'Science, I think. Anyway he was halfway through his studies when war broke out. He and David signed up at the same time but David came back and he didn't. What his poor parents must have gone through doesn't bear thinking about, does it.'

'You knew Monty Ghent well?'

'Oh yes. My daughter, David's mother, passed away when he was fifteen and my son-in-law, his father, married again which meant that David spent a lot of time here with me before the war.' She smiled fondly at the memory. 'He often brought Monty with him to see me. He was such a polite, quiet boy. Very studious. When I think of what happened to him . . . '

Albert saw that her eyes were shining with tears and he sat quietly, allowing her time to compose herself. After a while she dabbed her eyes with a delicate lace handkerchief, took a deep breath and gave him a brave smile.

'I'd like to speak to your grandson. If Patience confided in him he might know something about the friend she used to visit in Cheadle. Does David live near here?'

Esther shook her head. 'He's in London studying law. He's going to be a solicitor,' she said with grandmotherly pride.

Albert's spirits sank at this new obstacle that had appeared in his path. But all was not lost.

'May I have his address? I'd like to send one of my colleagues in London to speak to him. If he served with Patience's husband he might be able to help me find her family. They need to be told about what happened.'

Esther gave a gracious nod. 'Of course,' she said before reciting an address in Bloomsbury. 'I'm only sorry I can't be more help.'

'While Patience was living here did she visit her brother in Manchester? Or maybe he came here to see her?'

'He never came here and she never mentioned visiting him. Perhaps they didn't get on.' She lowered her voice. 'I asked her once what he did for a living and she said he worked for the government but there was something about the way she said it, almost as though she was ashamed.'

'Do you know his name?'

'It was Joseph, I think.'

'What was Patience's maiden name?'

'She did tell me once but I can't remember.' She closed her eyes. 'Now what was that chemist's shop called?' She opened her eyes again and sighed. 'I'm sorry, I can't remember. If you ask in Withington someone's bound to know, I'm sure.'

'Did you ever meet the Ghents, Monty's family?'

'I can't say I did but David used to visit them regularly before the war.'

'Do you know whether he's seen them recently? Did he ever visit Patience while she was there?'

'Not as far as I know. I'm sure he would have mentioned it.'

Albert paused before he asked his next question. 'Have you been told that the baby's missing?'

Her hand went to her mouth as if to suppress a silent scream. 'No. Poor little thing.'

'We're doing everything we can to find him.'

'Do you think he's still . . . alive?' He could hear the anguish in her voice.

'I hope so, Mrs Schuman, I really do.'

There was a long silence before she spoke again. 'I'll tell you one thing, Inspector. If Patience died because of some secret she was keeping — I'm sure it has something to do with that baby.'

23

Mallory Ghent drove home from church with his wife sitting silently in the back seat while Esme gazed out of the window. Over the past few weeks she had been distant, as though she was nursing some private and potentially explosive secret, but father and daughter had never been close so her thoughts were a mystery to him.

Though Jane Ghent still seemed preoccupied with the violent death of Patience Bailey, Mallory himself could feel no grief for the young woman who'd lingered around the house; always watching and, he suspected, always disapproving. She'd been too inquisitive for her own good. Once he'd even found her trying the door to his private place, although she'd pretended she'd wandered into the stable yard looking for toys that might have been left in the outhouse by previous generations. He knew it had been a lie — but now she wasn't around any more he had other things to worry about.

His wife had no inkling that he was pursuing Dora Devereaux and he wanted it to stay that way because it was his business and his alone. To his dismay Dora showed no sign of abandoning her relationship with Leonard Parms. He knew he had no right to be possessive but the thought of sharing her, of not being able to buy her exclusive company with gifts and trinkets, nagged at him like a physical pain.

Every time he closed his eyes and imagined Dora and Leonard together writhing in her bed, he wondered how it would feel to eliminate his rival forever. In his imagination he watched Leonard Parms draw his final breath and saw the horror in his eyes when he realised that offending Mallory Ghent had brought about his death, and as he enjoyed the mental picture he felt power coursing through his body. But he and Parms were gentlemen, prominent members of Mabley Ridge society, so whenever they met he treated him as a friend. He'd had plenty of practice at burying hatred behind good manners.

Once at Gramercy House he parked outside the front door and when Jane climbed out of the car he noticed her holding her stomach as though she was in pain. He didn't bother to ask her how she felt. Whenever Jane intruded on his thoughts he compared her to Dora and found her wanting. Dora was beautiful. Dora was vivacious, with a zest for life that filled him with new energy when he was with her. Dora was amusing and her imitations of his fellow Cottontots and their dull wives never failed to make him laugh. Jane hadn't laughed since Monty died and now she appeared to have assumed the role of invalid, barely eating and surviving on the beef tea Daisy brought her at regular intervals.

Dora had told him she couldn't see him that evening because, in her words, she had something tedious to do. Tedious was one of her favourite words and she could damn anything with those three syllables. He suspected the tedious thing was Leonard Parms and he was tempted to loiter outside her house to discover the truth. He couldn't help feeling like a lovesick schoolboy though he realised that such behaviour would hardly befit a man of his standing.

He needed a distraction so he turned to Jane. 'Tell Cook I'll be in for lunch,' he said tersely before leaving her side and walking round the side of the house to the stables.

The key was in his pocket. During morning service he'd put his hand in there to feel it and think of its comforting promise as the vicar droned on about loving your neighbour as yourself — a challenge in Mabley Ridge where the neighbours were business rivals all bent on outdoing each other socially and financially.

When he arrived in the cobbled stable yard he glanced back and saw that Esme had caught up with her mother. The two women were making for the front door, a double portrait of misery, and he waited until they were inside the house before tiptoeing past the kitchen door where he could hear pots and pans clattering and Cook singing a hearty hymn at the top of her voice: 'Onward, Christian Soldiers'.

After crossing the yard he unlocked the sturdy door beside the stables. Once the door had swung open silently he stepped into the gloom, careful to lock up behind him before he climbed the stairs to the upper room, aware that his heart was beating fast. He rarely had a chance to visit during the day and he was grateful for the light streaming in through the dusty skylight above his head as he breathed in the heady odour of death.

He stood for a while gazing on the tableau of dead flesh and with every breath he took he felt comforted. But there was a lot more to do before his work was finished.

★ ★ ★

As soon as she returned from church Esme Ghent left her mother and retreated to her room. Her father had left the car at the front of the house and she wondered whether he intended to go out again. He spent a lot of nights at his club these days — or so he claimed. Esme sometimes wondered — when she could be bothered to wonder about her parents at all — how her mother felt about his regular absences. Since Monty's death Jane no longer betrayed her emotions; it was as though something had died inside her when he was lost and she was no longer capable of feeling pain.

Her mother had gone straight into the drawing room and shut the door and Esme knew she'd be in there until lunch was served. When Esme reached her mother's age, she hoped her behaviour wouldn't be so predictable.

At least the police were no longer there, trampling all over the house and nosing into everyone's business, she thought as she reached the sanctuary of her room. She closed the door behind her and began to sort through her gramophone records; the ones Sydney Rich had given her. Sydney was older than the young men she'd known before the war, many of whom she'd grown up with, and she found it hard to believe how innocent she'd been before she met him.

She looked back on her naivety with embarrassment. Sydney had introduced her to the pleasures of sex and he knew the best music, the best restaurants, the latest cocktails — and other means of oblivion. Before she'd met Sydney her life had been restricted and humdrum, filled with dull girlfriends and even duller parents and relatives. Following the war young men were thin on the ground and many who'd returned were wounded or damaged in some way, not always with scars you could see.

All of a sudden Esme's musings were interrupted by a primitive cry of distress coming from downstairs followed by a loud keening; the same noise her mother had made when the telegram had arrived to tell them that Monty was dead. She abandoned the records and rushed out of her room, hurtling down the staircase to the drawing room. When she pushed the door open, fearful that something terrible had happened, she saw her mother slumped on the floor by the unlit fire, her face wet with tears and her body shaking with sobs. There was something in her hand; something that looked like a photograph together with a handwritten note, scrunched up in her fist.

Esme hesitated for a few moments, unsure what to do. 'Mother, what is it? What's the matter? Is it something to do with Monty?' she asked, her eyes on the photograph, wishing she could rip it from her mother's grasp and take a look at it.

Jane shook her head and tendrils of hair escaped their pins, giving her a wild look.

'What's that in your hand?'

Before she knew it her mother sprang up, grabbed a gold cigarette lighter off the mantelpiece and set the photograph and note alight, throwing them into the grate where they shrivelled to grey ash.

'What did you do that for?'

'It's better if you never know,' Jane replied, sinking to her knees.

24

Albert didn't feel like returning to the hotel after his visit to Didsbury. He found his room claustrophobic and he couldn't face the thought of sitting in the lounge pretending to read a newspaper. He needed to turn Esther Schuman's revelations over in his mind. Patience Bailey must have known the Ghents' late son Monty through her connection with Esther's grandson, David Cohen, and he couldn't help wondering why the Ghents hadn't mentioned this when he'd spoken to them. Perhaps they hadn't considered it important; or maybe there was another reason.

He'd contacted the police station in Withington and the sergeant there had supplied him with a name. Some years ago there had been a chemist's shop in the village run by a family called Jones. Albert's spirits plummeted at the mention of the all-too-common name, fearing that tracing Patience's family would take longer than he'd hoped. He pondered the problem for a while and concluded that her brother was probably his best hope. According to Esther Schuman he lived in Manchester and worked for the government so he was bound to find him eventually.

Whenever he needed to think in London he went for a long walk, making for the Thames to stare into its dirty grey depths, oblivious to the bustle of the city around him. There was no river in Mabley Ridge but there was the Ridge itself.

Before Jimmy Rudyard's murder it used to be a popular playground for young local adventurers but these days its reputation kept children away. According to Sergeant Stark, only those bent on self-destruction ventured up there now. A number of suicides had either hanged themselves in the woods or thrown themselves off Oak Tree Edge into the chasm below. Nevertheless Albert felt a sudden longing to go up there alone to contemplate the case.

When he arrived at the Ridge he took the path through the trees towards the stone circle. It was a path he'd trodden many times while he was investigating Jimmy Rudyard's murder and the action was automatic.

It took him a few minutes to walk there and when he reached the circle he stood in its centre and shut his eyes tight, wondering whether he'd imagined those faint voices in the breeze he'd heard during his last visit, distant and echoing as though they didn't belong to this world.

As he listened he thought he could hear them again but as soon as he opened his eyes the voices had gone. The brain could conjure all sorts of imaginings in a place like that, even bringing the dead back to life.

It was a relief to walk away from the circle and follow an unfamiliar path through the woods. In his opinion the whole area should have been searched for the missing baby but Sergeant Stark and his colleagues had seemed reluctant to consider the possibility that its abductor had left it to die in such a wild location like some Spartan infant abandoned in the wilderness. He hoped the local police were right in thinking that nobody would be that cruel. Even so, as he walked he looked around, alert for anything unusual; seeking some hiding place where a small body could have been concealed.

He took a narrow winding path which sloped steeply downwards and eventually found himself on the floor of what must have been a long-abandoned quarry. Cliffs of mossy rock rose on three sides, curtains of vegetation turning the small amphitheatre green in the dappled light filtering through the surrounding trees. The place smelled dank and he could hear water trickling somewhere, although he couldn't see the source of the sound.

All of a sudden he caught a flash of movement just out of his field of vision and when he turned his head he thought he saw a small figure, a child, vanishing into the rocks. He tried to follow but it had disappeared and he feared it had been a hallucination conjured by his overworked brain. A vision of Frederick perhaps — or Jimmy Rudyard. His head was aching and he shut his eyes, breathing in the scent of damp vegetation as reason told him that his guilt had made him mistake the shifting light for Jimmy's small, sad ghost.

He circled the quarry. The thick creepers hanging off the rock walls were cold and wet to his touch as he started to pull them aside. Then the blow came and he fell senseless to the ground.

He had no idea how long he lay there but when he came to the damp had penetrated his clothes and chilled his body. The raw stump, all that remained of his left hand after the shell had exploded in the trench, throbbed with pain and the rest of his body felt numb, apart from his head that ached as though a thousand soldiers were doing drill inside his brain.

He lay on the ground for a while, strange thoughts and visions flitting through his head. Flora was standing close to him, her face tilted towards his, inviting a kiss. Then she was lying on a bed reaching out to him and he experienced a sudden rush of desire, but with a great deal of effort he managed to block her out. Suddenly her face was replaced by that of Patience Bailey, distorted in death.

When he forced himself to open his eyes he discovered that he was in the centre of the stone circle, in the very place Jimmy Rudyard had been found. His last memory was of being in the quarry unless perhaps that had been an illusion; that and the ghost child.

He levered himself up, wincing with the sharp pains that shot through his body, testing his limbs and fearing he'd created phantoms out of nothing so that he could no longer believe what his senses told him. Tears pricked his eyes as he began to wonder what had made him volunteer to return to Mabley Ridge when he could easily have sent somebody else. Unfinished business, perhaps; the hope that, even after so much time had passed, he'd be able to identify the killer of little Jimmy Rudyard and bring him to justice?

At that moment that hope felt like vanity. He'd failed then and nothing had changed.

He struggled to his feet, sick and disorientated, wishing he wasn't alone there at the mercy of God knows what as the trees spun around him. He had the sensation of being watched and he suddenly felt afraid; the kind of fear he'd experienced when he knew enemy snipers were waiting ready to pick off any man unlucky enough to stray into their sights.

As he stumbled drunkenly out of the shelter of the trees and along the wide path leading to the road, he raised his right hand to his head and realised his hat was missing. He felt something wet and sticky and when he looked at his hand he saw it was red with blood. A small white building came into sight: the tearooms that catered for those ladies from Mabley Ridge who ventured outside the confines of the village, particularly in the summer months. He hesitated for a few moments before staggering towards it like a storm-tossed boat making for port.

25

When Gwen was living in Liverpool she'd often taken a stroll in Sefton Park with her sister on Sunday afternoons after church and dinner. Now years later when Sunday came round she was always eager to escape the confines of her lodgings, which increasingly felt like a prison furnished with chintz, china ornaments and antimacassars, although she'd never have dreamed of hurting Miss Fisher's feelings by putting her thoughts into words.

Miss Fisher was adamant that going near the Ridge was filled with risk, as though she imagined the place held more desperate criminals than the grim dockland courts of Gwen's native Liverpool. Gwen was surprised that her landlady was showing such concern when most of the time she kept her distance. But she made a solemn promise not to venture off the main road, a promise she had no intention of keeping as she set off wearing her most comfortable boots.

She needed to be alone. She needed to think about the letter she'd received from her sister the previous day. There had been no mistaking the coolness of Hannah's words. *I really would advise against visiting in your next halfterm holidays,* she'd said and later in the letter she'd even used the phrase *upsetting influence* which Gwen knew had come from the mouth of her

146

brother-in-law, Gareth. She could just hear him saying them, pious and mealymouthed in his disapproval of his erring sister-in-law. Gwen had never liked Gareth and he'd barely been able to tolerate her after what happened.

The walk up Ridge Lane seemed longer and steeper that day and Gwen's legs had begun to ache by the time she neared the little white tearooms beside the gate leading to the Ridge path. Yielding to temptation she made for the door.

The place was open and half-full of smartly dressed ladies — and the occasional gentleman — sipping from floral teacups and picking at dainty sandwiches and cakes. A table in the corner was free so she sat down and waited for the waitress to notice her and take her order. She was studying the menu when the door flew open, hitting the umbrella stand to the side of the entrance, and when she looked up she saw the inspector from London standing in the doorway, hatless, bleeding and dirty. She shifted in her seat, knowing that if he entered it would cause a stir.

A horrified silence fell over the tearoom as he stood there looking round, as though he was searching for a familiar face. When he spotted her sitting alone in the corner he beckoned to her with his good hand and she was suddenly aware that everyone in the cafe was watching her, hoping perhaps she would do something to cause a fresh scandal; something to be gossiped over in the village for weeks to come. Trying to hide her confusion, she made her way over to the

147

door to join him, her cheeks burning red as she noticed a hatchet-faced waitress in black scowling at her as though she suspected she was trying to leave without paying.

The inspector dodged out of sight and when Gwen emerged from the doorway she felt him touch her arm.

'I slipped in the quarry — fell and hit my head,' he whispered, looking round.

Gwen suspected he was lying but she imagined he had his reasons. 'You should get that cut seen to. I'll walk back to the village with you. We can call on Dr Michaels.'

'There's no need to bother him,' he said quickly. 'If you can just walk back to the hotel with me . . .' They barely exchanged a word as they made their way down the hill towards the village and there was something in his manner that told her not to probe too deeply into what had really happened. As they walked in silence, she couldn't help wondering whether there was somebody in Mabley Ridge who regarded him as an enemy; possibly a foe to be eliminated before he discovered some terrible truth.

She'd always been told that she had too much imagination, she reminded herself — rather like Peter Rudyard.

26

On Monday morning the pains that had prevented Jane Ghent from sleeping had subsided a little but she still felt weak and light-headed as she lay in bed clutching her stomach. Daisy had stayed up with her half the night, holding the bowl for her to be sick into, barely able to hide her disgust at the smell.

Daisy had suggested it was something she'd eaten but she'd hardly had anything the previous day and she hoped Daisy wouldn't pass on her suspicions to Cook, who could be a touchy woman at the best of times. Jane racked her brains, trying to think of anything she'd consumed that hadn't been shared by the rest of the household. All she could think of was the beef tea that she always drank before she retired to bed. Cook kept the packet in the pantry and Jane wondered fleetingly whether somebody could have tampered with it. But the idea was foolish; as foolish as the worries she had about Mallory disappearing mysteriously into the old storeroom by the stables whenever he was home and his furtive meetings with their gardener, John Rudyard, who'd turn up from time to time carrying something in an old sack. The storeroom was always kept locked and Mallory had given strict instructions that nobody was to go near because it was unsafe, which Jane knew was a lie.

Her husband hadn't been in to see why she wasn't at breakfast and she wondered if he'd already set off for the station. It was the start of the working week so the mill would be in full production again. Although the profits kept her in luxury, Jane hated the place and had visited it only once in the course of her marriage. She'd found it deafening and dirty and she'd been afraid of the wiry women with bold stares who'd worked on the clattering looms, tending them constantly like needy infants.

Another wave of pain engulfed her. Perhaps this was the next part of her punishment — the punishment that had started with Monty's death.

Daisy poked her head round the door. 'How are you, ma'am?'

Jane's reply was a low groan.

'Maybe I should telephone for Dr Michaels, ma'am,' Daisy suggested, although she didn't sound particularly concerned.

'No, Daisy. You mustn't bother him. Please,' Jane managed to gasp before collapsing back on to her pillows. If this was her punishment it was something that had to be endured.

The door shut, only to open again a minute later and when Jane opened her eyes she saw her daughter Esme standing by the bed looking at her with barely disguised distaste. Jane's head was hazy but, even so, she realised how the room must smell to a spoiled young woman unused to the sick bed. Esme had been a little too young to do anything useful in the war like volunteering to nurse the wounded. Until she lost her elder

150

brother her privileged life had shielded her from any form of suffering.

'I told Daisy she should send for Dr Michaels,' Esme said, backing away a little.

'There's no need for that. Can't you stop her?'

'Already done. He's on his way.'

'Is your father here?' Jane managed to ask.

'He left at half past eight.' Esme turned to go.

Jane dragged herself up on her pillows. She felt weak but this was important. 'Esme.'

'What is it?'

'I know you're seeing someone. Why won't you bring him to meet us?'

'Because who I see is none of your business.'

'You're my daughter. I need to protect you from . . . There are some bad men out there and . . .'

'Things have changed since the war, Mother. I'll see who I want to see.'

'Why won't you tell me who he is? Why are you keeping him away from us?'

Esme stormed from the room, slamming the door behind her, as another wave of pain gripped Jane's stomach and the tears ran down her pale cheeks.

27

Albert awoke on Monday morning with a headache. Gwen Davies had insisted on taking him to see Dr Michaels the previous evening and the doctor had cleaned and dressed his head wound, assuring him that it wasn't as bad as it looked. Because he'd lost consciousness, however, the doctor advised him to take it easy; advice Dr Michaels knew he'd most likely ignore.

Gwen Davies's ministrations had resurrected uncomfortable memories which had run through his head all night. When he eventually dropped into a fitful sleep, in the fleeting dreams that followed Gwen's face changed into Flora's and at first light he awoke suddenly, sweating and disorientated.

When he'd fallen and hurt himself in Wenfield the previous year Flora had tended his wounds. Her expert hands had been so gentle and he'd had no way of knowing those hands could kill as well as heal. Something about Gwen reminded him uncomfortably of Flora; some indefinable quality of self-sufficiency blended with the impression that she was harbouring some kind of secret.

He put a tentative hand up to feel the wound and was relieved to find the dressing still in place and that his pillow hadn't been stained with blood.

After he'd washed and dressed he forced himself to go down to the dining room for breakfast; as the man in charge of the investigation, he couldn't be seen to turn up at the police station late. Besides, he needed sustenance for what he knew would be another long day.

To his relief the dining room was quiet that morning and nobody stared at his white dressing. Since the war people had become used to seeing injuries and his newly acquired wound was trivial compared to most.

A waitress, a skinny girl with a permanently worried expression, hurried up to his table. 'There's a letter arrived for you, sir.'

She handed him a letter. It had a London postmark but he didn't recognise the handwriting so he knew it wasn't from Mary. He thanked the girl and as she scurried away he tore the envelope open.

A sheet of paper fell out and he saw the Scotland Yard letterhead with the words *This arrived addressed to you so I'm forwarding it on* written in a neat hand and signed by one of his detective constables. He shook the envelope and a letter fell out, postmarked Wenfield; his heart began to pound as he ripped at the flimsy paper.

How did she get away with it for so long? Who pulled the strings if not her lover?

There was no signature and the words were printed, suggesting that the author wished to remain anonymous. He imagined it was

153

somebody in Wenfield who had some connection to one of Flora's victims, which meant there were a lot of possibilities to choose from. There would be many people in that village who longed for revenge; people who were furious that she'd got away with killing so many before she was caught. He'd thought that nobody knew they'd been lovers — now it seemed he was wrong.

He screwed the letter up in his good hand, compressing it into a tight ball. He didn't want to be reminded of Flora. As far as he was concerned she was gone, although he couldn't feel the same about the son they'd had together. He often lay awake wondering whether the child was languishing in an orphanage somewhere or if it had been adopted by a loving family. The boy could be anywhere and Albert, his father, didn't even know his name.

On his way out of the hotel he dropped the letter into a waste-paper basket by the reception desk, eager to rid himself of any reminder of the most terrible mistake he'd made in his life.

Sergeant Stark was waiting for him at the police station and when he saw the dressing on Albert's head he asked him what had happened.

'I took a walk up on the Ridge. Slipped and hit my head.' He didn't want to discuss it but he feared Stark's curiosity wouldn't let the matter drop.

'Whereabouts?'

'In some sort of disused quarry. I just lost my footing. My fault for being so clumsy.' Albert tried to smile but found it hurt so abandoned the effort. 'Delicious lunch yesterday. Be sure to pass

154

my thanks to Mrs Stark.'

'I will.' He hesitated. 'Did you get to see Mrs Schuman yesterday afternoon?'

'Yes. She was very helpful.'

He relayed the gist of everything Esther Schuman had told him and saw the sergeant raise his eyebrows at the mention of Patience Bailey's connection with the Ghents' late son, Monty.

'So she got the job at Gramercy House through Mrs Schuman's grandson?'

'The grandson, David Cohen, was an old school friend of Monty's, although I'm surprised the Ghents didn't mention it. I really can't understand why Patience left Mrs Schuman's employment because she seemed more than happy to offer her and the baby a home for as long as she wanted it. Mind you, according to Dr Michaels, Patience wasn't the baby's real mother, which raises a lot of questions.'

Stark frowned. 'It's a mystery.'

'I need to talk to Patience Bailey's friend in Cheadle. Patience never told Mrs Schuman her name but I'm hoping David Cohen will know.'

'Isn't he in London?'

An idea was forming in Albert's head though it wasn't one he felt like mentioning yet. 'I'm going to pay the Ghents another visit. I'm wondering why they didn't say anything about their son's connection with the victim.'

'Perhaps they didn't think it was important.'

Albert sensed Stark was reluctant to bother the Ghents again, but he had no such qualms. 'I can see you're busy, Sergeant, so I'll go on my own,' he said and marched out of the station door before Stark could raise any objection. He could do without some obsequious local officer treating the Ghent family with kid gloves.

It had rained overnight and the pavements glistened with damp but it promised to be a pleasant day. Even so, there was a sharp breeze that made him keep tight hold of the hat he'd put on that morning. He was glad he'd had the foresight to pack his fedora because his trilby was still somewhere out on the Ridge. He told himself he should go back and look for it as soon as he had the chance, although he felt a nag of apprehension whenever he thought of that quarry with its shadows and dank, creeper-hung walls.

The fresh air helped to clear his head as he walked to Gramercy House. His meeting with Esther Schuman had convinced him that the Ghents knew more about Patience Bailey's history than they were admitting and he intended to get to the bottom of why the dead woman had relinquished her cosy situation in Didsbury for an unknown house in the middle of the countryside.

The door was answered by Daisy who looked at him suspiciously and said her mistress was indisposed and Dr Michaels was with her. Miss Esme was out and Mr Ghent had gone to his mill in Manchester.

'In that case I'll wait to see the doctor — ask him if your mistress is up to receiving visitors.'

As he stepped into the hall Dr Michaels emerged with perfect timing from the drawing

156

room, carrying his bag. He didn't look unduly concerned so Albert guessed the patient wasn't in any danger.

The doctor's thick lips twitched upwards in a smile of greeting. 'Good morning, Inspector. Fine morning. Any nearer catching Mrs Bailey's killer yet?'

'I'm hoping to make an arrest soon.' There was a selfsatisfied smugness about Dr Michaels that Albert found irritating. He was too confident and Albert wasn't sure whether this was a desirable trait in a medical man.

'Good. I don't like to think of the women in the village having to go about in fear of a madman. Mrs Michaels is refusing to leave the house unaccompanied. How's the head this morning?'

'Healing nicely, thank you,' Albert said, his hand travelling upwards automatically to touch his dressing. 'Is Mrs Ghent able to receive visitors? I'd like to have a word with her. Nothing arduous, I promise.'

Michaels slapped him on the back. 'Help yourself, old chap. She was up all night with a bad stomach, that's all.'

'What caused it?'

'Could be a chill; could be a touch of food poisoning. These things happen in the best-run households. She'll be right as rain by teatime.'

Daisy was holding the doctor's hat and when she handed it to him Albert saw him give her a wink, at which she blushed. As soon as Michaels walked out of the front door Albert spoke to her.

'If you'd tell Mrs Ghent I'm here.'

157

For a moment Daisy looked as though she was about to refuse. Then she disappeared into the drawing room, emerging a few moments later.

'The mistress'll see you but she says not to be long. She's not feeling too good.'

Albert found Jane Ghent stretched out on the chaise longue. Her flesh was pale and there were dark circles beneath her eyes. She looked exhausted and Albert suddenly regretted the intrusion.

'I'm sorry to disturb you, Mrs Ghent, but the doctor said you were well enough to speak to me.'

She gave a loud sniff. 'I sometimes think that man has no sympathy. He worked at a military hospital during the war, you know, and I think he saw so many terrible injuries there that he considers the rest of us to be malingerers.' She turned her head away and winced as though she was still in pain.

Albert took a seat opposite the chaise longue where he had a good view of the woman's face. 'I visited Esther Schuman yesterday — Patience Bailey's former employer. You were kind enough to give me her address.'

'I remember.'

'Mrs Schuman told me her grandson, David, was a close friend of your late son, Monty.'

She nodded.

'Did Mrs Bailey come here because of the connection?'

'I interviewed a number of candidates, none of whom seemed particularly . . . right. Then my late son's friend said he knew of a lady who might be interested in the post — a war widow with a child. She seemed most suitable.'

'You employed her on David Cohen's recommendation?'

'I've known David for some years and consider him entirely trustworthy. Monty was very fond of him.'

'Did you know the child wasn't Mrs Bailey's?'

Albert saw a look of disbelief on her face that couldn't have been faked.

'That's ridiculous. Why would she say somebody else's baby was her own? And if she was looking after it for a relative, why wouldn't she have said so?'

'Did David Cohen say anything to you about the baby?'

'No, he didn't. I haven't seen him since he recommended Mrs Bailey for the post. He's in London I understand.' She paused and looked up as though she'd suddenly had a brilliant idea. 'You don't think David could be the father, do you? If he'd formed an alliance with some girl and saw getting a respectable widow to take on the baby as the best way out of his predicament . . . '

It was a possibility Albert was beginning to favour and now Jane Ghent had put it into words it sounded perfectly feasible.

'Perhaps your husband might know more.'

'No.' She snapped the word, as though the idea of her husband's involvement horrified her. 'He barely knew David and he rarely spoke to Patience.' Her hand fluttered to her chest. 'I'd be grateful if you'd leave now. I don't feel well.'

Albert stood up. 'I'm sorry to have bothered you, Mrs Ghent. Thank you for your time.'

When he left the room he found Daisy hovering at the foot of the staircase. He wondered if she'd been eavesdropping and he was surprised when she hurried away without bothering to show him out. Then there was a cockiness about Daisy that suggested she wasn't the most deferential of servants. He took his hat from the stand by the front door and was about to let himself out when he heard a voice.

'Sir. Can I speak to you?'

He turned and saw a plump woman wiping her hands on her food-stained apron. Her cheeks were red with broken veins and her sleeves were rolled up to expose her chubby arms. She introduced herself as Mrs Foster, the cook.

She looked worried; more than worried, frightened, and he allowed her to lead him towards the back of the house, to a small, shabby room with faded chintz armchairs and battered pine furniture that she obviously used as her sitting room. She sat down, glancing at the door nervously, as though she feared being inter-rupted . . . or overheard.

'What can I do for you, Mrs Foster?'

For a while she didn't speak as though she was choosing her words carefully. Albert knew he had to be patient. If he rushed her she might change her mind.

'I think Mrs Ghent's being poisoned,' she said eventually, the words emerging in a breathless rush. 'She ate exactly the same as everyone else yesterday and they were all as right as rain.'

'Are you sure?'

'Of course I am. And nobody's ever made any complaints about my cooking.' Albert could tell she was indignant about the imagined slur on her professional ability. 'The only thing she had that the others didn't was her usual beef tea. I've thrown the packet away . . . just in case. I don't want to get the blame.'

'Of course not.' Albert wasn't sure whether the supposed poisoning was in the cook's imagination but something must have triggered her suspicion and he wanted to know what it was. 'What makes you think she might have been poisoned?'

She glanced at the door. The top half consisted of glass panes so anybody outside in the passage could be seen. 'It's Mr Ghent,' she whispered. 'I think something's going on.'

'You think he's trying to poison his wife?'

The woman lowered her voice. 'There's a door off the stable yard — used to be a storeroom but it hasn't been used since the chauffeur left. Mr Ghent had a new lock fitted a few months ago and nobody's allowed to go near it. I've seen him go in there and not come out for hours. And I'm sure he has a lady friend. A maid who works in one of the houses at the other end of the village has seen him going into a cottage near the cemetery and — '

Albert willed her to carry on. He'd learned as much from gossip in the course of his career as he had during formal interviews. But her words dried up so he had to prompt. 'Do you know who lives there?'

161

Mrs Foster's eyes flickered towards the closed door again. 'I've heard an actress has taken the place.' The word actress was said with a mixture of awe and disapproval. 'Although I've never seen her. I've heard she has other gentleman callers too . . . including Mr Parms who my friend works for.'

'So you're suggesting that Mr Ghent is in the habit of visiting an actress?'

Mrs Foster's mouth opened but she shut it again before she could say anything. Albert guessed she had no real evidence for her allegations and that she was beginning to regret being so candid. It was up to him to persuade her to keep on talking.

'Sometimes servants hear things that make all the difference to an investigation. You want to help me catch Mrs Bailey's killer, don't you?'

'Of course but . . . '

'It can be the smallest thing — something you don't think important. How did Mr Ghent get on with Mrs Bailey? Did you ever hear them talking?'

She shook her head. 'I never had much to do with Mrs Bailey or her little one but as far as I know her and Mr Ghent hardly said a word to each other.'

Albert smiled. 'Will you show me the locked door you told me about?'

Mrs Foster hesitated. 'I don't know if I should. Mr Ghent wouldn't like it.'

'Mr Ghent's not here. You don't know where he keeps the key by any chance?'

The cook shook her head. Then she stood up

162

and, after checking there was nobody about, she led the way to the back door and Albert followed her into a cobbled courtyard. She led him to a solid door a few feet away from the wide stable doors that stood half open to reveal a large and shiny vehicle parked in the shadows.

Albert tried the door. When it failed to budge he pushed harder but, despite his best efforts, it didn't give way under his weight. He examined the lock, which looked new and strong.

'Please, Inspector. Come away. You might be seen.' He heard panic in the cook's voice so, not wishing to alarm her, he did as she asked.

'What do you think is in there?' he asked as they made their way back into the house.

She stopped and looked him in the eye, a steady, fearful gaze. 'I've seen John Rudyard, the gardener, sneaking about in the yard with a sack. Now he's not a man to cross.' She clicked her tongue in disapproval. 'And that Daisy was hanging round there the other day. I know that silly girl's no better than she ought to be but I fear for her, I really do.'

28

The cottage on the road to the cemetery looked an innocent sort of place: pretty, half-timbered and slightly crooked with a rose bearing late pink blooms climbing up a trellis to the left of the front door. The diamondpane windows sparkled in the sunlight. It looked like a cottage from a fairy tale, although Albert knew fairytale cottages could harbour child-eating witches.

After Patience Bailey's body was found the cottage would have been visited in the course of routine door-to-door enquiries. But now Albert had discovered the connection between the woman who lived there and the dead woman's employer the occupant needed to be spoken to again.

The cottage was home to Dora Devereaux and Albert wondered if this was her real name or some glamorous-sounding pseudonym adopted for the stage. He'd met a few actresses in the course of his Scotland Yard career and found them a mixed bunch. Some were respectable married ladies while others, at the lower end of the market as it were, were the sort of women his mother used to warn him against. He was looking forward to finding out which category Miss Devereaux fell into.

She answered the door wearing a flowing silk frock, cut low at the neck to reveal a good deal of decolletage, and when Albert took off his hat and introduced himself her expression changed from one of polite interest to resignation.

'I suppose you want to come in,' she said, turning her back and walking ahead into the low-beamed drawing room. Albert followed, trying to take his eyes off her wiggling walk and focus instead on the bottle-blonde curls which suited her delicate features. He sensed she was conscious of the impression she was making as she sat back on a velvet sofa and patted the space beside her. Albert sat down in the armchair opposite.

'I've already had a visit from a very nice young constable. He asked me if I'd seen anything on the night that poor woman was murdered but I hadn't.' She shuddered. 'It's awful. You're not safe anywhere nowadays.' Her accent was upper-crust but every now and then Albert could detect some Northern vowels.

'Where were you that night?'

'At the theatre. Where else would I be?'

'Which theatre?'

'The Royal Hippodrome in Manchester. I'm in *Fielding's Follies*. It's a review.'

'You sing?'

She gave him a coquettish look. 'You have to have a lot of strings to your bow in my job.'

There was no mistaking the invitation in her last reply but Albert remained resolutely businesslike. 'What time did you get home from the theatre?'

'Around midnight, but I didn't see anything or I'd have told the constable.' She widened her eyes, the picture of innocence.

'Are you acquainted with a man called

165

Mallory Ghent? The woman who died worked for his wife.'

She studied her painted fingernails. 'Can't say the name's familiar. Still, I meet a lot of people.'

'He was seen calling here.'

'Whoever told you that needs spectacles.' The answer came instantly and Albert almost found himself believing her.

'Did you ever meet Patience Bailey, the woman who died?'

'No.'

'She had a baby with her. It's missing.'

She looked up, her face expressionless. 'There's no baby here, I promise you. You can search the place if you like.'

'That won't be necessary.' Albert stood up. 'Thank you for your time, Miss Devereaux.'

'Will you call again? I'd like to know if you find that baby. Do you think it's all right?' There was a hint of anxiety in her voice now as the mask of nonchalance slipped for a moment, showing a more human side. 'Not that it's any of my business, of course,' she added casually. 'But it'd be nice to know.'

Albert allowed her to show him out and as she walked ahead his instinct told him she wouldn't admit to any connection with Mallory Ghent unless she was confronted with more evidence, which he didn't have. Besides, he couldn't be sure it was relevant anyway.

He walked back to the police station, his mind on Mallory Ghent's locked room. It clearly worried the cook but perhaps she was allowing her imagination to run away with her. However,

Mallory Ghent had gone to the trouble of fitting a new lock, which suggested there was something in there he didn't want the world to see. Albert was curious to look inside yet he could hardly order a search of the home of a man of Ghent's standing without a very good reason. Besides, any local magistrate who was asked to approve a warrant would probably be Ghent's friend or business acquaintance, which meant Albert would have to tread carefully for the time being.

He arrived at the station to find Stark behind the front desk. He looked up as Albert came in and reached below the desk to pull something out.

'Someone from the hotel brought this down — came in the lunchtime post.' He produced a brown envelope and handed it to Albert who recognised it as coming from Scotland Yard again. He wished his colleagues there would be more selective when it came to forwarding his post but he supposed they couldn't know what was important and what wasn't.

He was aware of the sergeant watching him, eager to satisfy his curiosity, but Albert took the envelope into the office which was his for the duration and closed the door.

The first letter he'd received from London that day had been anonymous and he feared this one would be too. His hands were shaking as he tore at the paper and when he drew out the letter inside he saw that the single sheet had been signed at the bottom by Sam Poltimore.

Dear Inspector Lincoln,
I thought you'd want to know that the

prison chaplain at Strangeways has been in touch on the telephone. He asked for you and when I said you were unavailable he asked me to pass on a message that he'd like to speak to you in confidence and I said I'd let you know.

He went on to give a brief account of developments in a couple of their cases before signing off.

Hope the investigation is going well up North. Strange that it's in the same village where that poor little lad was murdered in '14. Any chance it's the same culprit?
Yours truly, Sam Poltimore (Sergeant)

Albert dropped the letter on to the desk and stared at it. If the prison chaplain wanted to speak to him it could only be about Flora . . . or what had become of her child. Now the tantalising possibility was dangled in front of him he suddenly felt apprehensive. Whenever he'd made discreet enquiries before he'd hit a brick wall of bureaucracy and awkward questions, and he wasn't sure what he'd say if he came face to face with the chaplain because the last thing he wanted to do was reveal his darkest secret to the world. On impulse he dropped the letter into the waste-paper basket. It was a problem he couldn't face just now.

29

Peter

The Shadow Man shows me things. Birds' nests and places where foxes hide with their cubs. He knows everything about the Ridge. He knows about the quarries and how the men used to haul the stone in carts down the cobbled paths. Sometimes he shouts at me to go away and leave him alone and he holds his head as though it's hurting. I don't like it when he does that and I asked him if he wanted Dr Michaels to come and see him but he used words me mam says are wicked; if I used those words she'd wash my mouth out with soap.

I didn't go back to school this afternoon 'cause I wanted to see the Shadow Man and take him some food 'cause he said he's hungry. I told our Ernie to tell Miss Davies I was poorly. At Sunday School they say you shouldn't tell lies but if I hadn't I wouldn't be able to go up to the Ridge and take the Shadow Man some of me mam's cake and he'd be hungry and Jesus fed hungry people so I'm sure He won't mind that I told a fib.

When I reach his special place I stand and wait then he appears out of nowhere and I give him the cake all wrapped up in greaseproof paper. I took it from the larder and I know that's stealing but he really needs it 'cause Mrs Pearce doesn't leave food for him any more and he might starve to death.

He's wearing his big army coat even though the weather's quite warm. And he's wearing a hat like the one the inspector from London wears. It looks new and I wonder whether he bought it — or maybe he stole it from someone.

He must be hungry 'cause he eats the cake so quick then he asks if I've got any more. When I say no he looks cross and I'm a bit scared.

'Have you heard anything about the lady in the cemetery?' he says. 'Do the police know who killed her yet?'

He speaks posh like a Cottontot and I want to ask him why but I don't dare.

'Did you know her then?'

The Shadow Man doesn't answer and he walks back to his cave. But when I try to follow him he shouts at me to go away.

'Go home and don't come here again. You're a bloody nuisance.'

I want to ask him what he was doing in the cemetery on the night the lady was killed but I don't dare so I run all the way home.

30

Peter Rudyard hadn't turned up at school that afternoon. According to his brother he'd felt ill when he'd gone home at lunchtime but something about the way Ernie said it made Gwen Davies suspect this was a lie.

She couldn't shake off the uneasy feeling that something was wrong at the cemetery lodge. She'd always been wary of John and Grace Rudyard. John had developed a reputation for violence since he'd returned from the war, especially when he'd taken too much drink, and she was sure Grace thought of her as an interfering do-gooder who had no idea how the world of the Rudyards functioned. However she wanted to find out what was wrong with Peter because she feared he knew more about Patience Bailey's death than he'd admitted.

As soon as the school day was over she walked to the cemetery lodge and knocked on the door, her heart beating fast. She'd brought some books with her, tied together with string for ease of carrying, and when Grace Rudyard opened the door and stood blocking the way, arms folded, she held them in front of her like a shield.

'May I speak to Peter please, Mrs Rudyard?' She tried to smile, fearing it looked more like a grimace of pain. 'Ernest told me he wasn't well. I do hope he's feeling better.'

Grace Rudyard eyed the books and sniffed.

Then she cleared her throat. 'Peter's not here.'

'Do you know where he is?'

'I thought he was at school.' She sniffed again. 'He'll be in big trouble when his dad finds out.'

Gwen's heart sank as she realised her intrusion had probably earned the lad a beating and she cursed her lack of forethought.

'Can you give him these, please? He tells me he's interested in wildlife and I promised I'd let him borrow them,' she lied, holding out the books like an offering. 'There's a copy of *A Midsummer Night's Dream* here for him too. My class are going to start reading some Shakespeare and I thought Peter would enjoy it.'

A slight smirk appeared on the woman's face and she looked at the books with distaste as she took them, as though she feared they were contaminated.

'Do you think Ernie or Maud might know where he is?'

'Doubt it. He's a law unto himself is our Peter.'

A baby started crying inside the house; Peter's little brother making himself heard. But Gwen didn't want to let Grace go just yet. 'Aren't you worried about him?'

'He'll turn up. He did the same on Saturday, remember, and then he came strolling in like nothing had happened. I've given up worrying.'

Gwen sensed that Grace was anxious to bring the conversation to a close. Peter's absence would have sent most parents frantic with worry but his mother seemed unconcerned, which surprised her. After losing one twin to murder, she would have expected her to be more protective of the other.

After she heard the front door of the lodge slam shut behind her, instead of returning to the road she took the path through the cemetery, walking between the graves and heading for the place where Patience Bailey's body had been found. Instinctively she turned her head to make sure she wasn't being watched from the lodge. When she saw no face in the window and no tell-tale movement of the faded curtains she carried on.

She made her way to the edge of the cemetery, to the area by the wall that had been neglected by John Rudyard's lawnmower, and looked around for some wild flowers to pick before realising it was too late in the season for the buttercups, tall daisies and poppies she usually gathered in a cheerful bunch; a tribute of sorts to the one she'd lost. All she could see was a pair of late roses blooming on a nearby bush and she picked them, scratching her hand as she did so but determined to ignore the pain.

As she retraced her steps she noticed a small patch of grass a few feet away that looked different from the ground around it. On closer inspection, it was clear that a rectangle of turf had been removed and then replaced, leaving a slight mound as though someone had buried an animal there in consecrated ground. A beloved pet, perhaps. She knew Peter liked to hold funerals for dead wildlife he found so she assumed it was the last resting place of some unfortunate bird or rodent until she remembered him saying how he liked to create elaborate little graves for the creatures he buried, edged with stones with a pious little cross made of sticks to mark the spot.

She hadn't time for speculation now. She walked past the site of Patience Bailey's violent death, now a grave occupied by old Mrs Potts marked by a dome of bare soil and a heap of fading flowers, making for another grave nearby, an opulent affair with a sparkling marble headstone. Here she knelt on the damp earth to lay the roses she'd picked in the centre of the grave before kissing her fingers and running them over the black letters incised in the white marble.

GEORGE SEDDING.
20 JUNE 1870 — 4 NOVEMBER 1919.

ALSO HIS SON, SAMUEL
WHO DIED IN THE SERVICE
OF HIS COUNTRY 15 MAY 1918.

ETERNAL REST GRANT THEM, O LORD.

She wiped her sleeve across her face, brushing away tears that had started to trickle down her cheeks. When she'd first met George Sedding in the library she'd thought him distant: tall, distinguished, immaculately dressed and much older than herself. But first impressions had deceived and soon she was escaping the farm to meet him whenever she had any free time. Because he was married theirs had been a clandestine love which had only added to the thrill and for those brief months she had known an intense happiness she'd never experienced before — until she was forced to leave the village and return to her family in Liverpool. As soon as her secret was discovered she was sent to her aunt in Wales and the lies everyone had told back then still made her blush with shame.

By the time she returned to Mabley Ridge to be near to George again it was too late. Gossip had it that his death had been caused by the shock he suffered when his eighteen-year-old son Samuel was brought back from France to die of his wounds at a nearby military hospital, but she knew she'd never get to know the truth of the matter. His widow still lived in the big house on the outskirts of the village that Gwen had never been allowed to visit and, as far as she knew, the woman had been quite unaware of her existence. Even so, she feared that if Mrs Sedding ever looked into her eyes she'd guess her secret right away. George's death had put a stop to what she'd been brought up to believe was a sin. And she knew there were many who'd say it had been a judgement on them both.

She scrambled to her feet and stepped away from the grave, unable to believe George was down there buried beneath the earth, lying beside his son who'd been little more than a boy when he died; a boy determined not to miss out on the great adventure of war.

Fighting back tears, she walked slowly back to the cemetery gates, watching the lodge in case any of the Rudyard family appeared. There was no sign of anyone — and no sign of Peter returning — but as she drew nearer she could hear a baby crying somewhere in the house, and hot tears began to run down her face.

31

Albert sat in his office going through a pile of statements. His apparent diligence was a pretence because he'd been unable to concentrate on anything since receiving Sam Poltimore's letter. After discarding the letter he'd had second thoughts and retrieved it from the waste-paper basket, stuffing it into the inside pocket of his jacket as though he hoped that by putting it out of sight the problem would go away. He glanced up at the office door with its etched glass top half, to make sure nobody was out there in the green tiled corridor to see him, before putting his head in his hands. He could feel the shiny scar tissue that ran down one side of his face smooth against his fingers. The war would never go away and neither would his memories of Wenfield.

He heard a swift knock and when Sergeant Stark poked his head round the edge of the half-open door he looked up, feigning alertness.

'Sorry to disturb you, sir, but I understand you visited that . . . er . . . actress.'

'Yes, I spoke to Miss Devereaux. She was at the theatre at the time we think Patience Bailey died and she denies knowing her or her employer.'

'Did you believe her, sir?'

Albert thought for a few seconds. 'No. I don't think I did.'

'One of the constables at Wilmslow went to

see her show. He said she was very good.' Stark edged into the room, shut the door behind him and lowered his voice. 'He said he saw Mr Ghent there with a few other gentlemen.'

This was hardly evidence. Albert needed more if he was to pursue Mallory Ghent as a suspect. 'Anything else?'

'There's been a break-in at a farm near the Ridge. Intruder helped himself to some food from the larder and a few bottles of ale.'

'I can't see what that has to do with our case.'

'Could be a vagrant, sir. And if we've got that sort hanging about he has to be a suspect.'

'There are a lot of poor unfortunates about who served their country only to be turned out with nowhere to go once the war was over, and I'm not inclined to make things worse for one of them by starting a manhunt with no evidence.' Albert snapped the words, irritated at Stark's assumptions. 'You didn't fight, did you?'

The sergeant's face reddened. 'No, sir. Afraid not.'

'Anything else?'

Stark consulted his notebook. 'A maid from one of the big houses near the cemetery says she's seen a man go in there after dusk. She didn't recognise him from the village.'

'Description?'

'She said he wears a greatcoat whatever the weather — like officers wear, she says — so she thought he might be a soldier.'

This caught Albert's interest. 'Anything else?'

'She said he was tall and scruffy. No hat. Probably youngish with long hair . . . like a tramp.'

178

'Why didn't the maid say this the first time anyone asked?'

'She says she didn't see him on the night Mrs Bailey died. Her lady and gentleman had people to dinner and she was too busy to look out of the window so she never thought to mention it.'

'Has she seen him there since that night?'

'She says not. But then she says she's had too much to do to be looking out of windows.' He hesitated. 'She did say something odd. Probably not to be taken seriously.'

'What was that?'

'She said he didn't seem to have a face.'

Albert, who had dismissed the Shadow Man as the product of Peter's overactive imagination, now wondered whether the maid's soldier was the same man. Peter made up stories and lived in his own world, distanced from reality, but if his Shadow Man was real, Albert needed to know.

'Did this man arrive before or after Mrs Pearce had been to leave her food?'

'After, she said.'

'Any word of Mrs Pearce?'

'Still trying to trace her sister but no luck yet.'

'Her son . . . is he definitely dead or was he missing in action?'

'The second, I think, sir.'

'Mrs Pearce has a husband?'

'He died just before the war, not long after her daughter passed away. They said he died of grief and they were buried in the same grave. They say that's why she leaves the food there . . . in the hope her lad'll go there to pay his respects to his sister and his dad and find it.'

'Is it possible this soldier the maid saw goes there to get the food? It's always been gone by morning, has it?'

'I believe so, sir,' Stark said.

'If Mrs Pearce's son's missing he might have deserted. He might be hiding out somewhere and his mother's in on his secret. He can't go home because he's afraid of the authorities finding out so she helps him by leaving food at the family grave.'

Stark looked at Albert as though he'd come up with a brilliant solution. 'Then where is she? Why's she gone missing?'

'Because she's with her son. They've gone off together to somewhere nobody knows them where they can start a new life with new identities. If we search Mrs Pearce's house I think we'll find she's packed up and gone.'

'In that case she's aiding and abetting a deserter.'

Albert banged his fist on the table, making Stark jump. 'If I'm right I say we leave them be. But someone should have another word with her neighbours.' He hesitated for a few moments. 'On second thoughts, I'll go myself.'

32

Sydney Rich had encouraged Esme to abandon her friends, the ones she described as dull, but now he was beginning to think this might have been a mistake.

She was always demanding reassurances about their future that he wasn't able to give, because the truth was she didn't feature in his plans. However he wouldn't end their relationship just yet, not until he decided to leave Mabley Ridge and move on. But before that happened he had unfinished business to attend to; business that would keep him in comfort for the foreseeable future.

He slumped on to his sofa because his foot was hurting again, throbbing as though he had walked much too far in uncomfortable shoes. He never tried to hide his discomfort when he was with Esme because it reinforced the persona of the wounded war hero he'd adopted since his return to Blighty.

He kicked off his shoe and massaged his instep until the ache subsided. Then he poured himself a Scotch, recalling a time when Esme's mother had drunk it with him, sharing a glass up on the Ridge, laughing as they took it in turns to sip the fiery liquid — until the day the boy died and the drinking and the laughter stopped.

Scotch had always been Sydney's favoured tipple, his refuge in times of stress, and as he stood up his head started swimming so he steadied himself on the arm of the sofa. Scotch didn't usually affect him like this but recently he'd been consuming rather a lot of it, along with the champagne and cocktails he'd shared with Esme. The way he saw it, he was doing the girl a favour by relieving the tedium of her Mabley Ridge existence. Now perhaps there was a price to pay for his excesses.

After a few minutes he began to feel better so he climbed the stairs, clinging to the banister to steady himself. Once he reached the landing another, much steeper staircase to his right led upwards to the attic, a place of eternal twilight lit only by a tiny casement window.

When he opened the door he was hit by the mingled smell of dust and mildew, but it was the only place private enough for his purposes. He flicked on the torch he kept by the door and made for the trunk at the far end of the room; the treasure chest that contained his deepest secrets. He paused for a while before lifting the lid which bore the initials CW in stencilled letters and when it creaked open he fell to his knees beside it.

After placing his torch on a battered chest of drawers nearby he rummaged through the trunk's shadowy contents. It was all in there: the evidence that would provide him with a good income and set him up for the future. He took out the letters and turned them over in his hands, gloating like a miser with his gold. It amused him to think of silly, innocent Esme falling for his stories . . . just as her mother had done before her.

He took out another photograph, a group of soldiers this time, posed stiffly; a souvenir of their comradeship in the trenches. He looked at the faces in the torchlight, concentrating on the two men who hadn't returned from France, not because of enemy action but because of what he'd done. They'd died shortly after he'd received the wound to his foot and their deaths had ensured nobody had ever discovered his deception. The chaos of war had provided a perfect cover for undetected wrongdoing and he'd been careful to cover his tracks. He kept telling himself he'd merely taken advantage of the situation, as he suspected many others had done; excusing his sins over and over again until he almost believed his own lies. He'd done what he'd done to survive and there was nothing wrong with survival.

His fingers came into contact with cold unyielding metal and he couldn't resist a smile as he drew the service revolver from the folds of cloth in the chest. He checked the bullets and found that they were all there, ready if they were needed.

He replaced the weapon and touched the rough cloth of the greatcoat that had kept him warm in the trenches. He'd held on to it because he needed to feel the scratchy cloth; he needed to smell the terror and remember.

If he forgot, he feared he might become a monster.

It was time to act but he didn't bother taking the Alvis to Gramercy House. It was too conspicuous and the element of surprise was everything.

He smoked as he walked there, lighting each cigarette with the glowing stub of the last. Smoking aided concentration and he needed all his wits about him if he was to pull this off.

He paused by the gates before making his way down the drive and when he reached the front door he ground the remnants of his cigarette beneath his shoe. When the door was answered by a young maid with an insolent manner he looked her in the eye.

'I want to speak to Mrs Ghent. Tell her it's an old friend.'

'The mistress isn't well. The doctor's with her. You'll have to come back.' She looked him up and down. 'Haven't I seen you with Miss Esme? You met her at the gates in a motor car.'

Sydney felt his fist clench and for a split second he was tempted to punch the girl's face. But he forced himself to walk away.

33

Albert rapped on the front door of Mrs Pearce's little terraced house, glad for once that the noise had brought the neighbours out on to their front steps. Two women in crossover aprons stood, arms folded, watching the spectacle.

'She's not in,' the thinner one said when he took a step back to look at the upstairs windows.

Albert introduced himself but the women still regarded him with suspicion.

'You're from London,' the bigger woman said accusingly. 'Weren't you here when the little Rudyard lad was found on the Ridge?'

Albert didn't answer. It wasn't something he wanted to be reminded of.

'Do you know where Mrs Pearce is?'

It was the thin woman who spoke. 'I told the young bobby who came she's likely gone to her sister's. And before you ask, no, I don't know her name. All I know is she lives in Northwich.' She sniffed. 'If you ask me Joan Pearce hasn't been right in the head since her lad went missing. Won't speak to no one and leaves food for him in the graveyard, she does, poor soul.'

'So I've heard. Is there a way in round the back?'

The woman looked at him as though he'd made an indecent suggestion and gave a small nod.

'Can you show me?'

The woman exchanged a look with her companion. 'You'd best come round.'

She led him to the back of the terrace into a wide alleyway with wooden gates each side leading to small backyards. He allowed the woman to walk ahead and she stopped at a gate less well kept than the rest. It was locked.

'You can climb over the wall can't you, lad?'

It was a long time since Albert had been called 'lad' but in spite of his injured leg he managed to scramble up the brick wall and let himself down into the yard. First he looked in the coal house and the outside privy, wrinkling his nose at the smell of stale urine, but could see nothing amiss.

Then he noticed that the kitchen window appeared to be crawling with black dots: flies. After taking a deep breath he put his shoulder to the back door, which turned out to be unlocked, and when it gave way he stumbled into the kitchen, fighting to regain his balance.

The woman was lying on the quarry-tiled floor, face down, her flesh discoloured and stinking. She'd been dead for some time and he shielded his nose and mouth with his sleeve as angry flies buzzed at his face.

Then he noticed the dried blood crusted on the floor and around her neck. Her throat had been cut.

Her coat had been flung over a chair and an empty wicker basket stood on the small kitchen table. Albert guessed that she'd deposited her offerings to her dead son and then returned home to meet her killer.

As he looked down at her sad corpse he knew

that this terrible act hadn't been committed in anger. And he feared that whoever had ended this harmless woman's life would kill again if he wasn't stopped.

187

34

When Albert returned to the hotel he took a bath but, try as he might, he couldn't get rid of the stench of death and decay in his nostrils. He didn't sleep well that night.

Mrs Pearce's body had been taken to the mortuary before her house was searched by a couple of constables under the direction of Sergeant Stark, although they'd found nothing that might help identify her killer. Dr Michaels had agreed with Albert's initial impression that the dead woman's throat had been cut, probably from behind causing a deep wound. It wouldn't have taken her long to die.

The next morning Albert sat at the breakfast table staring at the letter that had just arrived for him. It had a London postmark and had caught the last post the previous night.

Even though it was addressed to him at the hotel, the handwriting on the envelope was unfamiliar. However, it hadn't been forwarded from Scotland Yard so it was from someone who knew exactly where he was, which narrowed down the list of suspects. He tore the envelope open and took out a sheet of cheap lined notepaper.

The address on the top was his own and one glance at the signature told him that it was from Mary's mother, Vera.

Mary isn't well, it began after the usual

salutation. *She's suffering with her chest something awful and is in bed with a frightful cough and she won't eat.*

Since Frederick's death his wife had suffered many bouts of illness and he'd often wondered whether it was a symptom of her grief. However, for Vera to write like this, the situation must be serious.

I'm staying with her but you should come home, the letter continued. *She needs you.* It was signed *Yours truly, Vera Benton (Mrs).* In other circumstances the touch of formality would have made him smile but the letter's message banished any thoughts of levity.

As he ate his bacon and eggs in the hushed hotel dining room he could almost see Vera's face, set in her usual expression of disapproval. She'd blamed him for not being supportive enough when little Frederick had succumbed to the influenza that had consumed his small body and he could imagine her whispering poison into her daughter's ear: if he hadn't been so neglectful, if he hadn't stayed late at Scotland Yard to work on the murder of a shopkeeper in Southwark and put his work before his family, Frederick might have reached the hospital sooner and survived. In truth he didn't need Vera to blame him because he'd blamed himself often enough.

He sometimes felt that the injuries he'd received in France had been a punishment — then, when his affair with Flora had ended in disaster, he'd wondered whether it was all part of a pattern. Perhaps he was destined to pay a heavy price for his sins.

The letter dominated his thoughts as he pushed his empty, greasy plate to one side and sipped his tea until eventually he came up with a neat solution to his problem. Esther Schuman's grandson, David Cohen, lived in London and Albert wanted to speak to him. Abraham Stark was capable of dealing with routine matters and carrying out his instructions so he was confident he could leave the investigation in the hands of the local police for a couple of days while he made enquiries further afield. Mrs Schuman had provided her grandson's address in Bloomsbury so he could pay him a visit and then go home to see Mary.

At eight o'clock he walked into the police station and was greeted by Sergeant Stark, who told him there'd been no developments overnight. When Albert told him that he was returning to London it was hard to read Stark's thoughts, but Albert suspected he'd be relieved to be rid of the interfering detective from Scotland Yard for a while. The station in the small, normally law-abiding village was Stark's kingdom and if Albert had been in his place he knew he'd resent the stranger who'd descended from London to take charge although, to give Stark his due, on both occasions Albert had been there he'd encountered nothing but co-operation. Perhaps Stark was a better man than he was.

After asking one of the constables to look up the times of the trains, he sat down at his desk, only to be interrupted by a tapping on the door.

'Lady to see you, sir,' said a fresh-faced

190

constable who ushered Gwen Davies into the room and retreated.

Albert stood up, uncharacteristically flustered. Gwen suited the hat she'd chosen and her eyes sparkled despite the earliness of the hour. He felt the blood burning his cheeks as he invited her to sit.

'I'm on my way to school,' she said, slightly breathless. 'But I wanted to see you. I was in the cemetery yesterday and I noticed something odd.' Her voice tailed off as though she was having second thoughts about her visit. 'It's probably not important.'

'What did you notice?'

'It was a little mound in the grass as though the earth had been disturbed and the turf put back. I could be mistaken but . . . it wasn't far from where that poor woman was found.'

'What were you doing in the cemetery?'

Her face reddened and she shifted in her seat. 'I was . . . visiting the grave of someone I used to know.'

Albert sensed her reticence so he didn't press the matter, although he was curious to know what she was trying to hide. Gwen Davies didn't seem to him like the sort of woman who harboured secrets, but he'd been wrong before.

'You thought the earth had been dug deliberately?'

She gave his question a few moments' consideration before nodding slowly. 'Yes, but as I said, I can't be sure.' She paused. 'At first I thought it might have been one of Peter's funerals.'

Albert raised his eyebrows enquiringly.

'He holds little funerals for dead birds and creatures he finds but he told me he always decorates the graves with stones and a cross. Look, perhaps I'm wasting your time.'

'You could never do that,' Albert said quickly, immediately regretting his boldness. He gave her a reassuring smile. 'As far as witnesses are concerned, I'd say you were the reliable sort.'

'Thank you,' she said as though she wasn't sure how to take his clumsy compliment. 'Peter wasn't in school yesterday afternoon and when I called after school with some books for him he wasn't at home.'

'Where was he?'

'His mother didn't know. She thought he was at school. I couldn't help worrying but if he hadn't returned home his parents would have reported it, wouldn't they?'

'I'm sure they would.'

Albert stood up. 'I'd like to see that spot in the cemetery if you'd be good enough to show me.'

'Now?'

'Why not? Unless you're late for school.'

'No. I've got plenty of time.'

She hesitated for a few moments before leading the way out of the office. When Albert reached the front desk, he told Abraham Stark he was going to the cemetery and wouldn't be long.

As he was almost at the station entrance a constable appeared from a side room waving a sheet of paper. 'Those train times you asked for, sir.'

Albert took it from him and muttered his thanks. Gwen's arrival had driven all thoughts of Mary from his mind; now, with this reminder of his return to London, the slight swell of optimism he'd felt with this possible fresh lead vanished like sun in a sky filled with clouds.

Albert walked to the cemetery by Gwen's side, watching as she nodded politely to the people she passed. Even though she'd only been there a short time, the schoolmistress was already a well-known figure in the life of Mabley Ridge. Then he remembered she'd worked on a nearby farm during the war years; one of many young women who'd volunteered to work the land to free men for military service. He wondered whether the grave she'd been visiting belonged to somebody she'd known from that time. It was none of his business but he was curious by nature.

When they reached the cemetery gates Albert glanced automatically at the lodge, only to see that the door was shut and there was no sign of life behind the grubby lace curtains. Gwen walked on slightly ahead of him down the central path between the graves and tall memorials to the village's wealthier inhabitants, some topped by weathered stone angels with wings spread wide staring down mournfully at the scene. His eyes were drawn as always to Jimmy Rudyard's humbler memorial but he forced himself to look away.

Gwen headed for the back of the cemetery and stopped in the shadow of a large yew tree where she pointed at a small hump of earth covered by

193

a rectangle of turf which looked as though it had been dug up and replaced, leaving a fringe of bare soil around the edges. The more Albert studied it the more it looked to him like a tiny clandestine grave, recently dug and well concealed.

'Shall I see if Mr Rudyard's in?' Gwen said with an audible lack of enthusiasm.

'No. It's best if I handle this. Will you go back to the police station and ask Sergeant Stark to arrange for someone to come with a spade?'

She wavered for a second or two before hurrying away, half running, half walking back down the path towards the gates.

He had an ominous feeling about the disturbed patch of ground Gwen had showed him because he knew that if the killer had buried the mother in the newly dug grave then it was likely the baby had met a similar fate. He tried to put the thought from his mind but the image of little Jimmy Rudyard kept flitting through his head.

As he walked past the place where Patience Bailey had been found, he averted his eyes even though the grave looked completely different now that Mrs Potts had been laid to rest there. Instead he studied the headstones on the nearby graves, searching for any erected since Gwen had first arrived in Mabley Ridge to work the land, although he hardly liked to acknowledge what he was doing.

One recent grave stood out; only a year old and marked by bright white marble as yet unstained by time and the northern weather. The name inscribed on the headstone was George Sedding; he'd died on the fourth of November 1919, almost a year after the war's end. A couple of drooping roses lay on the marble chippings covering the tomb and Albert saw there was a note attached. He picked up the flowers and examined the note. There was no name, only a cryptic message: *I will never go but I will always come to you and talk of Michelangelo. With all my dearest love.* There was no signature.

When he heard voices he returned to the spot near the wall and waited. Gwen was walking down the path towards him, dwarfed by Constable Mitchell who'd shown her into Albert's presence earlier that morning. Mitchell glanced at her every now and then, a concerned look on his face as if he felt it his duty to protect her from any unpleasantness. He was carrying a spade across his body like a sceptre of office and Albert raised a hand in greeting as he waited for them to join him.

'Perhaps Miss Davies should leave this to us,' Albert said once the pair were within earshot.

'No.' The word was said with determination. 'I'd like to stay if you don't mind.'

'I warn you this might not be pleasant.'

She took a step backwards on to the path but she stood her ground so he didn't argue.

'Go on, Mitchell. Make a start. And be careful.'

Mitchell sliced the turf off the top of the little mound, revealing the soil beneath, alive with worms. At Albert's signal he started to dig and when the hole was about three feet deep Gwen

Davies gave a little gasp.

It was a small arm, mottled and filthy with soil.

'Sir, shall I . . . '

Mitchell's voice was shaking. But Albert told him to carry on — very carefully.

It didn't take him long to uncover the small body, discoloured by time and burial. It was a baby — around six months old, Albert guessed — and Albert's first instinct was to take the little thing in his arms and protect it, even though it was beyond protection — beyond everything. It was dressed in what looked like a nightgown which must once have been white and a thick towelling nappy and its little hands were clenched above its head as if it was reposing in sleep. As far as Albert could see there were no signs of violence but it would be Dr Michaels' job to tell him if he was right.

'Go and fetch Dr Michaels,' he said quietly to Gwen who had backed away at the smell. She obeyed at once, running fast out of the cemetery as though Patience Bailey's killer was after her.

35

Tears pricked Albert's eyes as he gazed down into the little grave. He had hoped, prayed, that Patience Bailey's baby had somehow survived and now he despaired at the heartlessness of the killer. To kill the mother was one thing but to slaughter an innocent baby and bury its body was nothing short of evil. And the fact that his own unknown son would be around the same age as the dead infant made him turn away, unable to bear the sight.

It seemed an age before Gwen returned with the doctor. Michaels' manner was businesslike, but Albert wondered whether he was hiding his emotions behind a professional façade. Perhaps it was the only way to deal with such an event, he told himself as he wiped his eyes with his handkerchief. A breeze had got up and was blowing the dry soil around so he pretended he had some grit in them, although he was sure the doctor could see through this minor deception.

Gwen joined Albert as Dr Michaels performed his examination.

'It looks as if this little one was buried with some reverence, unlike his mother,' she said.

'That's true. Look, if you want to go . . . '

She said nothing for a few seconds. Then, 'Would you like me to tell the Rudyards?'

'Thank you but that's a job for the police.' Albert glanced towards the doctor. 'Perhaps it would be best if you went, Miss Davies. Besides, I wouldn't like you to be late for your pupils. Thank you for your help.' He knew his words sounded formal but that was his intention. As he watched her walk off towards the gate, he sighed with relief. The emotion of finding the tiny corpse had left him drained and he couldn't summon the energy for conversation.

Arrangements were made to transport the baby's body to the mortuary at the Cottage Hospital to join that of Joan Pearce, and Albert waited until it was taken away because if he'd left while the child was still lying in the cold earth he would somehow have felt as though he was abandoning it. Constable Mitchell was barely able to keep his emotions in check and when Sergeant Stark arrived Albert saw him give the young man's shoulder a comforting pat. Albert suspected that this was the first time Mitchell had encountered the death of a child in the course of his duties and he couldn't help remembering how he'd felt when he'd seen the lifeless body of Jimmy Rudyard in the mortuary; overcome with a father's grief even though the child was no relation of his.

Albert asked Mitchell to visit the cemetery lodge to tell the Rudyards what had happened — if they hadn't already observed the activity from their windows. There was relief on Mitchell's face as he hurried off and Albert felt as though he'd done his good deed for the day.

'I can't understand why the killer buried mother and child separately. Why not throw them both into the newly dug grave? It was convenient and burying the little one would have meant more work,' he said to Stark as they walked back to the police station. His leg was aching from standing so long and his limp was worsening. He suspected that he'd been unwise to scale Joan Pearce's backyard wall the previous night, but he tried to ignore the pain and carry on.

'Who knows what goes through someone's mind when they do something like that,' Stark replied, almost in a whisper.

They walked the rest of the way in silence and it wasn't until they were standing beneath the blue lamp which hung above the entrance that Albert spoke the words that had been forming in his mind since he'd left the cemetery. 'The trouble with monsters, Stark, is that they look exactly like everybody else. You'd have trouble picking one out in an identity parade because they could look like the man you walk past in the street every day without a second thought — or the woman.'

'Surely a woman couldn't do something like this?' Stark sounded shocked at the suggestion.

Albert was on the verge of saying that the most disturbed killer he'd ever met had been a woman, and he'd fallen in love with her, before he stopped himself just in time. Flora had bobbed into his thoughts again like a cork on water, impossible to submerge for long.

'Women kill, Stark, take my word for it.'

'I'll give you the odd one poisons her husband but this sort of thing . . . '

'I'm keeping an open mind, and so should

you. You're a local man so you know the people around here better than I do. Can you think of anyone who's capable of this?'

Albert could see Stark's mind working, turning over each possibility. 'It's got to be someone who knows how to conduct a burial, sir.'

'John Rudyard?'

'He's fond of his drink. And he hasn't been the same since he came back from the war. People have seen him walking up Ridge Lane carrying something in an old sack . . .'

'Suspicious?'

'I've often thought we should keep a weather eye on him.'

Albert listened carefully. The Ghents' cook had mentioned Rudyard sneaking about with a sack. Perhaps he should have brought him in for questioning but he suspected he'd avoided the confrontation because of the guilt he felt at not being able to bring Jimmy's killer to justice.

'Then there's that lad of his — Jack,' Stark continued. 'He's taking after his dad, so I've heard. Beat up another lad, he did. Waited for him down an alley in the dark — not that we got involved. It was all settled between themselves, like.'

This was a possibility Albert hadn't considered. He'd been thinking of Jimmy Rudyard's siblings as children — as they had been when he'd last been there in 1914. 'Being a hot-headed young man who gets into fights when he's had a pint or two doesn't make him a murderer. He wasn't old enough to go to war, was he?'

Stark shook his head. 'No. But he's seen lads coming back changed and that's upsetting enough for some. Sent some wild, it has. And not only the lads. 'Live for today' — that's what some say nowadays. Enjoy yourself while you can and damn the consequences, if you'll pardon my language.'

Albert could hear a disapproval verging on bitterness in Stark's voice and knew he might have a point. However, he doubted if this new permissiveness went as far as wanting to commit murder.

When they entered the station Stark took up his usual post behind the front desk, the reassuring face of the police station, while Albert retired to his office at the back. Dr Michaels had agreed to perform the postmortem in an hour's time which meant his hopes of travelling to London that day had been dashed. David Cohen would have to wait until tomorrow.

36

Albert walked the short distance to the hospital with Stark at his side, solemn as an undertaker's mute. Dr Michaels had promised to conduct the baby's post-mortem first and then Joan Pearce's immediately afterwards. It was the baby's he was dreading most. As the doctor worked on the small discoloured corpse, Albert averted his eyes for most of the procedure but he judged from the length of time the doctor took that he'd been thorough. When it was over the doctor covered the little body as though he could no longer bear the sight of it.

'Well?' Albert prompted.

'I'm pretty sure it's not murder, gentlemen. I might ask for a second opinion but as far as I can see this poor child died of natural causes. There are definite signs of pneumonia and no indication of violence.'

'Are you sure?' The question was out before Albert could stop himself.

'As sure as I can be.' The doctor sounded irritated at having his judgement questioned. 'But, as I said, if you want a second opinion I know a very good man at Manchester Royal Infirmary who — '

'I'm sure that won't be necessary, Doctor,' said Stark quickly.

'On the contrary, I would like the doctor's

findings confirmed if that's all right with you, Doctor.'

Dr Michaels nodded graciously. 'Of course.' He hesitated. 'Is there any suggestion the murdered woman's baby was sick? She lived with the Ghents, I believe.'

'I'll send someone to ask but nobody's mentioned it.'

'In which case it's strange. Somebody in the household would have noticed if the child was so unwell, surely.'

Albert knew the doctor was right. And if Patience Bailey's child had been ill, what would have made her take it out at night into a cold cemetery wearing nothing but a thin nightgown? No blanket or shawl had been found in the grave, or in the pram that had been abandoned by the cemetery wall, yet there had been no suggestion from the Ghents or Mrs Schuman that Patience had been a neglectful mother.

Whatever had drawn Patience Bailey to the scene of her death must have been urgent if she'd taken such a risk with the baby's health; or perhaps he'd died at Gramercy House and she'd gone there to bury him before anybody asked any questions. She might have been planning to explain his absence away, saying he'd gone to relatives.

Whatever the explanation, Albert needed to know.

37

The results of Joan Pearce's post-mortem were much as Albert had expected. The woman's throat had been cut with some violence, most likely on the same night that Patience Bailey had been buried alive. As Albert looked down on her corpse, he wondered about the manner of her death. If she had been attacked from behind as the doctor claimed, then either the killer had been lying in wait for her and she was taken by surprise, or she'd known and trusted him enough to turn her back on him.

According to the doctor she had been killed with a sharp knife, possibly a kitchen knife of some kind, but no such bloodstained weapon had been found at the scene so it looked as if the killer had taken it away with him.

Albert was certain Joan Pearce's murder and that of Patience Bailey were linked but at that moment he had no idea how. Besides, for the next couple of days he'd be forced to leave the investigation to Stark and the locals because he felt some of the answers he was seeking were to be found in London.

The following day he rose early to be at Exchange Station in time to catch the London train. But first he called in at the police station to ask Constable Mitchell to telephone his colleagues at Withington to check whether they'd managed to trace any members of Patience

Bailey's family as he'd requested.

As he waited for the local train into Manchester he studied his fellow passengers on the platform. Most had the prosperous, well-fed look he'd come to associate with the so-called Cottontots.

Near him stood a man in his forties wearing a smartly tailored suit and carrying a neatly rolled umbrella — an essential accessory in the Manchester climate. He had receding hair and a chin to match and he kept consulting the watch dangling on a thick gold chain from his waistcoat. After a while the man was joined by Mallory Ghent, who nodded nervously in Albert's direction before turning his back as though he had no wish to be associated with him. Albert shuffled nearer to the pair, straining to overhear their conversation.

'Morning, Ghent. Theatre tonight?'

'Sorry, Parms, love to but I've got something arranged. Business. You know how it is.'

As the train pulled up the two men moved out of earshot, heading for the first-class carriage, and Albert began mining his memory. He'd heard the name Parms before and it took him half the journey to remember that, according to the Ghents' maid Daisy, Mr Parms had been seen visiting Dora Devereaux's house near the cemetery. Like everyone else in the village he'd been interviewed as a matter of routine, but he'd claimed to know nothing so he hadn't been questioned further. However, Albert had stored the tenuous connection at the back of his mind. Sergeant Stark might be reluctant to bother the wealthier citizens of Mabley Ridge but he had no such qualms.

He decided to buy an early lunch in the buffet car of the London train, eating so quickly that he was troubled by indigestion for the rest of the journey. When he arrived at Euston Station he tried his best to ignore the discomfort as he crossed busy Euston Road which teemed with taxis, trams and delivery lorries, some powered by horses and others by motors. After the fresh air of Cheshire he was conscious of the petrol fumes mingling with the smell of horse dung and the smoke from the capital's chimneys. He was home again.

Bloomsbury was convenient for the station and he wondered how often David Cohen made the journey up North to visit his grandmother. Since he was a student Albert wasn't sure of finding him in, but he thought it worth calling in on his way to Scotland Yard, just in case.

Cohen lived in a small side street, not far from St Pancras church with its strange caryatids and classical portico, and when Albert arrived at the address he found it to be a run-down Georgian terraced house that had seen better days. The stucco was flaking off and the sash windows were in dire need of a coat of paint. He knocked at the door and waited.

It was a while before the door opened to reveal a blowzy-looking woman in a dirty kimono of embroidered red silk. Her dark hair was carefully coiffed and a cigarette holder dangled between her lips, although the cigarette protruding from the end was unlit. Albert raised his hat politely, introduced himself and asked whether Mr David Cohen was at home.

The woman looked him up and down appraisingly before asking if he had a light. Albert took his lighter from his pocket and when the woman's cigarette was lit she inhaled the smoke deeply with a sly half-smile on her lips.

'What's he done?'

'Nothing as far as I'm aware. I'm hoping he might be able to help me, that's all.'

The woman didn't look convinced. 'I've had trouble with lodgers before and if he's been a bad boy . . . '

'It's nothing like that, I promise,' said Albert, suddenly fearing that his visit might be about to lose David his digs. 'His grandmother told me he served in the war with someone I'm trying to trace, that's all. I assure you Mr Cohen's done nothing wrong. Is he at home?'

The woman inhaled again and blew the smoke out between her pursed scarlet lips before replying. Albert noticed fine lines around her lips and eyes; she was older than she wanted to appear. 'He's a student so he don't keep working hours like some of my gentlemen. Top floor. Wipe your feet before you come in.'

Albert did as he was told and he was aware of the landlady watching him as he climbed the uncarpeted stairs. At first the banisters were mahogany, a relic of the house's former status, but when he neared the top of the house they became plainer as they led to what had once been servants' quarters. It was here in the attic that David Cohen had his lodgings and when

Albert reached the very top landing and knocked on the door it was opened by a dark-haired young man of medium height with intelligent brown eyes and a mouth that smiled readily.

'Mr Cohen?'

The young man nodded nervously, as though he feared Albert was some kind of official come to make life awkward for him.

'It's nothing to worry about. My name's Inspector Lincoln and I'm investigating the murder of Patience Bailey up in Cheshire.'

Albert had expected the news to come as a bombshell but Cohen nodded sadly. 'My grandmother wrote to tell me. It's been a terrible shock. Patience was such a nice girl. Wouldn't harm anybody. Have you any idea who . . . ?'

'That's something we're still working on, I'm afraid. May I . . . ?'

David Cohen had been standing in the doorway blocking Albert's view of the room beyond but now he stepped back to let Albert in, murmuring his apologies as though the thought of Patience Bailey's death had made him forget his manners.

David hastily moved some books off the worn sofa in the middle of the room to allow his visitor to sit down before settling in the armchair opposite and sitting forward, like a child waiting to be told a story.

'I've spoken to your grandmother. She told me that you persuaded her to take Mrs Bailey on as her companion.'

'That's right. Vic Bailey, her husband, served under me and I felt obliged to do all I could to help his widow. She had no job when the war ended, you see, and I felt I couldn't leave her in straitened circumstances.' He swallowed hard. 'Her husband saved my life; spotted an enemy sniper and tackled me to the ground out of harm's way. I owed him my life so giving Patience employment as Grandmother's companion seemed the least I could do. The old girl fusses terribly but her heart's in the right place. I can't see her as a harsh employer somehow.'

'Me neither.' The two men exchanged a smile and for the first time Albert saw a resemblance between grandmother and grandson. 'Just for the record, where were you last Tuesday evening?' It was a question that had to be asked.

'I was out with friends at the local pub.' He looked around the room. 'A man needs to play as well as work and an evening in this place isn't exactly a cheerful prospect. I have a gramophone but even so . . . You met my landlady?'

'I did.'

'She sleeps directly below me and she entertains gentleman callers. Some of the noises coming from her room can be rather . . . embarrassing, if you know what I mean, so I prefer the company of my fellow students to staying in all night — studies permitting of course.'

'You haven't asked about the baby.'

David frowned. 'Grandmother says he's missing. Is there any sign . . . ?'

'I'm afraid a baby boy's body was found buried near where Patience Bailey was discovered. According to the post-mortem the infant died of natural causes.'

209

There was no mistaking the shock on David Cohen's face. 'But if Patience was murdered then surely the baby . . .'

'The investigation isn't over, not by any means. No doubt everything will begin to make sense in due course but in the meantime I'm hoping you'll be able to help me.'

'Of course. Anything.'

'Please tell me everything you know about Patience Bailey — her background, her family, her sweethearts, everything.'

'She was brought up in Withington not far from my grandmother's place. Her parents ran a chemist's shop but they both passed away some years ago. Patience was only married to Bailey for about eighteen months before he died and he was devoted to her — used to write to her all the time from the trenches. He told me she had a brother and a sister. The brother works at that big prison in Manchester.'

'Strangeways?' Albert felt his heart beating faster.

'That's it. She told me once he lives near Strangeways with his family but I don't think she ever visited him; I suppose being near a prison isn't to everyone's taste. Mind you, I had the impression they weren't close anyway. All I know about the sister is that she went to London to follow the bright lights.'

'Do you know their names?'

'The brother's Joseph and the sister . . . I think her name's Constance.' He gave a sad smile. 'Patience and Constance — qualities we should all aspire to, eh, Inspector. I remember Patience telling me that Constance was very beautiful — a real glamour girl, she said. The type who should be in the moving pictures. Unfortunately I've never had the pleasure of meeting her so I wouldn't know her if I bumped into her in the street.'

'Patience left your grandmother's employment to become companion to Mrs Jane Ghent in Mabley Ridge. You were friends with Monty Ghent, I believe?'

David's expression suddenly became guarded. 'Yes, Monty and I were good friends. We went to school together. Manchester Grammar.' He paused. 'Monty was my best friend, Inspector. We were posted to different positions so we didn't see much of each other at the front. Then I heard he'd been killed . . . ' He was fighting hard to keep the emotion from his voice. 'But that's war, isn't it. Poor Monty's lying in some grave in France and I'll never see him again but you have to get on with life.' He looked at Albert's hand and the scarring on his face. 'You had a bad time yourself, I see.'

'At least I survived,' Albert said quietly. 'What can you tell me about Patience's baby?'

David appeared to be surprised at the sudden change of subject. 'His name was Lancelot — like in King Arthur and his knights. A rather fanciful name if you ask me.'

'You realise Vic Bailey couldn't have been the father?'

'Maths may not be my strong point, Inspector, but I'm well aware of that.'

'So who was the father?'

'Search me. I thought it impolite to ask.'

'Can you tell me why Patience moved to Mabley Ridge?'

'She seemed happy at Grandmother's and the old girl didn't mind about the baby in the least so I must say the move rather surprised me. All she told me was that she fancied living in the country and she thought it would be better for Lancelot. Just shows how wrong you can be.'

'You got her the job with Mrs Ghent.'

'I suppose I did. I still visit Monty's family sometimes when I'm up North so I must have mentioned to Patience that Mrs G was looking for a companion and she asked me to put a word in.'

'We know Patience wasn't Lancelot's mother. Who was?'

David sat in silence for a few moments, as though he was wondering how much to share.

'Please. Whoever the mother is, she should be told.'

David stood up and went to the small window that looked out on the nearby rooftops. He stood in silence for the while before turning to face Albert. 'I really didn't know for sure that the child wasn't hers but I suppose it explains a lot.'

'What do you mean?'

'Patience had a close friend called Barbara Nevin. She came from a respectable family and, according to Monty, her parents were very strict so if she'd fallen pregnant — and I'm not saying that's what happened — it wouldn't surprise me if they sent her away to have the baby and threatened to have it adopted by strangers. I can just imagine Patience volunteering to take the child on and make sure he was taken care of, which would at least mean that Barbara would have some contact. As a widow, it would be no problem for Patience to have a baby in tow and that would explain why she wanted to move away to a new place because people in Didsbury would have started doing their sums. She told my grandmother she was looking after the baby for a friend but I think Grandmother suspected it was really hers.'

'But you knew it wasn't?'

'Patience had been devoted to her husband so I can't see her taking up with another man so soon after his death. And she was very . . . moral. In fact if I was being uncharitable I would describe her as a little prudish. Not that she didn't have a good heart — just a keen sense of right and wrong.'

'What was Monty's relationship with Barbara?'

David considered his answer for a while, reminding Albert that he was a lawyer in the making. 'They were sweethearts. His family knew nothing about her but I'm sure that in time . . . if he'd survived . . . Mind you, I know one thing for sure. If the baby was Barbara's Monty couldn't have been the father because he died just before the end of the war. Again, the sums are all wrong.'

'Tell me about the relationship between Patience and Barbara?'

'They'd been close friends since they'd worked together as VADs in the war. They both

213

worked at Stockport Infirmary for a while; Barbara as an auxiliary nurse and Patience as a dispenser — she was brought up in a chemist's shop after all. She wanted to do her bit while Vic was away fighting.'

Flora had been a VAD in her local military hospital and for a brief moment David's mention of Barbara's work revived the memory. Then he composed himself, hoping David hadn't noticed the look of shock that must have appeared on his face.

'Did you play Cupid and introduce Monty to Barbara?'

'I can't deny it.'

Albert guessed that David had been brought up not to lie to the police. 'What's Barbara like?'

'She's small with fair hair and a turned-up nose. Pretty girl and sweet-natured — kind. Lives in Cheadle — that's a village not far from Didsbury. When Monty and I were on leave I used to ask Patience out for walks in the park because I felt responsible for her somehow, and on a few occasions she came along with Barbara and I brought Monty. They seemed to hit it off right away.' He smiled. 'They were rather jolly walks, Inspector. Making the most of the time we had and living for the day. A chance to forget about the horrors we had to go back to with a couple of nice girls.'

'So you and Patience . . . '

'Like I said, she was Vic Bailey's widow so it wouldn't have seemed right.'

'But Monty and Barbara . . . ?'

'You'll have to ask her, Inspector. I know she'll

214

be absolutely devastated to hear about Patience. She lost Monty and . . . Then there's the baby. If she is the mother she'll be . . . I don't know how she's going to face it.'

Albert knew that feeling — enduring the news of death after death until it numbs the soul. 'You haven't told her about Patience yet?'

He shook his head. 'I did think about contacting her but, to tell the truth, I didn't know what to say. Probably pure cowardice on my part. Perhaps I should have . . . '

'I'd like to tell her myself. I promise you I'll break the news gently.'

'If the baby is hers, how do you tell a mother her child's dead?' David Cohen was no longer trying to hold back his tears. They were coming fast now, trickling down his face.

'There's no easy way but I'm a policeman so it's something I've had to do before. All part of the job.'

David Cohen gave him a pitying look. 'You'd think with the war being over . . . '

'I don't think it'll ever be over, Mr Cohen. Not truly.' David walked to the window and stared out at the rooftops and Albert watched him in silence, giving him time to come to terms with what he'd just learned. Then he spoke.

'I'll need Barbara's address. Does she still live with her parents?'

'As far as I know, although it's a while since I've seen her. You will be discreet, I trust? If the baby was hers and her parents happen to be within earshot then I imagine the subject won't exactly be a welcome one.' He tore a scrap of paper from a notebook lying on the table by the window, scribbled down an address and handed it to Albert. 'You will give her my best wishes, won't you?'

'Of course.'

'And tell her I'll come and see her when I'm next up there.'

There was an anxiety in the young man's voice which told Albert that Monty Ghent hadn't been Barbara Nevin's only admirer. He took his leave, wondering whether to catch the tram or the tube to his home in Bermondsey. He decided on the tram. It was slower and would give him more time to think.

38

According to Esme Ghent's friends, playing hard to get was the only way to keep a man's interest — and she wanted to keep Sydney's interest more than anything else in the world.

Last time she'd seen him he'd been distant, as though he had something on his mind. And he still asked about her mother each time they met, making the questions sound casual, even playful. What did Jane Ghent do all day? Who were her friends? Were there any men sniffing around? When she'd quizzed him he'd made the excuse that he was just interested in her family because everything about her fascinated him. But she suspected there was more behind his interest, although she could hardly ask her mother what it was. Or perhaps she would. Why not?

Her mother was still complaining of pains in her stomach and her father was spending so much time at his club in Manchester that she hardly saw him. He often telephoned her mother early in the evening to say he wouldn't be home and on one occasion Cook had looked puzzled when she received the news that there'd only be two for dinner. When Esme's curiosity got the better of her and she asked if something was wrong, Cook said she'd seen Mr Ghent in the village earlier, although she did admit that she might have been mistaken.

Not that Esme saw much of her father when

he did deign to turn up. He kept disappearing into the door next to the stables which was always kept frustratingly locked. She wanted to know what was in there and she wondered whether Sydney knew how to pick locks because Sydney seemed to know everything.

Her mother had taken to her bed again, holed up in the room that was once performed by eau de Cologne but now smelled of vomit, so Esme crept out of the house. Sydney had promised to meet her by the gates in the Alvis and she wondered where he was planning to take her. Into Manchester for lunch at the Midland perhaps; she really hoped so because she'd put on her new shoes, which were hardly suitable for a walk on the Ridge. Sydney seemed obsessed with that sinister place, but Esme was tiring of their alfresco picnics and love-making on the damp car rug.

Sydney turned up at eleven as arranged and as soon as she saw him her planned aloofness vanished in the thrill of the moment. He offered her a cigarette from the packet and she took it gratefully, her eyes meeting his as he lit it with his gold lighter. He'd told her it had been a present from someone who'd once been special to him but he'd never divulged the identity of the giver.

'Can we go somewhere nice?' she asked as she climbed into the passenger seat. 'Lunch in Manchester, perhaps?'

'Manchester's out. Sorry.'

'I fancied the Midland.'

Sydney shook his head. 'It's full of fat

218

businessmen talking about the price of cotton. I thought we'd go back to my place? I've found the recipe for a new cocktail. You'll love it.'

Esme tried to hide her disappointment. She wanted to show off the new dress she was wearing. She wanted to walk into the Midland's plush restaurant on Sydney's arm and be addressed as madam by obsequious waiters. She wanted to be treated as a grown-up. 'As long as we don't end up on the Ridge again.'

'No danger of that. Looks like rain.'

He lit another cigarette and she felt the need to fill the silence with talk. 'Cook says the village is swarming with police again. Some old woman's been murdered.'

He sucked on the cigarette and blew out a perfect smoke ring. 'I heard someone saying they've found that baby too.'

'Dead?'

'Well, it wasn't dancing a jig.' His lips turned upwards in a slow, mocking smile. 'You're not frightened are you? You don't think there's a lunatic going around killing women and you're going to be next?'

'You seem to think it's funny.' Even though she hadn't had much time for Patience Bailey in life, her death, and that of her baby, had been no joke.

He started the engine and pulled away. 'Someone once called murder one of the fine arts, darling. Or you can think of it as a game — the brilliant artist of murder pitching his wits against the collective denseness of our renowned police force.'

219

'Stop the car and let me out.'

'Don't be a silly girl.'

'Stop the car.'

The car shuddered to a halt with a screeching of tyres, throwing her forward so that her head almost hit the polished wood of the dashboard. She scooped up her handbag from the footwell and climbed out inelegantly, slamming the door behind her to make a point. His words had frightened her and she wasn't sure whether she wanted to see him again. On the other hand the excitement she felt when she was with him made all the other men she knew — those who'd survived the war — seem desperately dull in comparison.

As she marched back towards Gramercy House she began to realise that she'd overreacted — perhaps he'd just been teasing her and she'd played right into his hands. She turned her head to see if he was still there but he'd gone.

39

Mrs Ghent was indisposed again, lying in bed with a sick bowl beside her. Daisy knew she'd be the one who'd have to deal with it but her late mother had always said that some unpleasant things had to be faced for the greater good.

She waited for Miss Esme to go out before she checked on Cook who was taking her afternoon nap, snoring in her chair. She had taken the key from Mallory Ghent's desk first thing that morning, reasoning he wouldn't miss it while he was at the mill. When she'd finished she planned to replace it exactly where she'd found it. She'd done it before and he hadn't suspected a thing.

Her hands shook as she turned the key in the lock, which clicked smoothly. She knew it was kept well oiled because she'd seen John Rudyard, the gardener, with the oil can. The door opened silently and she saw a narrow staircase rising ahead of her, the treads bare splintery wood. She tried to visualise Mallory climbing these stairs but failed; these were servants' stairs, not masters'. When she closed her eyes she could almost smell his pomade and feel his hands on her breasts. He was so much older than she was, far older than the boys she'd fooled around with before she came to Gramercy House, but he was rich and money excited her more than the thought of firm young flesh.

She knew Mallory would soon be free and if

Miss Esme didn't like how things were going to be, she could go off with her man in the Alvis; the one who hung around the house trying to look into the windows without being seen. The man who'd asked for the mistress that day, saying he was an old friend.

She climbed the stairs, her heart pounding as she opened the door at the top. She was the only one who knew Mallory Ghent's secret and that gave her the advantage.

She slipped into the room and allowed her eyes to adjust to the gloom before tiptoeing past the horrors on display and helping herself to what she needed.

40

Albert felt guilty that he hadn't gone straight home as soon as he'd arrived in London; and the knowledge that he probably wouldn't have made the journey if he hadn't needed to speak to David Cohen made him feel even worse. Still, he was there now so it was time to make amends.

He took his door key from his pocket but then had second thoughts and knocked instead. Mary wasn't expecting him and he didn't want to surprise her by barging in without warning, especially as she wasn't well.

He waited for a while, listening for sounds from within. Eventually he heard footsteps tapping on the linoleum and the door opened to reveal Mary's mother, Vera, wearing a disapproving scowl on her face. She was a large woman with a cascade of chins beneath a face mottled by time. Her faded crossover apron strained across her midriff and she folded her beefy arms in a gesture of challenge.

'About time too,' were her first words. 'She's been asking for you.'

'How is she?'

'Good of you to ask,' she said with heavy sarcasm, keeping him waiting on the doorstep. 'No better. I wanted to fetch the doctor but she won't have it.' Her expression suddenly softened. 'Maybe you can talk some sense into her. She won't listen to me. Keeps saying she'd rather be with little Freddy. The Reverend Gillit says he's so happy but . . . '

This was the first time Vera had appeared to be anything less than enthusiastic about the Reverend Gillit's influence over her daughter.

'You've been encouraging her in this Gillit nonsense, haven't you?'

Vera stood aside to let him into his own house and he shut the door behind him.

'He gives her a lot of comfort. Which is more than her husband does.'

'I do my best.' Albert was well aware that he'd dealt with Frederick's death by burying himself in his work. Even so, he felt obliged to defend himself against his mother-in-law's accusations of neglect. 'Where is she?'

As if on cue, he heard the sound of coughing from the direction of the kitchen and experienced another stab of guilt. At least, he thought, Mary had no idea about Flora and what had happened on his last trip up North in 1919, and what she didn't know couldn't hurt her. There had been a time when he'd been tempted to tell her — to tell the world — but circumstances had put a stop to that.

Vera led the way into the back kitchen where the range was lit. It was stifling hot in there and, mingled with the odour of cooking stew, he could detect a faint smell of the sickroom. Mary was stretched out on the old chaise longue that had once graced the front parlour. They had acquired it third hand when they'd been setting up home and now the fabric was frayed and shiny with wear. She looked up as he walked in, a handkerchief held to her mouth. When she lowered it he saw it was stained with blood-streaked mucus.

He hurried to her side and knelt on the quarry-tiled floor. 'We should call the doctor.'

'I don't want a fuss,' she said weakly. 'And the cost . . . '

Albert stood up, took Vera by the arm and shepherded her from the room. 'Fetch the doctor. Now.'

'But she said — '

'Now.'

He returned to Mary's side and took her hand. In spite of everything that had happened she was still his wife and he felt responsible for what happened to her.

Half an hour later the doctor arrived in his motor car, a spectacle guaranteed to bring the neighbours to their doorsteps. Dr Hughes was a large florid man in his fifties who carried a shabby bag and still wore a traditional frock coat that looked as if it dated from his days as a medical student. Albert knew he'd want paying as soon as he'd finished so he took some money from the tin on the sideboard in the parlour and returned to the kitchen to hear the doctor's verdict.

'What you need is rest and fresh air, Mrs Lincoln,' Hughes announced with confidence. 'I recommend a sanatorium in the countryside.'

'How soon can you arrange it, Doctor?'

Albert looked at his wife and saw panic in her eyes. 'The cost, Albert . . . '

'You mustn't worry about that.'

225

He led the doctor into the hall and spoke in a whisper. 'It's tuberculosis, isn't it?'

'I'm afraid so. The only remedy is plenty of fresh air. A cure can't be guaranteed of course but . . .'

'I understand. But we must do whatever we can.'

'Of course. I'll call again when I've made the arrangements.'

The doctor gave him a sympathetic look. Dr Hughes wasn't renowned for his empathy so Albert knew the situation was bad and he experienced an unexpected pang of sadness.

As soon as the doctor had gone Vera took charge, putting a kettle on the range to make beef tea for the invalid while Albert examined his pocket watch. He needed to call in at Scotland Yard. There were things he had to do.

At that moment he heard a sharp rap on the door and Vera hurried to answer, tutting at this latest disturbance to her day. When she returned it was with a plump man with a small moustache that gave him the look of a prosperous rodent.

He saw Mary push herself upright on her pillows and smooth her hair, her eyes eager as though she was greeting a lover. Vera too was simpering, something Albert had never witnessed before.

When the man noticed Albert standing there, the obsequious smile vanished and was replaced by a nervous grin.

'Mr Lincoln. How good to meet you at last. I've heard so much about you.' The man held out his hand and Albert noticed it was smooth, unmarred by any form of manual work.

'Reverend Thomas Gillit. Your good lady attends my little meetings. I'm sure you'd find them a great comfort too . . . after your loss.'

The man's lips formed a slight smirk and he looked into Albert's eyes as though he knew all his innermost secrets. For a split second Albert had a fleeting impression that he was referring to Flora but he knew Gillit meant Frederick and it was his own conscience that had brought Flora to the forefront of his mind. He tried hard to control the anger that was welling up inside him like bile. 'I'm sure I wouldn't — and I'd be grateful if you'd stop encouraging this nonsense.'

'I see you're not a believer. But answer me this — how can hope be nonsense? If you came to one of our meetings . . .'

'Get out of my house.'

'No, Albert. I want the reverend to stay.' Mary collapsed in a fit of coughing and Vera rushed to her side.

'If the lady wishes me to stay I'd be neglecting my duty if I was to leave, Mr Lincoln,' Gillit said with a hint of triumph.

'Please stay, Reverend,' said Vera, gazing at the man like a lovesick schoolgirl.

Albert had had enough. He left the house, slamming the front door behind him. Mary had made her choice and he'd do his duty to her. Nothing more.

★ ★ ★

An hour later he arrived at his office in Scotland Yard where Sam Poltimore greeted him like a long-lost friend. He felt his spirits lift even though the recent events at home still reverberated round his head; the three united against him as though he was a hostile outsider.

'We're missing you, sir,' said Poltimore. 'How's it going up there?'

Poltimore listened carefully while Albert brought him up to date with the investigation. Albert knew he'd miss his sergeant when he finally retired and he was tempted to ask him to return to Cheshire with him. But Sam Poltimore was an uxorious man who hated straying far from home. As far as he was concerned, Cheshire might as well be the Zambezi or the Antarctic.

'I can't imagine anybody killing a little baby like that,' Sam said, genuinely upset. 'You don't think it's the same bastard who killed that poor little kiddie back in 'fourteen?'

'I'm not ruling anything out, Sam. I'd like to take a look at the Jimmy Rudyard files if I may. There might be something I missed at the time — a name that cropped up then that's come up in this new case.'

Without further comment Sam made a telephone call requesting that the Jimmy Rudyard file be brought to Inspector Lincoln's office as soon as possible.

When he'd replaced the receiver, Sam looked Albert in the eye. 'I took that call from the prison chaplain in Manchester. Are you going to get in touch with him?'

'I don't know, Sam.'

'If I were you, I'd leave well alone.'

Albert knew it was good advice, but he wondered if it was advice he'd be able to follow.

41

Peter had been distant in class, more distant than usual if that was possible, and when the school day was over Gwen asked him to stay behind, telling him she needed to talk to him about his arithmetic homework. In reality she was anxious to find out what was on his mind. Sometimes she longed to take the boy in her arms, to reassure him that it was all right to make up stories and see things differently from other people. However she was his teacher and she knew it wasn't her place.

'Is something the matter, Peter?'

He didn't answer.

'What were you doing on Monday afternoon when you weren't at school? You weren't ill, were you?'

'I can't say, Miss. It's a secret.' He gave her a sly look. 'I've seen you kneeling by that posh grave, Miss. George Sedding. I've seen you put flowers on it and I've seen another lady come and throw them off. But I won't tell no one.'

'Then we've both got a secret to keep,' she said, her heart beating so loudly she was sure he'd be able to hear it.

Reluctant to leave it at that, she walked back with him to the cemetery lodge. When he said he'd see her tomorrow she assumed he'd go straight in but when she looked back over her shoulder she saw him flitting down the road, half walking, half running, with a determination that made her worry for him. If he'd become involved in something dangerous, her instinct was to keep him safe.

She wanted to see where he was going so she decided to follow some way behind. After a while she realised he was heading for the Ridge, his hands in his pockets and his satchel still on his shoulders. He seemed so engrossed in his task, whatever it was, that she was sure he had no idea she was there.

When he turned on to the path leading to the Ridge she hesitated, reluctant to be there alone, before telling herself that it was her duty to ensure Peter's safety. His twin brother had died up there and, should Peter find himself in danger, she wanted to be ready to come to his aid.

She tracked him through the trees, wishing her footwear was sturdier, and watched him flit like a ghost through the dappled green gloom. He obviously knew where he was heading, which was more than she did, and she was suddenly afraid of losing sight of him and getting lost in that wild place. But it was too late to turn back now.

Gwen watched him vanish through a gap in the rocks and when she followed she found herself in a passage leading to a circular amphitheatre with steep rock walls towering all around. She guessed it was a quarry, long disused, with greenery and moss growing on every rock face. Peter stopped in the centre and called out. 'I've got it.'

She pressed herself against the damp stone of the quarry entrance, trying to make herself invisible, and all of a sudden a figure emerged from nowhere: a man in a tattered army greatcoat with a trilby hat on his head.

Showing no fear, Peter ran to him and opened up his satchel, producing a paper bag which the man snatched hungrily, pulling out its contents — bread and cheese by the look of it — and devouring it as though it was the first meal he'd had in years. She knew from the pictures Peter had shown her that this was the Shadow Man he'd spoken of so often, and this was her chance to clear up the mystery of his identity once and for all. On the other hand, in that isolated spot with no help nearby she feared she'd be at his mercy if things went wrong.

As she took a step back her foot slid on some loose shale and the noise echoed through the quarry, reverberating off the stones. Peter and the stranger swung round to face her and when the man walked towards her slowly she saw to her horror that he had no face. In place of his features was the blank white of what looked like a handkerchief with two holes cut in for eyes. Then, to her relief, Peter put his hand on the man's arm. 'That's Miss. She's all right.'

Gwen could hear her own heart thumping as she stared at the man with no face and she asked the first question that came into her head: 'Who are you?'

42

Albert had spent the night at home, listening to his wife coughing through the wall. Mary and her mother were sharing the bedroom which used to be theirs and Albert couldn't help feeling excluded. Vera made it clear that he wasn't wanted and that she thought him a failure as a husband. If Vera had her way Albert would no longer have the right to make any decisions about their future but he'd insisted that Mary should have the best treatment available. If she needed to go away, he'd pay for it somehow. He owed her that much.

First thing the following morning he travelled back to Mabley Ridge, leaving Mary asleep and asking Vera to say his goodbyes for him. As the train sped north the blue sky gradually turned greyer and a few drops of rain hit the train window as they approached Manchester.

After dropping off his bag at the hotel he made for the police station where he found the post-mortem reports waiting for him on his desk. He had to give Dr Michaels his due, he didn't delay like some he'd dealt with over the course of his career. Then he supposed the medical profession had more suspicious deaths to deal with in London — although little Mabley Ridge seemed to be doing its best to catch up.

With the deaths of Patience Bailey and Joan Pearce, he feared that a disturbed killer was at large in the area; a killer who could bury a woman alive and cut an elderly widow's throat. From past experience he knew that the culprit would probably be someone who appeared quite harmless; someone's neighbour or relative who was leading a hidden, darker life; perhaps someone wealthy and outwardly respectable. His mind turned to Mallory Ghent's locked room and his frequent absences from home. Then there was Leonard Parms, who'd been seen visiting Dora Devereaux whose cottage happened to be opposite the cemetery; although he knew it was sheer prejudice that made him hope one of the village's more prosperous residents would turn out to be responsible for the recent atrocities.

It was more likely the solution was to be found in the heart of the village — or even up on the Ridge. Somebody had attacked him up there that day and he was as sure as he could be that it wasn't children who were up there seeking adventure in that wild forbidden place. His assailant had been tall and strong — perhaps strong enough to bury a woman and her child.

He leaned back in his chair and closed his eyes. Then after a few moments he heard Stark's voice.

'Telephone call for you, sir. Withington Police Station. That's near — '

'I know where it is, Sergeant. Put it through if you please.'

Albert waited a few seconds, his hand hovering over the receiver, and when the phone rang the sudden sound made him jump. Since the war loud noises had alarmed him and when he answered he was still shaking.

'This is Constable Magson, Withington. You were asking about a family called Jones who used to have a chemist's shop.' The man's accent was thick and he sounded as though he was nearing retirement.

'What have you got for me?'

'As a matter of fact I remember the Joneses. Quiet family. Kept themselves to themselves as they say.' There was a pause then Magson lowered his voice. 'I hear one of the lasses has been murdered.'

'Do you remember Patience?'

'I do. Sweet little lass. Used to sit behind the counter with her mam after school.'

'I'm trying to trace her relatives.'

'The mam and dad are no longer with us, God rest their souls, but there were four children in all.' There was another pause, longer this time. 'Or rather three. One of them died in an accident when he were little. Drowned.'

The words made Albert freeze. Any mention now of a young child's death brought up images of Frederick in his mind: the small lifeless body; the unimaginable grief.

'The Joneses used to live on Vicarage Road,' Magson continued. 'So I went to have a chat with an old neighbour of theirs. One of the lads in the station's married to her daughter and she was only too glad to share a bit of gossip.'

'Did she mention the brother's accident?' he asked.

'It happened in Platt Fields Park lake but

235

that's all she knew. The family didn't shout it from the rooftops if you know what I mean.'

'I understand the brother works at Strangeways?'

'So I've heard. I take it he's been told.'

Albert felt a pang of conscience. This should have been his priority as soon as David Cohen had told him where Joseph Jones could be found. 'I've only just found out where he is and I'm about to telephone the governor to arrange a meeting,' he said, thinking of the chaplain's request to see him.

'Someone's got to break the news, but I don't envy you.'

'Was the other sister mentioned?'

'Oh aye. Constance her name was but they used to call her Connie. She was a year younger than Patience and no better than she should be, according to my informant. Always wearing make-up and flirting with boys. She went away when the war started and I don't think it was to do her bit. Word has it she went to live in London.' From the way he said it she might as well have settled in Sodom or Gomorrah. 'But no one round here's any idea what became of her.'

As soon as he'd finished talking to Magson Albert called Sam Poltimore at Scotland Yard and asked him to make enquiries about a Constance Jones who may or may not be in London. London was a big, impersonal place and Jones was a common name so unless Joseph knew how to get in touch with her, Constance might be destined to remain ignorant of her sister's fate.

He looked at his watch, relieved that it was too late now to venture into Manchester and seek out Joseph Jones at Strangeways Prison. It would have to wait until tomorrow. When tomorrow came he'd still be reluctant to go there and he toyed with the idea of sending someone else, Stark for instance, but he was in charge of the case so it was his place to interview the victim's brother. Although he'd faced worse things in his life there was nothing he dreaded more than being so near to the place where Flora's life had ended.

The chaplain who'd probably witnessed her death had asked to speak to him but his instincts told him he should stay well away.

43

While it might be too late to visit the prison there was still time to see Barbara Nevin in Cheadle. If she was indeed the mother of little Lancelot, as David Cohen had implied, someone needed to tell her that her child was dead, along with the friend who was caring for him. Albert felt that someone should be him.

On the advice of one of the constables he caught the train to a station not far from the village and walked the short distance into Cheadle, which was a pleasant village with an old stone church standing next to a pub and a long village street leading to a little green in front of a grand house and a tall literary institute. A notice on the green announced that it was soon to be the site of a new memorial to commemorate those who'd died during the war. Such memorials were springing up in many towns and villages and Albert wondered if the names carved on them would ever be forgotten in time. He would always remember his dead comrades and he, and many others, bore scars that would stay with them throughout their lives, be they long or short. But once his generation had gone he wondered whether people would prefer to forget, although he was sure of one thing — the horrors of that war would never be repeated, so maybe some good would come out of it all.

Barbara lived a short distance from the High Street, in a small square of fine brick villas clustered around a central area of grass. Some boys were playing cricket there, lost in concentration, and Albert watched them for a while before approaching Barbara's front door, gathering courage for what was to come.

The door was answered by a waif-like maid who looked no more than sixteen and he was shown into a handsome front drawing room. Barbara's family were clearly well-to-do and he wondered whether she and Monty Ghent would have married had he survived the war. Then again, like Flora, Barbara had worked as a voluntary nurse so perhaps she yearned for a career of her own rather a lifetime as somebody's wife.

David Cohen's description of Barbara had been remarkably accurate. She was small with fair hair and a smile of greeting that lit up the room.

'An inspector from Scotland Yard. Oh dear, what have I done? And before you ask how I know, David Cohen telephoned to say you'd called on him and wanted to speak to me about Patience.' The smile suddenly vanished. 'You don't have to break the news, Inspector. David's already told me.'

The cheerful greeting had been a brave attempt to cover her true emotions and now the mask had slipped and her eyes were glazed with unshed tears. 'I can't believe anybody would want to hurt Patience. I'm sure she didn't have any enemies so it must have been a maniac. You hear of these things, don't you?' She sat down heavily on an armchair and stared out of the window. 'David didn't mention the . . . baby. Is he all right?'

Albert's heart lurched. David had broken half the news but he'd left him to tell her the worst possible thing a mother could ever hear. He searched for the right words, something that would soften the blow, but he couldn't think of any so he had to be direct.

'I'm sorry. It appears that the baby died of natural causes either before or shortly after Patience was killed. I'm so sorry. Would you like me to fetch someone . . . your mother?'

She shook her head and straightened her back. 'No, thank you. I'm quite all right.'

'Are you sure?'

She looked sad but not unduly distressed, which surprised him.

'What do you need to ask me?'

'You knew Patience before she went to live in Mabley Ridge.'

'That's right.'

'She visited you here regularly, I believe. Did she mention anybody in Mabley Ridge — someone she was afraid of, perhaps?'

She breathed in and her body shuddered. 'The only person I can think of was the gardener, Mr Rudyard. She didn't like him. Said he made her nervous.'

'Did he ever threaten her or . . . ?'

'No, nothing like that.'

'Did she say anything about her employers?'

'Oh yes, she used to talk about the Ghents

quite a lot. She thought Mr Ghent had a mistress. She wasn't too happy about that.' There was a long pause. 'She felt sorry for Mrs Ghent. She said she'd never got over Monty's death.'

'That's understandable. Was there anybody else in the household Patience didn't get on with?'

'She wasn't too keen on Esme, Monty's younger sister. Said she was spoiled. I fear there's going to be a great chasm between we women who did our bit in the war and learned to deal with unspeakable things, and those who were too young to serve. There's going to be a generation coming up who live for nothing but pleasure whereas the rest of us saw things that . . . '

'You were a VAD, I believe?'

'That's how I met Patience.' She smiled at the memory.

'Where did you work?'

'Initially at a place in Derbyshire, in a village called Wenfield, not far from New Mills. Tarnhey Court it was called.'

The name hit Albert like a blow. Flora had nursed at Tarnhey Court and after the big house was no longer needed for the war effort it had been handed back to its owners, the Cartwright family. He had interviewed Sir William Cartwright when he'd been investigating the Wenfield murders, along with his son, Roderick, who'd had secrets of his own. At one stage they'd even come under suspicion.

'I know Tarnhey Court,' he said quickly. There was a question he couldn't resist asking, although resurrecting the memories seemed like picking at a sore. 'Did you know Flora Winsmore?'

She hesitated before answering. 'Yes, I knew Flora. I read about her in the newspaper. I still find it hard to believe. Although there was something . . . '

He sat forward. 'What?'

'At first she seemed nice . . . quite ordinary. Then . . . There was this doctor called Dr Bone; he had a reputation and none of the nurses wanted to be alone with him but Flora was flattered by him and . . . anyway I heard that one day he caught her alone and . . . something happened. Nothing was said, of course, but she was never the same after that. Not that it excuses what she did.'

'Of course not. You didn't stay on at Tarnhey Court?'

'My mother and father wanted me nearer home so I moved to Stockport Infirmary. Patience was working in the dispensary there. That's where we first met.'

Albert longed to hear more about Flora but asking more questions would only arouse Barbara's curiosity. 'I'd like to talk about Mabley Ridge if I may. Did Patience say anything else about the Ghent household?'

'She said the maid, Daisy, was a sly little thing who had her eye on Mr Ghent, although I don't know if that was true.'

Albert stored this unexpected piece of information away in his memory and moved on.

'Did you ever visit her there?'

'A couple of times. She met me off the train and we walked up to the tearoom near the Ridge. But most of the time she came here. It seemed easier.'

'While you were in Mabley Ridge you didn't go to the Ghents' house?'

She hesitated. 'It didn't seem . . . appropriate.'

'Can you tell me anything about Patience's family?'

'Her brother's a prison warder in Strangeways.' A worried frown passed across her face. 'Does he know yet?'

'I'm going there to tell him tomorrow. Have you ever met him?'

She shook her head again. 'They didn't have much to do with each other. I don't think they'd ever been close.'

'What about her sister?'

It was a few moments before she answered. 'She didn't mention her much. Connie I think her name is.'

'Did she tell you anything about her?'

'She said she was a . . . tart. And before you ask the only thing I know is that she's in London somewhere and that she had ambitions to go on the stage but, as I said, Patience didn't speak about her much. To tell you the truth, I think she was a bit ashamed of her.'

'I understand you were close to Monty Ghent.'

She bowed her head so that he couldn't see her expression, then drew a small lace handkerchief from her sleeve and dabbed her eyes before blowing her nose delicately. Albert

243

could tell she was fighting back her tears and he wanted to assure her that it was all right to cry in his presence if she needed to, although he imagined her parents would have different ideas. He had the impression that this was a household where respectability had to be maintained at all costs.

'Were you . . . going to get married?'

Another nod. 'We were in love, Inspector. There's nothing wrong in that, is there?'

'Nothing at all.' He paused. 'We know the baby didn't belong to Patience.'

This time the tears came, cascading down her cheeks as her body shook with bitter sobs. Albert produced his own handkerchief and handed it to her, waiting until the sobbing subsided before he spoke.

'Would you like to see him? I'm sure it can be arranged,' he said, remembering the small, discoloured corpse. If she was the baby's mother it would be the worst thing she'd ever be likely to experience but at least she'd be able to say her goodbyes.

She looked puzzled. 'No. Why would I?'

It suddenly dawned on Albert that he might have got this completely wrong. 'I thought . . . '

She caught on quickly. 'You thought the baby was mine?' She gave him a bitter smile. 'No. I've never given birth to a child and, as things are, I'm not likely to in the future. Monty was the only man I've ever loved and am ever likely to love.'

'So where did the baby come from? Patience visited you here quite often. She must have

244

explained it somehow.'

'She always claimed it was hers but I saw a lot of things during the war so I'm not completely naive. I thought it might have been her sister's and that she might not have been telling the truth when she said she had no contact with her. If her sister had got herself into trouble . . . Well, family is family, isn't it. I'm sorry. I only wish I could help you but I can't. You say the baby died from natural causes?'

'That's what the doctor says. He wouldn't have suffered.' He didn't know the truth of his last statement but thought it would provide a small crumb of comfort.

She wiped her nose with his handkerchief and looked up at him, her eyes swollen and red. 'You've got to find out who killed Patience. The more I think of it the more I'm sure her sister has something to do with all this. Patience always said she was an evil, manipulative bitch.'

44

The Shadow Man knew it had been a mistake to trust Peter Rudyard but the boy had promised to help him so he'd taken the risk. However, in his innocence Peter had unwittingly led the schoolteacher to his hiding place.

The woman had sworn not to betray his secret and at the time he'd believed her. Now he'd had a chance to think it over, he wondered if her promise had been made out of fear; and fear is no guarantee of compliance, as he knew only too well. He'd been afraid once and his terror had turned him into a criminal.

If word got out that he was living up there he knew they'd come looking for him and he was bound to become the prime suspect for the recent murders. He'd already had one narrow escape when the policeman from London came sniffing round his special place, but he'd dealt with him and he'd kept the policeman's hat as a souvenir of his rare bit of good fortune. He liked the hat because it reminded him of those happier days before they began to hunt him like an animal.

The light was fading but the darkness held no dread for him, not any more. When he'd first begun living up on the Ridge he'd felt there were ghosts all around him; the ghosts of the workers who'd laboured in the quarries and ancient mines and the ghosts of the suicides whose unquiet spirits haunted Oak Tree Edge where they'd chosen to end their lives. There was even the little ghost of Peter's twin brother and whenever he found himself near the standing stones at dusk he sensed the presence of his small, sad wraith. In his clearer moments he understood that these hauntings were produced by his mind. Then at other times he cowered in his cave covering his ears against the sound of gunfire, eyes tightly shut and his body paralysed with terror. Sometimes he cried. Peter had seen him cry and had taken his hand and held it until he stopped.

Seeing the old woman in the cemetery so soon after his arrival in the village had been a rare stroke of good fortune. He'd been visiting the grave of his beloved grandmother when he'd seen Mrs Pearce arrive with her basket and hidden himself behind a large tombstone. He'd watched her place something on a grave some distance away and as soon as she'd gone he'd hurried over to investigate and found a package wrapped in greaseproof paper containing bread, cheese and ham. He'd hardly been able to believe his luck when she returned every night with more; sometimes apples, sometimes slices of pie. Unwittingly she'd fed him for weeks and he'd come to regard her as his guardian angel.

On the night of Patience Bailey's death he'd got to the cemetery later than usual because he'd had one of his turns and been unable to leave the sanctuary of the Ridge for an hour or so. When he'd eventually arrived his mind had been conjuring snipers behind each headstone and for

247

a while he'd cowered behind a memorial with his hands clamped against his ears to block out the noise of gunfire. He cursed the episodes he'd experienced since that dreadful day at the front — and he couldn't help wondering whether he'd have been able to save Patience that night if he'd been more alert to what had really been happening around him.

Then there was a possibility that filled him with dread. In his confused state had he mistaken Patience for an enemy soldier and killed her? But could he have killed his unwitting benefactor Mrs Pearce with realising it? He thought not but he couldn't be absolutely sure . . . not when the waking nightmares over-whelmed his mind and body.

Although Peter had brought him as much food as he could lay his hands on, it wasn't enough and hunger was gnawing at his stomach, which meant he'd soon have to venture out. At times he'd been tempted to go to the one place he knew he'd be taken in and fed; but if he went there they'd come for him and then his only future would be death by firing squad. He'd seen men die like that during the war. They'd called them cowards but the Shadow Man knew this wasn't true.

Pulling the hat down to shade his face and hugging his greatcoat around his thin body, he set off down the road, praying he'd meet nobody on the way, although on the few occasions he had been spotted people had taken him for a vagrant passing through. Some had given him a few coins, assuming his makeshift mask hid some terrible disfigurement acquired in battle, but nobody had ever asked questions.

By the time he passed the cemetery it was dark and he looked across at the lodge as he always did, but there was no sign of Peter in the lighted windows. He wondered where the teacher lived; in those awkward moments of conversation it had been hard enough to explain his situation without making small talk as well. Now he wanted to know.

He walked on beyond the edge of the village into the countryside and came to a small brick farmhouse, isolated from its neighbours by fields of grazing cattle. Perfect.

Sneaking round the back, his spirits soared when he saw the kitchen window was unlit. He tried the door and, to his relief, it opened smoothly so he stepped inside, listening for the sound of footsteps. He made straight for the pantry and, after stuffing two pork pies and some bread and cheese into the pockets of his greatcoat, he crept out again, thankful that he hadn't been forced to break a pane of glass in the back door. Theft was always best when it went undetected.

He avoided the main village street as he hurried back with his head bowed and his hat pulled down to conceal his masked face. Then when he neared the gates of Gramercy House his footsteps slowed to a halt.

From where he stood he could see the house clearly. The curtains hadn't yet been drawn so, unable to resist, he crept down the drive, keeping to the side so the trees and bushes concealed his approach. As he drew nearer he could see the drawing room lit up like a stage beyond the glass.

A woman was lying on a chaise longue, reposing like an invalid with a blanket draped over her body, and he could see a fashionably dressed girl standing in the doorway wearing her coat, hovering there as though she was anxious to get away. When the girl left the room he stepped back further into the shadows. Then a few moments later he heard the front door slam and the girl marched down the drive straight past him. She was only a few feet away — so close he could have reached out and touched her — but she had no idea he was there because he'd perfected the art of making himself invisible.

From the shelter of the bushes he watched as she stood by the gate, examining her watch with increasing frequency, and when the Alvis drew up with a screech of brakes the glow of a nearby street light gave him an excellent view of the man who emerged from the driver's seat and offered the girl a cigarette.

His stomach lurched because he knew who the man was — and what he was. He didn't know what name he was using now but back in 1918 he'd been known as Lieutenant Charles Woodbead and the thought of such a man being with the girl made him feel sick. The Shadow Man had seen him kill — and his victims hadn't been the enemy. If anybody deserved to pay for his many and various sins it was Charles Woodbead.

45

The following morning Albert received another letter from Vera, just to keep him up to date, she said. Mary seemed a little better and the doctor was calling later. But she didn't want to go to the sanatorium because it would mean leaving London and the comfort of the Reverend Gillit's meetings. As far as she was concerned, going away would mean abandoning their little Frederick. Albert was tempted to screw up the letter in fury but instead he left it in his hotel room, stuffed inside a drawer out of sight.

When he reached the police station he found a message from Gwen Davies lying on his desk. Could he meet her at lunchtime in the Primrose Tearoom in the centre of the village? Since she gave no reason her request intrigued him and as he sat in his office going through statements from various witnesses he kept checking his watch, wondering what she had to tell him.

His interviews with David Cohen and Barbara Nevin had opened up a new range of possibilities, mainly concerning Patience Bailey's estranged sister, Constance. He also needed to speak to the brother, Joseph, at Strangeways Prison. One moment he was determined to arrange the interview, the next he was tempted to delegate it to Stark or maybe to Constable Mitchell, whose intelligence and common sense continued to impress him. However he knew this would be cowardice. He had a job to do.

Eventually he yielded to the inevitable and telephoned the governor. Arranging to speak to Joseph Jones that afternoon proved to be a simple matter and as soon as the appointment had been made he felt better. He'd made no mention of the chaplain; he would gauge the situation once he was there. He knew he was unlikely to see any reminder of Flora there . . . and yet he wondered whether he'd be able to resist asking the governor about her last days.

He hoped the meeting with Gwen Davies would take his mind off his afternoon appointment at the prison, and when lunchtime came he told Stark he was going out, although he didn't say where. Gwen had wanted to meet in private on neutral territory; he guessed that whatever she had to say she didn't want shared with the entire station.

As he walked to the tearoom he found he was looking forward to seeing Gwen again. The fact that she reminded him a little of Flora should have caused revulsion but it didn't; just a sad longing for the stolen happiness he'd experienced in that short period before his world fell apart. He forced himself to think of Mary, expecting to experience a pang of guilt, then to his horror he realised that if the worst should happen and her illness proved fatal, he probably wouldn't grieve for her as a husband should.

The tearoom in the centre of the village had chintz curtains and dark oak furniture, chipped in places through years of wear. Albert remembered it from his first time there in 1914 and it hadn't changed one iota. In spite of the proprietor's attempts at gentility, the Cottontots and their wives took their tea elsewhere.

Gwen was waiting for him at a table for two in the corner and he sat down opposite her, signalling to the waitress — a young girl wearing a black dress and crisp white apron that looked too big for her. The white cap perched precariously on the girl's unruly curls slipped a little and she adjusted it before taking their order. Gwen chose Welsh rarebit and a pot of tea and Albert asked for the same. His mind hadn't been on food but he suddenly realised he was hungry.

'Is there something you want to tell me?' he asked as soon as the waitress was out of earshot.

'I thought it would be better to talk away from the police station. It's something I think you should know but I would like it dealt with . . . delicately. It's Peter Rudyard.'

'What about him?'

'For a while now he's been talking about a Shadow Man but I presumed it was just another of his stories.'

A battered leather briefcase stood on the floor by her feet and she hoisted it on to her knee and opened it. She took out a sheaf of child's drawings, remarkably detailed and, in Albert's untrained opinion, showing promise of future artistic prowess. She shoved them over the table to Albert and he saw that each depicted a tall man wearing what looked like an officer's greatcoat. The figure had no face, only a blank oval with two dark holes where eyes should have

253

been. In most of the drawings it was bareheaded with longish lank hair framing the blank face but in two of the drawings it wore a hat remarkably similar in style to the one Albert had lost.

'This is him? This is the Shadow Man?'

'That's what Peter drew.' She sighed. 'Perhaps I shouldn't believe everything he tells me but there's something about him that makes me want to protect him.'

'That's understandable.'

'The Rudyards aren't a happy family, Inspector.'

Albert sat in silence for a while before he spoke. 'If you ask me I don't think it was ever a happy household, even before Jimmy's murder.'

'It can't be easy, living so close to the dead like that . . . in the cemetery, I mean. It's enough to give any child nightmares, let alone a sensitive, imaginative soul like Peter. An obsession with death and funerals isn't healthy for a boy that age, wouldn't you agree?'

Before Albert could answer the food arrived and he ate hungrily. Gwen, on the other hand, picked at her food as though there was something on her mind. Eventually she spoke.

'This Shadow Man — Peter says he's seen him up on the Ridge.'

Albert stopped eating. Someone had attacked him up there — could it have been Peter's Shadow Man? 'Is he real or just a figment of Peter's imagination?'

She didn't answer.

'When I was injured on the Ridge . . . When you looked after me . . . '

'You told me you'd slipped on some rocks in the quarry.'

'That's what I said but I think someone attacked me.'

'The Shadow Man?'

'I don't know.'

'Will you organise a search of the Ridge?'

'If this Shadow Man is real — and if he is the killer — he could be miles away by now.'

'If he does exist, who do you think he is?'

'Some unfortunate soldier damaged by war and then thrown away like rubbish once he was no longer needed as cannon fodder.' Albert saw a look of shock pass across Gwen's face. But he couldn't help betraying his feelings.

They ate the rest of their lunch in silence, Albert watching as she forked the food into her mouth, delicately at first then faster as though hunger had got the better of her.

Once their plates were empty she spoke again. 'The Shadow Man's real. I've met him.'

'Why didn't you say this before?'

'I didn't know if I could trust you not to go straight up there and arrest him.'

'Any reason why I shouldn't?'

'Because I don't believe he killed either of those women.'

'How can you be sure of that?'

'You'll have to take my word for it. I know a broken man when I see one and he's no murderer.'

'Then why is he in hiding?'

'Just because someone doesn't want to be found it doesn't mean they're a killer.'

She stood up, sending her chair clattering backwards and making everyone in the tearoom turn to stare. This would be all round the village by teatime.

Before he could stop her she'd marched out, setting the bell on the door ringing to fanfare her departure. Albert sat for a few moments before following but when he reached the High Street she was nowhere to be seen.

As he walked back to the police station he knew that he couldn't put off his visit to Strangeways any longer.

46

The governor allowed Albert to use his office for the interview. It was a room not unlike his own office at Scotland Yard, only considerably larger in acknowledgement of the governor's status. As Albert sat waiting for Joseph Jones to be brought to him, he eyed the filing cabinets he could see through the open door to the outer office. One of them would contain details of Flora Winsmore, former prisoner in the women's wing.

He wondered how she'd coped with her last days on earth. Had she thought of him and the love they'd shared before the horror of what she'd done was revealed? What had happened to the child she'd given birth to inside the prison walls? Had she any inkling of what had become of their baby boy or had she been as ignorant of his fate as he was? He longed to ask her all these questions but now it was too late. He'd kept well away while she was awaiting her execution, thinking it was for the best. Now he wasn't so certain.

He had ten minutes to ponder the situation before he was joined by Joseph Jones. He was a dapper man of medium height with neatly cut whiskers and piercing blue eyes. Albert had only seen Patience Bailey in death, lying on a cold slab in the mortuary, but nevertheless he recognised a resemblance between brother and sister.

Jones stood to attention and didn't move until Albert shook hands and invited him to sit. Even then he looked awkward, as though he was reluctant to relax in the presence of a superior officer.

Albert smiled to reassure him. 'I'm sorry that we're meeting under such tragic circumstances, Mr Jones,' he began. 'Please accept my condolences for the loss of your sister.'

'Patience chose her own path,' was the unexpected reply.

'You weren't close?'

'No.'

Albert sensed that the interview wasn't going to be an easy one. The man sat upright and there was no show of feeling for the sister he'd lost.

'You've been told that Patience was murdered?'

'Yes.'

Albert paused to allow him to say something more but he waited in vain.

'Have you been told how she died?' Surely the horrific manner of her death would elicit some emotion.

'Yes.'

'She was buried alive. A terrible way to go.' Albert watched the man's face and he still couldn't see any flicker of grief.

'Indeed. But no worse than a lot of my comrades.' For the first time he looked Albert in the eye. 'Where did you get that lot?'

Albert told him: battle, date and regiment. It was something seared on his memory. With that Jones appeared to unbend a little.

'What about you?'

There was a short pause before he replied. 'Came through unscathed. I was lucky.'

Not entirely unscathed, Albert thought. People returned with scars invisible to the eye; scars of the mind that made it impossible for him to mourn his own sister. He'd seen it time and time again, and there was no help for such men.

'What can you tell me about Patience? When did you last see her?'

'At her wedding in 'sixteen,' he answered. 'October the twenty-third it was.'

'You haven't seen her since then? You didn't get in touch with her when her husband was killed?'

'He wasn't killed. He was reported missing in action, believed killed.'

'Same thing, surely.'

'Is it?' He pressed his lips together as though he wasn't prepared to say any more on the subject.

'You think Victor Bailey might still be alive?'

'It's possible. You hear things, don't you.'

'What have you heard?'

'Came across a comrade of his — said he thought he'd scarpered. She had a baby didn't she?'

Albert was about to correct him but he decided to let him carry on.

'Our Patience wasn't one to go with any Tom, Dick or Harry, you know. She wasn't a harlot like — ' He stopped, as if he'd thought better of what he was about to say. Then, 'I think Vic Bailey deserted and came back. I think Patience was covering for him.'

Albert sat back in his seat. This was something he hadn't considered. David Cohen had seemed absolutely sure that Corporal Bailey was dead; he'd even considered it his duty to look out for his NCO's widow. Unless David had been lying, and been in on the secret all along.

A new possibility occurred to him. What if the Shadow Man Peter Rudyard had drawn was Vic Bailey, who'd travelled to Mabley Ridge to be near his wife? Perhaps David Cohen had arranged it that way — after all there was nowhere for a man on the run to take refuge near his grandmother's house in Didsbury because there were always too many people around — neighbours, servants, shopkeepers — all too ready to notice anything or anyone out of the ordinary. But Mabley Ridge, especially the Ridge itself, was full of hiding places and if Jones was right, Bailey was a deserter — and deserters were punished severely in times of war.

'The baby was found dead, buried near to Patience's body.'

Jones didn't respond.

'You have another sister, I understand?'

'Who told you that?'

Albert was taken aback by the sharpness of the man's question.

'An old neighbour of yours in Withington supplied the information.' He had no wish to bring David Cohen into the conversation unless it became absolutely necessary. 'Her name is Constance, I believe. I hear she went to London.'

Jones stood up and his chair made a loud

scraping noise against the floor that set Albert's teeth on edge. 'That whore could be in hell as far as I'm concerned.'

'I take it you have no love for Constance.'

'Like I said, she's a whore.'

'Why don't you sit down and tell me about her?'

Jones hesitated for a few moments before doing as he was asked. Albert waited for the man to speak and eventually his patience was rewarded.

'Connie left home at sixteen; broke my mother's heart. Got lots of fancy notions in her head about going on the halls. Always showing off to all and sundry when she were a lass.'

'And you've no idea where I can find her?'

'I haven't heard from her for years and that suits me fine.'

'Why?'

'She killed my little brother.'

Albert tried his best to conceal his surprise and left a long silence, hoping that Jones wouldn't be able to resist filling it by expanding on his statement. The tactic worked.

'She nagged our mother to let her take our little brother to Platt Fields Park in his pushchair. She was eight, he was two. She came back with the pushchair but it was empty. He'd drowned in the lake.'

'An accident?'

'She'd always been jealous of little Isaac being the youngest and the centre of attention. In my opinion she took the opportunity to be rid of him.'

'Did anyone see what happened?'

'Connie was too clever for that. She waited till there was no one about and said he wandered into the boating lake when she took her eye off him for a moment. My parents believed her because it was easier to do that than face the fact that their own flesh and blood was a murderess. But it was all lies if you ask me. When she went away I swore to have nothing more to do with her as long as I lived.'

'Did Patience feel the same?'

'Patience was soft-hearted. Never realised how wicked people can be.'

'But you do?'

'You face the reality of human evil every day when you work in a place like this, Inspector.'

'Did you fall out with Patience over Constance?'

'You could say that. Patience never thought she'd done anything wrong. Neither did our parents.'

'So Patience stayed in touch with her sister after she went to London?'

'She never said anything to me but I wouldn't be surprised.'

'I need to speak to Constance.'

Jones pressed his lips together in a stubborn line. 'I can't help you.'

Albert knew he was lying so he persisted. 'If you have any idea where she is, please tell me.'

There was another long silence before Jones replied.

'Somebody said they'd seen her performing at the Royal Hippodrome in town. Singing and dancing.' He made these sound like deadly sins. 'She was calling herself something different.'

'What?'

'I think it began with a D. As if the name she was born with wasn't good enough for her.'

'Not Dora Devereaux by any chance?'

'Could be,' he said noncommittally as if confirming it would bring his wayward sister back into his life.

Now there was another possibility Albert had to consider. Victor Bailey might not have been the attraction in Mabley Ridge; it might have been the presence of Patience's own sister, Constance.

'Could the baby have been Constance's? Would Patience have helped her by pretending it was hers?'

'If she did that she was a fool.'

'Can you think of anybody who'd want Patience dead?'

'Only Constance.'

'Why would that be?'

'If the scales finally fell from Patience's eyes she might have threatened to expose Constance as a murderess.'

'Or if Constance wanted her baby back and Patience refused to hand it over?'

'Surely the baby was Patience's.'

'The doctor who examined her body thought otherwise. He said Patience had never given birth. She was looking after that baby for somebody.'

As Albert waited for the revelation to sink in he looked round the office, wondering how much longer the governor would give them.

'The doctor's wrong.'

'You live nearby, I believe?'

'That's right.'

'You have children?'

'Indeed I do. Three girls and a baby boy.'

'How old is the baby?'

'Seven months.'

'The same age as the baby Patience had with her. Your little ones will be distressed at the death of their Aunt Patience.'

'They didn't know her. She was nothing to them.'

Albert was well aware that nobody really knows what goes on in other people's families but he was surprised by Joseph Jones's coldness.

'I'll make sure you're informed about the funeral arrangements — unless you'd like to make them yourself . . . as her nearest relative.'

'As I said, I'm sure that husband of hers is still alive. The funeral arrangements should be up to him.'

'And if he's dead? Or if he was the one who killed his wife?'

'That's no concern of mine, Inspector. I have a family of my own and I can hardly be held responsible for the mistakes my sisters make.' He made a move towards the door as though he was keen to get away.

All of a sudden Albert didn't want him to go. 'You had a prisoner here — Flora Winsmore. She was hanged about six months ago.'

'Why? What's she to you?'

'I arrested her.'

264

'In that case you must be as pleased as I was that justice was done.'

'How was she before . . . ?'

'No trouble, according to the matron. They usually come to terms with the inevitable at the end.'

'She had a baby?'

It was hard to read the expression on Joseph Jones's face; a mixture of disapproval and something else Albert couldn't quite fathom. 'Indeed.'

When it was clear he would say no more on the subject, Albert thanked him, careful not to betray the turmoil he felt inside. Unexpectedly he felt near to Flora at that moment and yet she was never so far away.

Albert watched as Jones left the room. He'd taken a dislike to the man and his self-righteousness had irritated him. But he had provided two useful pieces of information — Connie Jones might be living in Mabley Ridge under a different name and Patience Bailey's husband might be alive after all. If this was true, it changed everything.

Before he left the prison he said his farewells to the governor but instead of leaving his office straight away he hovered in the doorway.

'Is it possible to have a word with the chaplain?' The question was out before he could stop himself. 'I believe he telephoned Scotland Yard recently saying he wanted to speak to me so as I'm here . . . '

The governor looked apologetic. 'I'm sorry, Inspector, he went away yesterday. He's visiting an old friend down south — a bishop I believe,' he added as though he expected Albert to be impressed. An awkward silence followed, then: 'You arrested Flora Winsmore, I understand.'

Albert's heart lurched. He'd had no idea the connection was common knowledge. Perhaps Flora had spoken of him. Perhaps she mentioned him when she'd given birth to their child — or when she finally met her brutal end.

The governor was waiting for Albert to reply but he said nothing. The memory of Flora and what had happened to her in this very place was too much to bear.

47

Esme Ghent felt restless. Earlier she'd crept into her father's study to conduct a swift search of the great oak desk that dominated the room like an altar. She'd seen him hide the key there once and had stored the information in her memory for future use. Once she'd found what she was looking for she returned to her bedroom to consider her next move.

She put a record on the gramophone — jazz because Sydney had told her it was the only thing to listen to — and paced the room, pausing at the window from time to time to look out, hoping to see Sydney walking up the drive even though she knew he was unlikely to appear. He never called for her at the house and she was beginning to wonder whether the excuses he made had any truth in them.

Esme wondered if she should go down and ask her mother how she was feeling but she told herself that it was Daisy's job to fetch and carry for her. Then she remembered it was Daisy's afternoon off and Cook was out visiting her sister. The servants seemed to have a great deal of time off these days. Things had changed a lot since the war and she sometimes wondered if they were taking advantage.

The record finished and once she'd put another on she moved around the room trying out a few dance steps, dreaming of when Sydney would take her to a nightclub in Manchester. She bit her lip. The boredom was stultifying and she longed for something to happen. She'd already tried to telephone Sydney's house but there'd been no answer and now the jazz on the gramophone was getting on her nerves. She picked the needle off the record, then decided that music was better than silence so she replaced it carefully at the edge and waited for the trumpet to start again, turning up the volume to mask any noise she would make. There was something she'd been longing to do for a while and now was the perfect time.

She left her room and stood on the landing for a while listening for any sound from the servants' rooms upstairs, just to make sure that Daisy hadn't returned to the house. Esme didn't trust Daisy, although her father seemed to like her. She'd found them whispering together on more than one occasion and they'd sprung apart as soon as she'd walked in. Her father claimed that he'd been giving the maid instructions but she'd seen the smirk on Daisy's face; recently she'd grown in confidence, almost to the point of insolence, as though she was privy to some secret which gave her power over her employer. If Esme had her way she'd dismiss her, but she had no say in the matter and her mother was too weak these days to do anything about it.

She crossed the landing on tiptoe and crept down the stairs, shutting the front door behind her before walking round the house to the stable yard. Mallory Ghent had given strict instructions that the room by the stables was out of bounds, claiming that it was dangerous, although he hadn't specified what the danger was. Esme hadn't believed him for one moment. There was something in there he didn't want her or her mother to see and she needed to know what it was.

After unlocking the door she saw a narrow staircase ahead of her, lit only by a dusty skylight above. Her shoes clattered on the bare wood as she made for the door at the top and when she pushed the door open her hand was shaking. She wondered fleetingly whether it was the after-effects of the white powder Sydney had given her but she didn't care because she was having fun and after the dark years of war, fun was what everyone needed.

The door swung open noiselessly and it took a few moments for her eyes to adjust. In the feeble light trickling through the dusty window she could make out strange twisted shadows in the centre of the room.

They were writhing as if in agony, creatures so realistic in their pain that she couldn't help crying out. She could see badgers, cats, weasels and squirrels, all armed with guns and bayonets, slaughtering each other in what looked like trenches. Their desperate eyes were made of glass which glinted in the pale shards of light and some limbs had been separated from bodies, lying scattered while black crows hovered on outstretched wings over the scene, dangling from almost invisible wires like angels of darkness.

She heard a sound behind her and swung round.

'You're not supposed to be up here.' Daisy was addressing her as though she was a disobedient maidservant and Esme bristled with indignation.

'I'll tell my father of your impertinence.' A smug smile spread across Daisy's face. 'Why don't you do that, Esme?'

48

Albert had asked Mitchell to contact the Royal Hippodrome; he needed to get his facts straight before he made his visit.

He was annoyed with himself for not spotting the resemblance between Dora Devereaux and Patience Bailey when he'd first interviewed her but the two women had led such different lives.

Dora was at home when he called, although her maid was reluctant to admit him because she had company already. When Albert made it clear that he was there on police business, the girl backed down and scurried off to tell her mistress he wanted to see her.

He was kept waiting in the hall for a few minutes before he was shown into her presence and as he entered the drawing room he saw a figure hurrying past the window; a figure he recognised as Leonard Parms, who'd chosen to leave discreetly by the back door.

Dora greeted him, standing with her hand extended like a queen receiving the homage of her subject. If Albert hadn't been watching her closely he would have thought she was confident. But he'd had a lot of experience of reading people, both the wrongdoer and the innocent victim, and he could tell she was frightened.

Dora Devereaux — or rather Connie Jones — had played enough games with him so he came straight to the point. 'Why didn't you tell

271

me Patience Bailey was your sister?'

'You never asked.' She pouted like a little girl and slumped down on to her velvet sofa.

'I've spoken to your brother, Joseph.'

'How is the old prig?'

'I can't say he sends his regards. He told me one or two interesting things about your past.'

'You don't want to believe everything he says. Did you know he got out of being conscripted because he said he had a bad heart? It was all lies. There's nothing wrong with his heart. If you ask me, what he had was a bad attack of cowardice.'

'He told me he'd fought.'

'There you are, then. He's a liar. What did he say about me?'

Albert didn't answer the question. He hadn't liked Joseph Jones but he wasn't going to discuss his statement with a suspect.

'I want to talk about Patience.'

As if on cue she produced a delicate handkerchief and dabbed her eyes. The performance wasn't convincing. 'I felt awful that I couldn't tell anyone she was my sister but we'd agreed to keep it secret, you see.'

'I don't understand why.'

'I've renounced my old life, Inspector. Besides, I didn't know anything about her murder because I was at the theatre that night so why dig up the past? Connie Jones is dead. I'm a new person now.'

'Patience was still your sister.'

'We weren't close.'

He could tell she was putting on an act for his

benefit and he found it hard to believe that underneath it all she wasn't grieving; although she was determined not to show it.

'I've checked with the theatre. You told the police you were there on the night your sister was murdered but you weren't. You'd done the matinee and it was your night off.'

A brief flicker of panic passed across her perfect features. 'Sorry, of course. I remember now. I was . . . er . . . seeing a friend.'

'Who?'

'I'd rather not say.'

'Very well. Let's return to your sister, shall we. Did she come to Mabley Ridge because you were here?'

When she didn't answer the question he spoke again. It was time to get to the truth.

'The baby was yours, wasn't it?'

Her eyes widened. 'What makes you think that?'

'Because it's the only thing that makes sense. You found you were in trouble and asked your widowed sister to help out by saying the baby was hers. I think she left Didsbury to come here to be near you — and to be a mother to your child.'

Albert heard a wail of raw grief as Connie flung herself forward, sobbing. It must have taken a considerable effort to keep up the act but now the mask had cracked and she was giving full vent to her feelings. Her body shook and she howled out her rage while Albert waited for her tears to subside. He'd seen grief like that before when his own son had died. Mary had been inconsolable. In a way she still was.

After a while she gave a great shuddering sigh and looked up at him, her eyes bloodshot and her make-up smudged. 'I want to see him,' she whispered.

'That might not be a good idea.'

'I need to say goodbye to him. Please.'

Albert nodded and sat down beside her, touching her hand. It might not have been a wise gesture but it seemed the right thing to do. 'Tell me what happened. I need to understand.'

'I was working in London and I found I was in the family way. The father was married so . . . Anyway, I wrote to Patience and she had an idea. The lady she was working for, Mrs Schuman, has a grandson who knew Monty, her friend Barbara's sweetheart who died in the war. Monty's mother lived in Mabley Ridge and she needed a companion. Somebody in London had already put me in touch with the man who runs the Royal Hippodrome and I was offered a season so this village seemed an ideal base. Roderick, who owns the theatre, found me this cottage and a . . . friend's paying the rent so . . . '

'Roderick?' A memory stirred in Albert's head.

'Roderick Cartwright. He's a lovely boy but not the marrying kind if you know what I mean.' She slapped her hand over her mouth, realising she'd been indiscreet. After all, if Roderick's sexual preferences were discovered he could go to jail.

'I know Mr Cartwright. I met him last year when I was up this way on a case.'

She looked horrified. 'Please say you're not

going to arrest him. It'd be too unfair.'

Albert shook his head. 'As far as I'm concerned Roderick Carter's private life is no business of mine.'

She sniffed and fanned herself theatrically with a fluttering hand. 'That's a relief.'

A short silence followed then her face clouded. The subject of Roderick Cartwright had momentarily distracted her from her grief but now her face crumpled again. 'I want to see my baby now,' she whispered.

'I'll see what I can do.'

Albert asked if he could use her telephone and went into the hall to call the hospital, shutting the door carefully behind him. He didn't want her to overhear.

Half an hour later they were walking side by side into the mortuary at the rear of the Cottage Hospital. Connie had washed her face and without her heavy make-up she looked as pale as a ghost.

As the sheet was lifted from the little body he heard her gasp and fought his inclination to put a comforting arm around her shoulders. Then, unexpectedly, he heard her laugh.

Dr Michaels, who was standing to one side holding the sheet that had been draped over the baby's corpse, gave a puzzled frown when Dora kissed Albert on the cheek. He'd seen lots of different reactions to grief in his time but never this sort of jubilation.

'It's not him,' she said breathlessly. 'That's not my Lancelot. He's nothing like him.'

'If the baby isn't yours, whose is it?'

Connie lowered her gaze, fingering the silk of her dress; a mauve dress, the height of fashion that seemed to Albert inappropriate for the occasion. 'I don't know. But it isn't my Lance. He has a good head of hair.'

Albert said nothing for a few moments while he took this in. If Connie was telling the truth — and having seen the relief on her face when the little body was uncovered, he had no reason to doubt her — perhaps the dead baby had no connection with Patience Bailey's murder. Perhaps it was a secret child, born out of wedlock and hidden because of its mother's shame. Shame was a powerful force in small communities like Mabley Ridge.

They left the mortuary and once they'd reached the hospital gate Connie stopped walking, cleared her throat and looked straight at him. She wore an expression of complete honesty but he reminded himself that she was an actress. She made her living by pretence.

'I haven't told you the whole truth, Inspector.' She gave a nervous smile. 'I can't go on calling you Inspector. What's your name?'

'Albert.'

She took a deep breath. 'I'd arranged to meet Patience that evening.'

She paused and he waited for her to continue. Eventually she lowered her voice as though she didn't want to be overheard. 'I'd asked her to meet me on my night off 'cause I wanted to see little Lance. She sent a message back telling me to get lost because she was angry about me and Mal — Mr Ghent. I've been seeing him as well, you see. It's hardly my fault if gentlemen find me attractive, is it?'

She looked at Albert as though she was hoping for agreement, an absolution from her sins. But his expression stayed neutral; he wasn't one to judge.

'I was getting a bit worried about Mal,' she continued. 'I thought he was getting obsessed with me. I mean, I had Leonard to consider, didn't I. He pays the rent for my cottage and I've been scared that if Mal kept badgering me Lenny'd find out and get hold of the wrong end of the stick.'

'Would it be the wrong end?'

She didn't answer the question but Albert saw her blush.

'Let's get back to Patience. You asked to see her and she refused.'

'She agreed eventually.'

'Why?'

Connie gave a theatrical shrug. 'How should I know? Fit of conscience? I am his mother after all.'

'Who's Lance's father?'

'I'd rather not say,' was the quick reply. 'He's in the Cabinet and it might be embarrassing for him.' She lowered her lashes and gave Albert a sly smile.

'I take it he knows about Lance.'

'Of course.'

'And he pays towards his upkeep?'

'He's a gentleman.'

Albert understood. Little Lance was a source of income for Connie Jones, that and the rent paid for by Leonard Parms.

'Does the father know he's missing?'

The answer was another blush and a shake of the head. Albert saw that it had been a foolish question; why would Connie cut off a Cabinet minister's guilt money like that before it became absolutely necessary?

'Tell me what happened on the night you were supposed to meet your sister.'

'She telephoned me about ten o'clock that morning to say she'd meet me after all. I suggested the graveyard 'cause it's handy for me and I thought there'd be no one about. I mean, who'd go to a graveyard after dark?' She paused for a moment. 'She did say something odd.'

'What?'

'She said she knew a secret that would turn the village upside down. And before you ask, she never told me what it was.'

'Did she telephone from Gramercy House?'

'I suppose so. The Ghents have a telephone, although I've never called it . . . for obvious reasons.'

Albert's mind was working overtime. Anybody at Gramercy House could have overheard the conversation — with the possible exception of Mallory Ghent who would, presumably, have been hard at work at his Manchester mill.

'Can you remember her exact words?'

Connie closed her eyes tight in an effort to recall the conversation. 'She said she wanted to ask my advice — she said I'd know what to do.'

'Did you go and meet her?'

'I intended to but Lenny arrived just as I was

getting ready to go out. I couldn't turn him away, could I?'

'So you didn't see her at all?'

'No. Lenny stayed all evening. I could hardly chuck him out,' she added with a hint of defiance.

'Will he back up your story?'

'I'd rather you didn't bother him. He's got a wife and . . .'

'I'll be discreet. I promise.'

Connie touched Albert's arm and he flinched at the unexpected sensation as though she'd struck him.

'What are you going to do to find my Lance? That kiddy's not him so he must be somewhere. Someone must have him.'

Albert couldn't answer her question because he had no idea.

49

It took Esme some time to take it in. Somebody, most likely her father, had taken dead and broken wild creatures and preserved them to form a hideous tableau. A badger skewered a fox with a bayonet while a rat lay bleeding, caught for eternity on vicious barbed wire. There was a small deer too, dismembered by the blast from a grenade, its limbs lying scattered in a hideous pattern. More badgers lay limbless as if they had died in agony and a pheasant, its neck broken at a cruel angle, dangled over the edge of the recreated trench as if it had been caught by a sniper's bullet. She thought she knew where Mallory Ghent had obtained the corpses because she'd seen John Rudyard, the gardener, hanging around the stable yard with bulging sacks, although she guessed there were many folk in the countryside who'd be happy to provide such horrible things.

Taxidermy had been her grandfather's hobby and as a young child she'd hated visiting his house with all the dead creatures posed beneath dusty glass domes. Her father had been taught the techniques as a boy and now he'd put this knowledge to use again — his way of resurrecting the dead and giving them eternal life. As for the origin of the weapons, since the war ended there were a lot around, brought home as souvenirs to be hidden in trunks in forgotten attics.

'He says it's his tribute to your Monty. A sort of memorial,' said Daisy behind her.

Esme had almost forgotten the maid was there and she spun round to face her. There was no deference in Daisy's manner now. They were equals. 'You knew about this?'

'I know everything that goes on around here. Like I know about that man of yours — the one with the Alvis.'

'I could have you dismissed.'

To Esme's surprise the girl began to laugh and all of a sudden she realised the balance of power in the household had shifted — and it had shifted in Daisy's favour. Sly Daisy was behaving more like the mistress of the house with each day that passed, growing in stature while Esme's mother shrank and diminished on her chaise longue in the drawing room.

'Your mother doesn't look well.'

'Dr Michaels is treating her. She'll get better.'

'I wouldn't trust Michaels to treat a cat.'

'Then my father will call in a specialist from Manchester.'

'Your father has other worries. The world's changing and you need to get used to it.'

Daisy stalked out and Esme listened to the sound of her retreating footsteps on the stairs. Esme had noticed the maid's shoes were soft leather and fashionable; the sort of shoes she herself would wear.

She stood in the gloom with the animals' broken bodies and cried.

★ ★ ★

Esme didn't know how long she stayed in that terrible room, numbed by her discovery, trying not to look at the animals suspended in their dreadful moment of death. The place smelled of chemicals and the shelves at the side were filled with jars and bottles, all carefully labelled; substances her father used in the preservation process. One jar in particular contained a white powder, not unlike sugar in appearance. A skull and crossbones was prominently displayed on the label beside the word Arsenic.

She wondered whether to telephone Dr Michaels but that would be tantamount to an accusation. If her father was poisoning her mother, the situation needed to be dealt with within the family because the consequences of involving the authorities would be dire. But Esme had to end it and she was sure that, once her father found out that she knew what he was up to, he'd stop.

She had eyes and ears and she'd known about his actress, Dora Devereaux, for a while, although his relationship with Daisy had come as a shock. At that moment she hated him for his betrayal of her mother. Maybe it was even worse than betrayal.

There was one person whose advice she could ask; someone who wouldn't go running to Sergeant Stark crying attempted murder.

Eventually she left, locking the door carefully behind her, and returned to the sanctuary of her bedroom. The gramophone sat on the chest of drawers by the window but this time she ignored it. She was in no mood for music.

After a while she made her decision. She crept down to the hall, picked up the receiver and asked the operator for Sydney's number.

50

The Shadow Man was a troubled soul and it worried Gwen that she'd told Inspector Lincoln about him.

Her aim had been to convince the inspector that the man wasn't responsible for the recent murders, that he was an innocent, damaged by war and forced by circumstances into a wild and uncomfortable existence. But her revelation had only made things worse. Peter's unfortunate friend had become a suspect and she felt responsible.

Wanting to make amends in some small way for her indiscretion she'd bought food from the village shop at lunchtime and the large pork pie, the apple pie, the bread, ham and cheese had sat concealed under a tea cloth in her basket in the classroom store cupboard all afternoon.

When school was over for the day, she asked Peter to stay behind on the pretext of asking him to clean the blackboard. In fact she wanted to visit the Ridge and she needed Peter to go up there with her.

To her relief there were no policemen up on the Ridge searching for Peter's friend, which meant that Inspector Lincoln hadn't ordered an immediate manhunt, although she feared time was short.

The basket weighed heavy on her arm as she walked towards the quarry with Peter. She wanted to make up to the man for betraying him. Being with the inspector had made her feel reckless with the result that her tongue had run away with her. She thought she'd abandoned that kind of recklessness when she'd left Mabley Ridge that first time to conceal the results of George's infidelity. She knew the inspector was married because he'd mentioned his wife, so she knew she should leave well alone — just as she should have done when she'd first met George Sedding.

As they neared the quarry she felt apprehensive at the prospect of another encounter with the Shadow Man. There was something disconcerting about speaking to someone who chose to hide their face and she couldn't help wondering what hideous disfigurement his mask concealed, although she would never ask because it was none of her business. He was injured fighting for his country and that was all she needed to know.

Once they'd reached their destination Peter called out and after a few moments the man appeared out of nowhere, standing like a statue on a ledge, framed by greenery. Then he leaped down and Gwen noted the grace of his movements. Whatever his injuries were, they hadn't affected his agility. As he approached she held out the basket to him and he snatched it without a word of thanks, pulling the tea cloth aside and rummaging amongst the offerings of food as though he hadn't eaten for days.

When he lifted his mask a little to take a bite of pork pie Gwen caught a glimpse of his chin but she could see no scars on his flesh.

As soon as he'd satisfied his immediate hunger he turned towards her and said thank you with a formality that surprised her.

'I was grateful to the old woman,' he said unexpectedly, his voice slightly muffled by the handkerchief. 'She must have thought it was her son who was taking the food and I feel bad about raising her hopes like that but . . .'

'The needs of the living outweigh those of the dead,' Gwen said.

The answer was a sad nod.

'Perhaps you should speak to the inspector about the murders,' she said. 'You might have seen something.'

'No. No police.'

'They need to speak to you. Please.'

'They don't even know I'm here.'

She knew it was time to make her confession. 'They do. I told the inspector I'd seen you.'

Up until then he'd been calm, almost meek, but suddenly his anger erupted like a volcano. With a wild roar he threw down her basket and ran off, vanishing through the gap in the rocks into the dense woodland.

'You shouldn't have told on him, Miss. Why did you do that?'

'I'm sorry,' was all she could think of to say as tears burned her eyes. She felt like a Judas, a betrayer. Then she started to wonder why he was so frightened of the police. Perhaps her first impressions had been wrong. Perhaps he wasn't just an innocent man fallen on hard times because of the war. Perhaps Peter had been in danger from him all along.

She was about to follow the man when she heard the sound of voices raised in anger some distance away. She put a protective hand on Peter's shoulder but the look he gave her wasn't one of trust; it was disappointment.

She ordered him to stay where he was and dashed towards the quarry entrance. She'd recognised one of the voices and her worst fears were realised when she saw the Shadow Man struggling with a man she recognised at once as Albert Lincoln. The inspector was forcing the Shadow Man's arm up his back and the mask had been ripped off and lay like a dead dove on the ground alongside the trilby he'd been wearing. At last the face that had been hidden was revealed; Gwen was surprised to see that it appeared to be unblemished by violence and war. He was a good-looking young man with fair hair, an open freckled face and a generous mouth and her first thought was that it wasn't the face of a murderer, although she was sure looks could deceive.

'Who are you?' she heard the inspector ask as he clung to the man to prevent his escape.

'I can't tell you.'

The inspector relaxed his grip and Gwen saw him hesitate, torn between his duty and sympathy for his captive. 'Is your name Pearce? Was it your mother who left food for you in the cemetery?'

The man shook his head. 'Let me go. I don't know anything.'

Gwen could hear the terror in his voice.

'Do they know you in the village? Is that why

you've been wearing that mask?' The question was out before Gwen had time to wonder whether it was wise to interfere.

The inspector looked at her as though the same thought had occurred to him.

'You're known here, aren't you?' she heard him say. 'You lived in Mabley Ridge before the war and you knew you'd be recognised. I'll find out who you are sooner or later so you might as well tell me.'

The man collapsed on the ground like a puppet whose strings had been severed. Peter had joined her and she could feel his small hand in hers as they waited for the answer.

'My name's Ghent. Monty Ghent.'

51

Albert had been passing the village school just as Gwen Davies emerged from the door carrying a basket with Peter Rudyard by her side. They'd looked like a pair of conspirators and curiosity had made him follow at a distance.

When he saw they were heading straight for the Ridge he hung back hoping they wouldn't spot him, grateful that the bends in the road provided some cover. Then he loitered in the shelter of the tearoom and watched them walk down the footpath towards the woodland. It was only when they reached the trees that he emerged from his hiding place and followed.

They were making for the quarry where he had been attacked and he closed in on them slowly, pressing himself against the damp rocks when Peter called out. Then as the man appeared on the ledge he rushed forward, shouting a challenge.

To Albert's surprise the man only put up a half-hearted fight and soon gave up the struggle, surrendering himself to the inevitable.

Albert had been so sure he was either Mrs Pearce's missing son or Patience Bailey's husband that when his name was revealed he couldn't hide his amazement. Monty Ghent, the young man everybody, including his own family, knew for certain was dead, lying beneath French soil for eternity, was very much alive and he couldn't help wondering whether David Cohen and Barbara Nevin had been in on the secret. If they were, Patience was bound to have known too. But had she died to prevent that secret coming out?

Albert had no choice but to take his new prisoner down to the village police station. Even if he was cleared of any connection with the recent murders, he was presumably a deserter. He'd known men accused of cowardice in the face of the enemy whose minds had been too damaged to continue fighting, although their bodies still appeared unscathed, so he was reluctant to judge Monty Ghent until he knew all the facts.

Albert took his handcuffs from his pocket and locked them on Monty Ghent's thin wrists, imagining how he must have suffered while he'd been hiding out tantalisingly close to home yet unable to enjoy the lavish comforts of Gramercy House.

As they walked back to the village Gwen Davies and Peter Rudyard formed a little procession behind. When they reached the gates of Gramercy House Gwen drew level with Albert and whispered in his ear.

'He might be guilty of desertion but I know he didn't murder those women.'

'How can you be so sure?'

'Because he told me and I believe him. Look, if he tells you everything he knows, will you promise me you won't hand him over to the authorities? Please.'

'You should know I can't promise anything.

Besides, once he gets inside that police station it won't just be me who knows he's here.'

He saw despair on Gwen's face — and disappointment as though he wasn't the man she'd judged him to be.

52

Sergeant Stark loomed behind the station's front desk as they walked in.

'Now that face definitely rings a bell.' He stared at Monty, frowning in an effort to place him. After a while the frown vanished, to be replaced by a look of triumph. 'It can't be. He's dead. Killed in action.'

'This is Monty Ghent,' said Albert, putting the sergeant out of his misery. 'And he's alive . . . obviously.' He removed the handcuffs and his prisoner stood with his head bowed. He looked dirty, defeated and disorientated and Albert's instinct was to take him back to Gramercy House to be reunited with his family and take a hot bath and a good meal. But he was a police officer so he wasn't in the business of allowing law-breakers to go free — and Monty Ghent had undoubtedly broken at least one law, possibly more.

'I'm sorry I stole food from those farms,' was the first thing Monty said once he was sitting opposite Albert and Stark in one of the station's back rooms. 'But when Mrs Pearce stopped leaving that food I was starving. Of course I'll pay the farmer for it if . . . ' He paused and looked straight at Albert. 'And I'm sorry I hit you that day at the quarry. I panicked.'

'Apology accepted but you didn't have to hit me so hard — and steal my hat.'

Monty mumbled another apology, head bowed so his words were barely audible.

'Did you wonder why Mrs Pearce stopped leaving the food?' Albert asked gently.

'Peter told me she'd been murdered but I didn't believe him because I couldn't think of anyone who'd want to kill her. I thought he was lying because he makes things up. Comes out with all sorts of nonsense about ghosts and monsters and knights in armour. He lives in a world of his own.'

'He wasn't lying about Mrs Pearce. She was found dead in her house. Her throat had been cut.'

Albert could tell Monty's look of horrified disbelief wasn't faked.

'You were at the cemetery on the night Patience Bailey was murdered. Buried alive.' He let the last words sink in, watching Monty's face closely. But all he saw was revulsion when the manner of her death was mentioned.

'I didn't see anything . . . as God is my witness. I can't tell you anything.' His body was starting to shake.

'Tell me everything you remember about that night.'

'I . . . I went out later than usual that night. I have . . . flashbacks sometimes and I think I'm at the front coming under fire.' He shuddered, pulling his coat around him for protection even though the room was warm. 'I stayed in the cave till it was over and then I felt hungry so I went to get the food. Then when I got to the cemetery the noises in my head started up again so I took cover behind one of the big memorials for a while. Afterwards I just took the food as usual and went back to the Ridge. I didn't see anyone. Honestly. It must have been late when I left because some men were coming out of the Rose and Crown but no one saw me.'

'You sure?'

'Yes.'

'And you saw nobody in the cemetery?'

'No. I told you.'

Albert sat back, knowing he could be telling the truth. By then Mrs Pearce would have gone home and Patience Bailey would be lying in the newly dug grave, invisible to the casual observer.

'Did Patience know you were still alive?'

Monty shook his head. 'Nobody knows. I wanted to tell David . . . and Barbara, but I didn't want to get them into trouble.'

'But you were going to tell your family?'

'Eventually — when I'd worked out how to do it. That's why I came back. I sometimes went to the house and stood outside in the dark, watching them through the windows. You don't know what it was like knowing they thought I was dead.' He put his head in his hands for a few seconds then looked up at Albert. 'I couldn't believe it when Peter told me Patience had been murdered.'

'Did you know she was at Gramercy House working for your mother?'

He nodded. 'I saw her through the windows. It came as a surprise to see her there but David knew her through her late husband and he knows my parents so I suppose . . . If I'd gone to the cemetery earlier that night I might have been able to save her.'

'You mustn't think that,' Albert said on impulse. This thought must have been churning in the young man's mind since he learned of Patience's death but Albert knew regrets were futile. There were times he thought 'if only' were the two most painful words in the English language. 'She went to the cemetery to meet her sister, Constance, the real mother of the baby she had with her.'

'Do you think her sister killed her?'

Stark had been sitting in silence but now he spoke. 'If she was desperate to get hold of that child and Mrs Bailey refused to hand it over . . . '

Albert gave him a look which silenced him but he didn't answer Monty's question.

'You say your family have no idea you're alive?'

Monty's eyes suddenly glistened with tears. 'I swapped my identity with some poor chap from my regiment who'd been blown to smithereens and I knew it'd mean they'd be told I was dead but I was desperate. I couldn't take it any more.'

Albert offered him a cigarette which he accepted gratefully. When Albert had lit it for him he inhaled the smoke deeply.

'I saw my mother through the window. She doesn't look well.'

'I heard Dr Michaels has been called,' said Stark, earning himself another look from Albert.

'And I really need to talk to my sister.' His expression hardened. 'If you're looking for a killer, that's where you should start.'

'Your sister? Esme?' Albert didn't bother to hide his surprise.

'Not Esme . . . the man she's been seeing. I don't know what name he's using here but his real name's Charles Woodbead. Lieutenant Charles Woodbead. I've seen him going into a house near the Ridge. He drives an Alvis.'

'You think we should speak to him?' Albert glanced at Stark and saw the sergeant was sitting forward, eagerly awaiting the answer.

There was a long silence before Monty replied. 'You should be arresting him. Charles Woodbead murdered two of his own men and I saw him do it.'

53

Esme couldn't bear to be cooped up in the house any more. She couldn't bear to see her mother retching into the bowl, growing thinner and paler by the day. Dr Michaels called it a bilious attack but Esme knew it was more than that. Her father was poisoning her mother with the arsenic she'd seen in that terrible room. She'd even visited the village library and consulted a book about poisons, just to be sure the symptoms fitted.

She also couldn't bear Daisy's increasing insolence and she'd told her mother to dismiss her. However Jane Ghent was far too weak to contemplate anything that might cause conflict; besides, servants had been hard to come by since the end of the war. Women wanted well-paid work in factories and offices, not a life of sleeping in someone else's house and being at another woman's beck and call. Times were changing and Esme wasn't sure if they were changing for the better.

She walked down Ridge Lane towards Ridgeside Lodge, hoping to find Sydney at home. He hadn't been answering his telephone but she needed to tell him about the room by the stables and ask his advice. He'd been through the war so he was bound to understand.

To her relief she saw the Alvis parked in front of the house and she smoothed her hair and checked her lipstick in the small mirror she kept in her handbag before lifting the door knocker. As she waited she experienced a flutter of nerves and her palms felt clammy as the possibility that he hadn't been in touch because he was growing tired of her crept to the forefront of her mind. Suddenly she couldn't think of anything worse than losing him and being plunged back into the dull routine of village life after glimpsing the world outside.

The door opened and as soon as he saw her he smiled. A few weeks ago she would have been taken in by the apparent warmth of his greeting but now she could see a coldness in his eyes.

'I just had to get out of the house. Got anything to drink?' she said with a nonchalance she didn't feel. She needed the warm numbness of alcohol to give her courage. Accusing your own father of attempted murder was a serious business.

Without a word a bottle of champagne was produced along with two glasses.

'Something the matter, darling?'

'You could say that.' She took a deep breath. 'I found something rather horrid at home. My father keeps stuffed animals in a locked room. They're arranged in some sort of battle scene and they look as if they've been blown to pieces with their legs and arms hanging off and . . . ' She shuddered. 'It's too gruesome.'

'You said you thought he was up to something.' Sydney opened the bottle with a satisfying pop and began to pour the champagne.

'That's not all. He's poisoning Mother.'

Sydney stood open-mouthed as the champagne dribbled on to the tray.

'I found some arsenic and I don't know whether to tell the police. He's fallen for some cheap little actress who lives in the village and — '

'You can't go to the police.'

The knock echoed through the house. Twice, three times, like a portent of doom. Sydney froze and for the first time in their relationship Esme thought he looked unsure of himself.

'Who's that?' she asked.

When the knocking started up again he returned the bottle to its ice bucket, staring at the door as though he was planning his escape.

'They're not giving up. Shall I answer it?'

'No,' he barked. 'Stay where you are. Did they follow you here?'

'Who?'

The charming war hero had been replaced by a hostile stranger.

'Answer the front door and keep them talking,' he ordered as he began to sidle out of the room.

She obeyed without question; obedience to his whims had become a habit. When she opened the front door she saw Sergeant Stark standing there with a young constable, their expressions serious. Whatever they were there for she knew it must concern Sydney. But she also knew the police often persecuted the innocent so she'd do her best for him.

'Is Sydney Rich at home?' Stark asked.

Before she could answer in the negative she heard a car engine start up. He'd made it to the Alvis.

The two policemen looked at each other and ran towards the car. Then the engine died and she heard Sydney swearing as the constable hauled him from the driving seat and pinioned his arms behind his back.

'Charles Woodbead, I'm arresting you in connection with the murders of Patience Bailey and Joan Pearce.'

The thing that hurt Esme most was that Sydney never looked back in her direction when he was escorted away.

54

Albert was horrified by Monty Ghent's revelations about Charles Woodbead. He himself had suffered in the war and he knew what pressures the men had been under, but for an officer to shoot two of his own men in cold blood because they'd inadvertently witnessed him shooting himself in the foot to get a passage home was a despicable act.

War, as Albert was only too aware, could provide a perfect cover for all manner of crimes and Woodbead might have got away with it if Monty Ghent hadn't been a third, unseen, witness. Woodbead hadn't realised he'd been watching from the trees at the edge of the clearing where it happened or he would have ended up with a bullet in his head as well, an enemy sniper being the perfect scapegoat to receive the blame.

Instead, in spite of suffering shell shock, the chaos of battle had allowed the traumatised Monty to swap identities with a dead comrade and make his way back to Blighty. There were those who would have called it desertion or cowardice in the face of the enemy; but witnessing Woodbead's crime had been the last straw that had tipped the young officer over the edge into despair.

Quivering and barely aware of what he was doing, by good fortune and the kindness of strangers it had taken him more than a year to find his way back to Mabley Ridge, sleeping rough and stealing to eat.

By the time he reached his destination he had recovered sufficiently to realise that going home to his parents wouldn't be the wisest move so instead he hid out in a concealed cave on the Ridge that he'd discovered during his childhood. It was part of some ancient mine workings and it had once been his secret place; somewhere he'd played with David Cohen when David had stayed with him at Gramercy House. He'd toyed with the idea of letting David and Barbara Nevin know he was still alive, but he'd been reluctant to burden his friend and his sweetheart with the dangerous knowledge. Besides, with those visions of battle which left him a shaking husk, he wasn't the same man he'd been when he'd known them.

Albert had sent Stark to pick up Woodbead, reasoning that if he was left alone with Monty he'd be more likely to open up if they could speak man to man: soldier to soldier.

'I'm scared I might have been responsible for Patience's death,' Monty said so quietly that Albert had to lean across the table to hear him.

'How's that?'

'If Charles Woodbead learned somehow about the link between me and Patience he might have assumed I'd told her what he did during the war. He might have killed her so she couldn't give away his secret. Maybe if I'd warned her about him . . . '

Albert, seeing the look of despair on Monty's

302

face, assured him he wasn't to blame and promised to let Barbara Nevin know he was safe. Monty shot Albert a grateful half-smile. He looked gaunt and ill and Albert wasn't inclined to make him spend the night in a cell. Stark might object when he found out what he planned but he was determined to deal with the matter in his own way.

'Let's get you home,' said Albert as he stood up, offering Monty his hand. Monty hesitated before taking it and when they shook hands Albert noticed that his fingernails were filthy and his grip weak.

They received questioning looks as they left the police station together but nobody dared to challenge the man from Scotland Yard.

The two men walked to Gramercy House in silence and when they reached the drive Albert asked the question that had been on his mind since Monty's revelation. 'Do you really think Woodbead killed Patience?'

'I can't think who else it could be.'

'What about Mrs Pearce?'

'Perhaps she saw him that night when she went to the graveyard to leave the food and he wanted to make sure she didn't give him away. To think I just took it . . . ' Tears began to roll down his face. 'If I'd known . . . '

His thoughts echoed Albert's. And yet Charles Woodbead couldn't have killed little Jimmy Rudyard in 1914. Albert had hoped to find a connection between that and the recent murders but it looked as though he was wrong.

'You don't have to see Woodbead if you don't

want to but we will need your testimony.'

Monty nodded. 'I realise that.' He paused. 'What'll happen to me? Will I be handed over to the military authorities?'

'Not if I've got anything to do it.'

The front door of Gramercy House was in sight. Albert allowed Monty to go on ahead while he hung back and watched as the door opened. He could tell by the expression of disgust on Daisy's face that she thought he was a tramp who'd had the temerity to come begging at the front door, then he saw her expression change when he told her who he was. She moved to close the door in his face but Albert stepped forward.

'He's telling the truth, Daisy. Let him in and tell your mistress he's here.'

Daisy, suddenly meek, did as he told her and Albert was at Monty's side when he entered the drawing room and took his mother in his arms.

55

Peter

The police have caught the Shadow Man and I know they'll hang him or shoot him at dawn because that's what he told me they'd do if they ever found him. Miss Davies was crying. I've never seen a teacher cry before.

Mam sent me to bed early and I can hear the baby screaming downstairs. It never used to scream but Mam says it's teething. I don't like the baby. I wish it had died instead of our Jimmy.

Ernie and Jack won't come to bed for a while so I kneel on the chair by the window looking out at the graves. I can see Jimmy's 'cause it's close to the house. Mam puts flowers on it and Dad tidies round it every time he mows. Sometimes I see Jimmy standing by his grave smiling at me like he's still alive but Ernie says I'm making it up. Nothing's happening in the graveyard 'cause it's not dark enough for owls and bats so I lie on my bed and when I close my eyes I can see Jimmy. He looks like me and I always know what he's thinking, even though he's dead.

I felt safe up on the Ridge with the Shadow Man but now he's been caught I don't think I'll go there any more. Jimmy says I shouldn't. He says it's a bad place.

I've got my eyes tight shut and I can see a

shadow next to Jimmy but it's not the Shadow Man — nothing like him. I told everyone I couldn't remember what happened the day he died and that was true. But now I sometimes see things . . . like the knight who got our Jimmy. I saw him with a lady before I ran away but if I told Mam she'd say I was lying.

At school today Miss Davies made us read that play about fairies again. It's stupid. There's a man who turns into a donkey and people rushing around putting stuff in other people's eyes so they fall in love. Our Ernie says it's daft too. I don't know why Miss Davies likes it so much.

When we read it out loud she made me play Oberon who's the fairy king. I didn't want to be a fairy king but I read like she asked. Then when I'd said, 'I do but beg a little changeling boy to be my henchman,' she made me stop and asked if anybody knew what a changeling was.

Robert from Verity Farm puts his hand up. He's clever and knows everything. 'It's a baby the fairies swap for a human baby, Miss.'

Robert's not the only one who knows things so I put my hand up too. 'Our baby's a changeling, Miss. It looks different now so the fairies must have swapped it.'

Ernie gave me a nudge that really hurt but Miss Davies smiled and asked me to go on reading. But I wasn't lying. Why does nobody ever believe me?

56

Esme stumbled home with tears streaming down her face, leaving dark rivulets in her face powder. Sergeant Stark, who'd always been a comforting presence in the village, especially for families like her own who had a lot of property to protect, had just hauled the man she loved off to jail like a common criminal.

She'd overheard the words 'arresting you for the murder of Patience Bailey', yet Sydney hadn't even known Patience. Why would he have killed her?

She wondered whether to go to the police station and find out what was going on but she told herself they'd soon realise their mistake and let him go. Besides, she'd never been inside a police station and she imagined they were frightening places, teeming with criminals in handcuffs.

She let herself into Gramercy House by the back door, hesitating in the passage next to the kitchen. She took the little mirror from her bag to check her makeup and when she saw the devastation she realised she needed to wash her face before her parents saw her and began to ask questions. She could hear no sounds from the kitchen, which surprised her because Cook was usually hard at work preparing the dinner at that time of day.

All of a sudden the door at the end of the

passage burst open and she saw Cook standing there, sleeves rolled up and breathless. Her face was glowing, not with the heat from the oven but with delight, as though she'd just received miraculous news.

'Oh Miss Esme, have you heard? He's back. He's alive.'

Esme saw tears in her eyes but she didn't like to assume they were tears of joy until she knew more. 'Who is?'

'Your brother. Monty. He's come back.'

Esme stood stunned for a few seconds. 'What do you mean? Where is he?'

'With your mother.'

Without another word she barged past Cook and burst through the door to the hallway, hardly aware of her legs moving towards the closed drawing-room door. Cook was wrong. Monty was dead.

But when the drawing-room door opened with a crash he was there, sitting on Mother's chaise longue, bending over her tenderly like an angel she'd seen once in a painting. He was thin and filthy and he smelled of rotting vegetation but, despite all this, she recognised him at once. Monty had come back to them. She flung herself on him, weeping hot tears as she clung to the coarse cloth of his greatcoat.

★　★　★

Monty was reluctant to let go of his mother's hand. She looked so fragile with her parchment skin and bloodshot eyes. In his father's absence he'd ordered the maid to call Dr Michaels again but she'd stared at him defiantly as though she considered him an imposter who had no right to tell her what to do. Fortunately Jane Ghent's condition had made Monty temporarily forget the damage war had done to him and it was with his old officer's confidence that he shouted at Daisy to do what she was bloody told, surprising himself as much as the girl.

'Let's leave Mother to rest,' he said to Esme, taking her elbow and leading her into the empty dining room.

'Where have you been?'

'Here and there. I've been lying low on the Ridge for the past few months. Never mind that now — I know all about you and Woodbead.'

'Who is this Woodbead?'

'The man you've been seeing.'

Esme looked confused. 'The police called my boyfriend Woodbead when they arrested him but they've got the wrong man. His name's Sydney Rich.'

'He's been lying to you, Esme. His name's Charles Woodbead and he's a murderer. I saw him shoot two of his own men.'

'You're wrong. He was wounded in France. A ricocheting bullet hit his foot.'

Monty put both his hands on her shoulders and looked into her face. 'He shot himself in the foot to get back to Blighty and then he shot two of his men who happened to witness what he'd done,' he said as though he was explaining to a child. 'I saw him do it too, although he didn't realise that at the time. If I hadn't got away fast he would have killed me as well. He's evil, sis. A bad lot.'

She was about to argue before she realised it was best to leave it until Monty was more his old self. She knew her Sydney and she was sure Monty had got it all wrong. Nevertheless there was one thing she couldn't resist blurting out; something that had been on her mind since she'd visited her father's secret room.

'If you're looking for someone who's evil look no further than our own father. He's poisoning Mother.'

'That's ridiculous.'

'He's fallen for an actress and he's trying to get rid of Mother. I think he's putting it in her beef tea because that's all she drinks these days.'

'What makes you think it's Father?'

'He keeps arsenic in the room next to the stables. I've seen it. Remember Grandfather used to make those horrible stuffed animals? Well, Father's been doing the same only worse. They're horrid . . . all twisted and . . . '

Monty felt tears welling up in his eyes. He'd come home expecting comfort and he didn't feel strong enough for this yet.

'I need something to eat,' he said before making for the kitchen where Cook was waiting to give him a hug and ask the questions that had been bubbling up inside her since his arrival. But Monty was in no mood to talk. He sat at the kitchen table shovelling the food she'd provided into his mouth like a starving man while she bustled about. He watched as she took a jar labelled beef tea from the pantry.

'This is for your mother,' she said as though she was reading his mind. 'I've tried bits and pieces to tempt her but this is all she wants these days, poor lady.'

Monty felt relieved that someone was looking after his mother and he trusted Cook implicitly. She'd been with the family for years, ever since his childhood.

'Does my father ever come in here?'

'Never. Master has better things to do.'

'Are you sure?'

She gave a puzzled nod just as the young maid opened the door then, seeing Monty there, shut it again quickly.

He heard the sound of excited voices from the direction of the hall but he couldn't make out what was being said because of the heavy door separating the world of the servants from that of the masters.

'That sounds like your father,' Cook said with a smile. 'Miss Esme must have telephoned him at the mill.'

Monty stuffed some bread into his mouth and sprang up. He rushed towards the hall, followed by Cook who was keen to witness the family reunion.

When the servants' door clattered open Mallory Ghent stared at his son in disbelief for a while. Then he shook his hand, a strangely formal greeting; he seemed too stunned for speech.

It was Esme who broke the awkward silence. 'Show Monty that room, Father. Show him the animals.'

The look of shock on Mallory's face was unmistakable. 'He doesn't want to see that.'

'Show him.'

Monty waited while his father fetched the key from his study then he followed him past the kitchen in silence, unable to get Esme's accusation out of his head. Perhaps he'd come back just in time to prevent a tragedy.

Esme followed a few feet behind with Cook bringing up the rear. Mallory stopped and turned, looking at Cook. 'I don't think it's appropriate for the whole world to see this.'

'Why not, Father? We don't have any secrets, do we?'

Mallory's expression was one of total defeat as he made his way across the stable yard. When they reached the room Esme propelled Monty inside.

'I made it as a memorial to you,' Mallory whispered as Monty stared in horror at the tableau. 'It was my attempt at resurrection — bringing these creatures back to life . . . like I wanted to bring you back to life.'

Monty closed his eyes tight. Even though the participants were animals, the twisted, broken bodies were all too real to him.

He heard a crash and the sudden, ear-shattering noise made him jump. Things were being smashed around him and he crouched down, sweating, his hands clamped over his ears. He gave a howl. It was starting again: the gunfire; the cannons; the death.

Then he felt an arm around his shoulders and heard Cook's voice. 'It's all right, Master Monty.

312

Open your eyes. It's only your father.'

It took a few moments for him to screw up the courage to do as she said and when he did he saw his father destroying his own handiwork, throwing the maimed animals against the wall with a violence that shocked even a man who'd witnessed the horrors of war. Mallory Ghent flailed about, hitting out at his creation as he wailed with pent-up grief.

'He's here, Father. He's alive. There's no need for this,' Esme called out.

Mallory Ghent fell to his knees on the dusty floor and wept, his body shaking, while Monty stood, frozen with shock. He saw Esme run past the destruction and pluck a jar off the shelf. He could see it was almost empty — and that its white label bore the word Arsenic.

'See. This is what Father's been doing. No wonder he's behaving like this. He's been found out.'

But Mallory, oblivious to his daughter's accusation, was still weeping when Cook took Monty by the arm and led him back to the kitchen making soothing noises. Monty had always been her favourite. When the telegram had arrived to say he'd been killed she'd mourned him as if he was her own.

Still supporting Monty, she pushed open the kitchen door and to her surprise she saw Daisy standing by the pantry holding the jar of beef tea in one hand and a small phial of something that looked like sugar in the other.

'What are you doing with that, Daisy. Put it down at once.'

'The mistress is asking for it,' came the swift reply.

By now Monty had recovered sufficiently to notice the defiance in Daisy's eyes. He rushed towards her and knocked the phial of white powder from her hand so that the thin glass smashed and the crystals spilled across the flagstone floor.

Then he wept.

57

Albert had heard of killers who lacked any human emotion but he'd rarely encountered one before. Killers usually wept or tried to justify their actions when they were finally caught. Even Flora had done that. But Charles Woodbead was as cold as a statue as he sat facing him in the small back room of the police station smoking his expensive brand of cigarettes.

'You've been taking a great interest in Mrs Jane Ghent. Why was that?'

'Jane and I go back a long way. We met in 'fourteen, a few months before war broke out. I was staying nearby in Wilmslow and we became . . . close. Jane was a passionate woman back then,' he said with a smile.

'And now her daughter's taken her place.'

'Esme, bless her, was just a means to an end. I wanted to get close to Jane again because I'm in possession of some . . . correspondence which might be embarrassing to a woman of her social standing. I need money and she was in a position to pay for my silence. And if she began to have second thoughts, I always had Esme as a bargaining tool. The silly girl would do anything I wanted.'

He made it sound like an everyday business transaction and Albert fought the urge to punch him. 'You were planning to blackmail Mrs Ghent.'

'Blackmail's not a pretty word, Inspector.'

'Neither is murder. I think Patience Bailey discovered your true identity and you killed her so she couldn't talk. You followed her to the cemetery where she'd arranged to meet her sister that night and you silenced her.'

'Prove it.'

'The old lady who used to visit the cemetery to leave food for her dead son saw you so she had to be dealt with too. If you'd known where Monty Ghent was you would have killed him as well but he kept himself well hidden up on the Ridge. We now have Monty Ghent's account of what he witnessed during the war so you might as well confess to your other crimes.'

Albert looked at him expectantly and saw him stub his cigarette out with unexpected violence. 'I didn't kill those women. You have my word as an officer.'

'An officer who shoots himself in the foot then kills two of his own men because they saw him do it.' Albert stood up, sending his chair clattering behind him.

'You can't prove a thing.'

Without a backwards glance, Albert limped from the room. Charles Woodbead made him sick.

58

While Albert had been questioning Woodbead, Connie Jones, alias Dora Devereaux, had turned up at the station to ask if there was any news about her little Lance, as she called him. With everything else that had been happening Albert had almost forgotten about the missing baby but the more he thought about it, the more he suspected it might hold the answer to the whole case.

Sergeant Stark was adamant that Monty Ghent should be handed over to the relevant authorities because he was a deserter — a coward. But Albert did his best to hide his irritation as he pointed out that, as Stark hadn't actually fought in the war, he couldn't know what unbearable pressures the soldiers had been under. Besides, he knew of many cases these days where such things were quietly forgotten; not an official amnesty as such but a case of least said soonest mended. The war had been over for almost two years — what would be gained by pursuing damaged men like Monty?

'I won't have Monty Ghent treated like a criminal,' he told Stark firmly. 'I've told him he can stay with his family. He'll be safe enough there.'

'But he's got to be a suspect for these murders,' Stark protested, his eyes gleaming with righteous indignation.

'If we put all the suspects in this case in the cells, the place would be full.'

Stark looked at him as though he'd just uttered words of treason and Albert suspected there'd be no more invitations to eat at the Stark house. Which was a pity, because Mrs Stark was such a good cook, but principles came before stomachs.

Albert decided to return to the hotel to eat and rest before resuming the questioning of Charles Woodbead. The man was still denying his guilt but Albert knew that if a jury believed Monty's testimony concerning the murders of the two hapless soldiers, then he'd probably hang. Even so, Albert wanted him to make a full confession — and to tell him why two innocent women had had to die.

When he reached the hotel two letters were waiting for him at the reception desk. The first was from Vera; the usual bulletin on Mary's health he was beginning to dread reading because the news was never good. The second letter was a plain brown envelope, addressed to him at Scotland Yard in sloping copperplate writing and forwarded on. He stuffed it into his pocket to read later.

As a child his mother had always told him to get the most unpleasant thing out of the way first so he tore Vera's letter open, only to find that the situation had worsened. *The doctor's very worried about her,* she wrote. *And the Reverend Gillit says that she will soon be with little Frederick which is a great comfort to her.*

Albert was tempted to tear the letter into

318

pieces. But he was sitting in the hotel lounge so he had no wish to draw attention to himself by making such a dramatic gesture. How dare Gillit put such ideas into her head? How dare he tell her to give up fighting for her life so she could be reunited with their son? Albert might not be much of a husband but he couldn't face the thought of losing her like that — and the burden of guilt that would inevitably follow.

He went up to his room where he sat on the bed and buried his head in his hands, trying to cry tears that wouldn't come. All he saw when he closed his eyes was Flora: Flora smiling; Flora kissing him tenderly; Flora hanging dead in the execution chamber. Then he wept.

Now that Charles Woodbead was in custody his excuses for not returning to London were running out. But he was reluctant to leave with so much business unfinished. When he'd come to Mabley Ridge he'd hoped to rectify the failure that had haunted him since that hot summer of 1914: his inability to solve the murder of Jimmy Rudyard. The truth was he felt as useless now as he had back then.

However his last interview with Woodbead had given him a small glimmer of hope. He'd now established that Woodbead had been in the area in 1914 when he'd become Jane Ghent's lover. The man was a heartless killer so it was quite possible that he'd disposed of Jimmy for some reason. Perhaps if the boy had seen him and Jane together and Woodbead thought he might betray them. He might have smothered the child to stop him making a fuss — or even for the sheer pleasure of killing. It would be a neat solution and one Albert intended to pursue.

He heard a tap on his bedroom door and he wiped his face with his handkerchief before saying, 'Come in.'

It was a chambermaid, smart in her white apron and starched cap. 'Sorry to bother you, sir, but there's a lady wants to see you down in reception.'

Stuffing the second, unopened letter into his pocket, he followed the girl down the grand main staircase and to his surprise he saw Gwen Davies sitting in a worn leather armchair near the door. She stood up when she saw him, nervously fidgeting with the edge of her sleeve.

'You wanted to see me, Miss Davies?'

She sat down and looked around to check that nobody was within earshot. 'It's Peter.'

'Again? You worry too much about that child.'

Her eyes met his. 'I think you have a soft spot for him yourself . . . after his brother's murder.'

Albert knew there was truth in her words. As soon as he'd seen Jimmy Rudyard's twin he'd felt some responsibility for him, justified or not.

'I know you can't rely on everything he says but he said something strange at school when we were reading *A Midsummer Night's Dream*. There's a speech early on by Oberon which mentions a changeling and I asked the class if they knew what a changeling was. One of the boys gave the right answer then Peter put his hand up and said the Rudyards' baby was a changeling — that he'd changed suddenly in appearance. His brother tried to stop him saying any more but Peter was in his own little world as usual.' She took a deep breath. 'Word has it that the baby we found buried wasn't Patience Bailey's Lancelot. What if . . . ?'

Albert caught on quickly. 'You're sure he wasn't making it up?'

'I can't be sure, but perhaps you should have another word with the Rudyards.'

Albert was tempted to ignore her suggestion. He knew he wasn't welcome in the Rudyard house but he was a policeman, used to intruding where he wasn't wanted. And if his suspicions about Charles Woodbead proved correct, he might soon be able to tell the Rudyards that he'd finally brought Jimmy's killer to justice.

'Do you have a picture of the missing baby?'

Albert kept a photograph given him by Connie Jones in his inside pocket. She'd paid for Patience to have it taken in a photographer's studio and the child, clothed in fancy white frills, stared at the camera with wide innocent eyes; no doubt watching some imaginary birdie. He'd promised to return it to Connie as soon as he'd finished with it, although he hadn't said when that would be. He took it out and studied it before handing it to Gwen.

'Come to think of it, every time I've visited the cemetery lodge Mrs Rudyard's been very careful to keep the baby out of sight,' he said.

'We can go now if you want,' said Gwen. 'You can demand to see the baby.'

Going there on Peter's word seemed fool-hardy; yet recently the boy had been right about a number of important things. Nobody had believed him when he said he'd found Patience Bailey's body but that had turned out to be true. And nobody had believed that the Shadow Man existed but he did.

'It might be best if I come with you. Peter'll talk to me.'

'Very well. Wait for me here.' He barked the words like an order and immediately regretted his abruptness. His experience with Flora had made him wary of any woman for whom he felt any spark of attraction. Perhaps he'd be like that for the rest of his life. Perhaps Flora had killed something in him as surely as she'd killed her victims.

He went to his room to fetch his hat and his notebook, every stair providing a reminder of his injuries as he hobbled up the staircase. He returned to find Gwen waiting impatiently by the hotel's front door and they walked down the High Street in silence because he couldn't think of anything to say to her. With Vera's letter still on his mind, he had no small talk. Everything else seemed insignificant in the face of death.

When they reached the cemetery lodge he hung back as Gwen knocked on the door. Dusk was starting to fall and he could see the flicker of gaslight in some of the windows.

'What do you want now?' Grace Rudyard said angrily as she opened the door. 'Our Peter's in bed and I'm not disturbing him for you or anyone else.'

Albert stepped forward. 'Sorry to bother you again, Mrs Rudyard, but somebody's made a statement you can easily disprove. I'm sure you understand I'm obliged to check and then I'll leave you in peace.'

The woman looked suspicious. 'What is it? What's this . . . statement and who's made it?'

Albert ignored the question. Instead he asked if he could come in and Grace stood aside reluctantly as Albert and Gwen entered the kitchen.

'Where's your husband?' said Albert.

'Rose and Crown, where he usually is at this time. If you want him, that's where you'll find him.'

'May I see your baby, Mrs Rudyard?'

'Why?'

'It's just to clear up a question that's been bothering me.'

'He's asleep and I'm not going to wake him up.'

'I don't need you to wake him. I just need to see him.'

Albert waited, confident that she'd refuse and wondering what he'd do when she did. He was quite unprepared when she began sobbing uncontrollably. The formidable woman had crumbled, leaving a vulnerable mother. He took a handkerchief from his pocket and passed it to her.

'I'm sorry, Grace, but I really do need to see the baby.'

She waved an arm in the direction of the parlour door and Albert touched her shoulder as he passed her. Gwen followed, walking on tiptoe.

The child lay in a battered pram, most likely used to convey each of the Rudyard children, even the twins who would have had to share its worn mattress. As Albert leaned over the sleeping baby he saw his own sleeping child. Frederick had always slept with his little arm above his head like that; he had made the same gentle snuffling noises, and Albert felt a sudden pain in his heart.

He took Connie's photograph from his pocket. There was no doubt about it: this baby was Lancelot, known as Lance.

He returned to the kitchen where Grace Rudyard was sitting stiffly in a hard wooden chair staring at the range.

'Tell me what happened, Grace,' Albert said gently, drawing up a chair to sit beside her. Gwen was standing by the door, breath held, listening.

'I heard a noise so I went outside to see what it was. I thought it was a cat or a fox at first but it turned out it was a baby crying over near the wall. John was asleep but I couldn't sleep . . . not after . . .'

'The baby we found buried — that was yours, wasn't it?'

She started to cry again, wiping her face with Albert's handkerchief which was now sodden with tears.

'He died. John said not to call Dr Michaels 'cause it'd cost too much.'

'When did he die?'

'That day, while the others were out he took sick and it happened so fast.' She glanced at Gwen, who'd bowed her head as though in respect for the dead child. 'John buried him.

Didn't want to go to the expense of a funeral — said it wasn't worth it for a baby.'

The words struck Albert with horror but he knew poverty forced people to make harsh decisions. The Rudyards had a lot of mouths to feed.

'So that night you found the baby crying in the cemetery?'

'He was lying on one of the graves all wrapped up warm in a blanket. I thought someone had abandoned him — some girl who'd got herself into trouble most like. It seemed like it was meant . . . a baby to replace my little Harry. I never saw that dead woman, honestly. All I saw was the little one lying there near where John had buried my little Harry. I picked him up to comfort him and took him home. That's the truth. It seemed like a miracle.'

Albert knew she wasn't lying. Patience Bailey's killer hadn't been able to bring himself to kill the child she had with her. Only a monster would have done that.

His superiors at Scotland Yard, some of them at least, would say he'd be neglecting his duty if he let Grace off so lightly. But the child had come to no harm and she had just lost her own baby so, in Albert's opinion, she hadn't been in her right mind on the night she'd found an apparently abandoned child so soon after losing her own. He remembered only too well how Mary had been when they'd lost Frederick; the last thing Grace Rudyard needed in her grief was to face the full force of the law. He waited for her sobs to subside before asking his next question.

'Please think carefully. Did you see anybody there in the cemetery that night?'

'No. Like I said, I only went outside 'cause I heard the baby crying late on.' Then she thought for a few moments, and her next words were spoken almost dismissively, as though she saw nothing unusual in what she'd just told him. It was just something normal; something she saw most nights.

But Albert knew it might hold the answer to the whole case.

He knew Grace would make sure the sleeping baby came to no harm so he left him where he was. As Connie would be performing at the theatre he reasoned he had no choice. The matter could be sorted out in the morning.

He escorted Gwen back to Miss Fisher's cottage and once he'd left her at the front door he returned to the police station, determined to say nothing about Grace Rudyard's revelations until things were clearer in his mind. Sergeant Stark was off duty and Albert assumed he'd be home with Mrs Stark, enjoying an evening by the fireside, smoking his pipe and reading the newspaper, the picture of domestic bliss. In his absence Albert took Constable Mitchell to one side and made his request and, although Mitchell expressed surprise, he obeyed without question before putting on his helmet. The Rose and Crown would soon be chucking out and it was time for his evening patrol.

Albert sat at his desk poring over the information Mitchell had just provided, checking and double — checking. Then he found the file on Jimmy Rudyard's murder and went through it again in detail, only to find that the same name kept cropping up again and again.

If his suspicions proved correct, the rigid certainties of Mabley Ridge's society were about to be turned upside down. But first he needed proof.

59

Peter

I heard someone at the front door so I got out of bed and stood at the top of the stairs 'cause nobody can see you up there in the dark. Miss Davies came in with the inspector from London and he talked to Mam for a long time but I couldn't hear what they were saying.

Then I heard the parlour door open, which was funny 'cause Mam always puts the baby in there till she goes to bed so we don't wake him up. I wondered why the inspector wanted to see the baby. Perhaps he just likes babies. Some people do but it's usually ladies. Perhaps they've found out he's a changeling like in the play but I've never heard of policemen arresting fairies who swap babies.

Now Miss Davies and the inspector have gone and Mam's crying. She cries a lot these days. Sometimes I can't sleep, what with that and Ernie's snoring and Dad telling Mam to shut up.

I'm fed up of lying in bed so I get up and look out of the window but I can't see nothing in the graveyard; only an owl and some bats. I wonder what it's like to be a bat. Do their wings get tired flying around like that?

I took some paper home from school today. Miss Davies said it was all right so it's not stealing. Last night I couldn't sleep and when I closed my eyes I kept seeing our Jimmy and the others who were there on the Ridge. It all keeps flashing through my head like pictures so I drew what I remembered. I'm going to show my picture to Miss Davies. She won't laugh at me.

Mam's still crying and she won't stop but I know if I go down and ask her what the matter is, I'll get shouted at . . . or worse. But something's wrong and Miss Davies was with the inspector so she might know what it is. If I ask her I know she'll tell me what it is because she's not like other grown-ups. It might be something to do with the murders so maybe I can help 'cause I'd like to be a detective like Sherlock Holmes when I grow up. Miss Davies gave me a book about him to read once and I liked it.

Dad's not back from the Rose and Crown yet and Mam's in the parlour crying her eyes out so she won't hear me if I sneak out. Jack and Ernie are snoring so I get dressed as quiet as a mouse and creep downstairs and out of the back door.

I don't know if Miss Davies'll be home yet but I read in a comic once that if you don't want to knock on someone's door you can throw stones up at their window. Miss Davies lives with Miss Fisher but I don't like her so I call her Miss FishFace.

I don't know which room's Miss Davies's but if I get the wrong one, I can always hide behind the hedge if Miss FishFace comes out. And if she catches me I'll say I know things about her and I'll tell on her if she gives me a hiding.

They used to say I was a liar but if I can prove our Harry's a changeling they'll have to believe me, won't they. I don't tell lies. I just know things other people don't.

When I pass the Rose and Crown I can see shapes behind the funny glass in the windows and the voices inside sound like a buzz, like that swarm of bees I saw in the graveyard once. I run past 'cause Dad's in there and I don't want him to see me if he comes out. Mam says he likes his ale and some nights I hear them shouting. Sometimes he hits her. Perhaps that's why she cries so much. And I know he's the Body Snatcher 'cause I've seen him with the sack.

When I get to Miss FishFace's house I stand outside for a bit. I can see lights on behind the curtains so I pick up a handful of soil from the front garden. Then I hear voices and at first I think it's Miss FishFace shouting at Miss Davies. But one of the voices is a man's.

I don't recognise the voices so I wonder if Miss FishFace has got burglars. Or perhaps Miss Davies is arguing with that inspector 'cause he's arrested her for something. I've seen her a lot at that Cottontot's grave — George Sedding who had the fancy funeral. I've seen her crying there so maybe she killed him. That's it. I've solved a crime . . . like Sherlock Holmes.

The front door opens and Miss FishFace rushes out like she's heard a noise. Then she sees me and I drop the soil.

'Is Miss Davies in please?' I say, all polite like.

'No. She isn't. What do you want?'

'I heard a man talking. Is it that inspector? Is he here?'

'No,' she says staring at me like I'm something

nasty she's trodden in.

'Who is it then?'

She doesn't answer the question. All she says is, 'Miss Davies isn't back yet.'

'Can I wait for her? I've got something important to tell her.'

'What about?'

'My brother Jimmy. I've remembered something and I need to tell her.'

She looks cross and I think she'll tell me to get lost or threaten to tell me dad then suddenly she turns all nice and tells me to come in. I've never been in her house before and it's all posh with nice red carpets and furniture polished so hard you can see your face in it. Me mam would love it.

'You can wait in the parlour,' she says like she's talking to a servant.

I do as she says and I think she's going to leave me there but she follows me in and shuts the door behind her. She's so close that I can smell her scent. It smells nice like flowers. Me mam never wears scent like that.

She tells me to sit on the settee. It's velvet and it looks as if it should be in a Cottontot's house, not that I've ever been in one. I wonder why she's not telling me off for calling so late. Our Ernie's been here and he says she's a right tartar.

I've got the picture I drew in my pocket and I wanted to show it to Miss Davies but now I want to go home. I stand up and say to Miss FishFace that I won't wait, thank you very much, 'cause me mam'll want me home.

But as soon as I'm on my feet she pushes me

down on to the settee, so hard it hurts my arm. I say I'll tell me dad but she takes no notice and her eyes go all funny — hard like gobstoppers — and when I stand up again and try to run to the door she grabs my arm. I try to wriggle free and she loses her balance and falls against a glass cupboard full of books. The glass smashes and she gives a little scream, like owls do when they're hunting, and there's blood everywhere gushing out bright red. When she sees it she gives another scream, quieter this time, and clutches her arm.

I wonder if I should fetch Dr Michaels but I need to get away. If she dies everyone'll call me a murderer but I didn't mean to do it and if I get home quick I can tell everyone I was in bed. Then it comes to me that if it was a burglar she was arguing with he'll get the blame.

I run for the door but before I can get there it opens and he comes straight at me. He tries to grab me but I get past him and run for it.

60

Gwen had the uneasy feeling that she'd let Peter down by sharing his words with the inspector. But she knew she'd had no choice.

Grace Rudyard had confessed to taking the murdered woman's baby to replace her own little one who'd died. It had been the act of a desperate, grieving woman and no real harm had been done, Albert said as they walked away from the cemetery lodge. When he concluded that nothing would be gained by placing Grace Rudyard under arrest she felt a glow of satisfaction that he trusted her enough to take her into his confidence, although she did wonder whether others would agree with his decision to leave the baby in Grace's care. Sergeant Stark had always struck her as a man who did things by the book and she hoped Albert wouldn't get into any trouble over his merciful act.

Gwen held her door key at the ready as she walked up the front path to the cottage, the tall plants each side grabbing at her legs and dampening her stockings. The parlour light was still blazing so she assumed Miss Fisher was still up. She wondered if her landlady would mind if she made herself some cocoa — although she was sick of cocoa. She was sick of Mabley Ridge with its fathomless gulf between rich and poor and its mean minds. She'd come back to be with George and now he was dead there was no reason to stay. All she had were memories of their time together and the occasional glimpse of his widow to remind her of her guilt.

When she stepped into the hall she expected to hear the gramophone Miss Fisher often listened to before she retired for the night, her music of choice being the operas of Wagner. Instead there was a heavy silence.

Feeling uneasy, she stood in the hallway faced with three closed doors and when she pushed the first door open it hit the inside wall with a force that sounded like a gunshot. In the gaslight she could see something glinting on the floor: shards of glass from the broken door of the bookcase that stood against the wall to her right. The glass had broken into vicious daggers and there were brownish-red stains on Miss Fisher's spotless rug.

Filled with dread, she rushed out and pushed open the door to the back parlour but the room was in darkness and appeared to be undisturbed. The third door led to the kitchen where, once again, the gaslight was burning. She called Miss Fisher's name and when there was no reply she stepped into the room and saw a large, raw leg of lamb in a roasting tin on the kitchen table, dripping with blood, ready for the oven the next day, although a pair of flies circled and landed every now and then on the meat like children let loose in a sweetshop who weren't sure where to begin.

She called Miss Fisher's name again as she made her way upstairs but there was no response. Miss Fisher's bedroom door was shut and Gwen hesitated; entering her landlady's inner sanctum seemed an impertinence too far so she knocked and when there was no answer she walked downstairs again. It wasn't like Miss Fisher to go out and leave the lights burning because she was a great one for thrift, although if she'd met with an accident she might have gone to find help, perhaps to Dr Michaels or to the Cottage Hospital. Miss Fisher seemed to have no qualms about walking out alone in the evenings.

Gwen reached the foot of the stairs where she noticed a scrunched-up piece of paper lying near the front door. Miss Fisher didn't usually tolerate untidiness so she picked it up and as soon as she'd straightened it out she realised that it was one of Peter Rudyard's drawings. It showed two people — a man dressed as a knight and a woman — who might have been locked in a struggle; or possibly an embrace. There was a small figure too, lying on the ground near the pair; and tooth-like shapes surrounding the little figure like the bars of a cage.

It was certainly Peter's handiwork, which meant he must have called and perhaps been turned away by Miss Fisher who regarded anybody beneath the age of sixteen as little better than vermin.

She looked round and noticed some brown smears on the dark-green lincrusta that covered the lower part of the staircase wall. After stuffing the picture into her pocket, she retraced her steps, climbing the stairs on tiptoe. She picked up the paraffin lamp that was burning on the

335

landing windowsill and pushed Miss Fisher's bedroom door open with her free hand, holding her breath. When she held the lamp aloft she saw that the bed was neatly made and the items of the dressing table were arranged with military order. Then she saw Miss Fisher lying on the floor, her arm outstretched towards the wardrobe.

Gwen placed the lamp carefully on the dressing table to light the scene and bent to examine her landlady, relieved when she moved a little and let out a groan.

'Miss Fisher. What happened?'

The answer was another groan. Then the woman managed to gasp one word. 'Boy.'

Gwen's eyes were drawn to the deep cut on her left arm, which was bleeding profusely, and she concluded that the woman must have fallen hard against the bookcase so that one of the shards of thin broken glass had penetrated her flesh, although she was puzzled as to why Miss Fisher had dragged herself up to her room instead of trying to get help.

'I'll fetch Dr Michaels.'

The woman's eyes snapped open and she grasped Gwen's arm with her right hand. 'No.'

Gwen was surprised by the strength of her grip and she suddenly felt a stab of fear. The word 'boy' echoed in her head as she remembered the discarded picture. There was a possibility she didn't want to consider; but she needed to know. 'Was Peter Rudyard here? Did he do this to you?'

Miss Fisher answered in a hoarse whisper.

336

'He'll pay for what he's done. Get towels. Stop the bleeding. Quickly.' The words were cold, like an order to a prisoner.

61

Monty Ghent lay in the bed he'd slept in since childhood, his body trembling as the sounds in his head grew louder: the noise of gunfire and the roar of cannon; the whistle to signal they were going over the top. In the cave there'd been nobody to hear him crying out in desperation but now he was home his family were there to witness his distress. He opened his eyes and saw his anguished father kneeling by his bedside.

'You're safe now, son,' his father whispered. Monty could feel the weight of his protecting arm on the blankets. 'You were having a bad dream, that's all.'

'It wasn't a dream.' Monty turned over to face the wall, his eyes stinging with tears for all the comrades he'd seen blown to pieces. He could see their severed limbs hanging from the barbed wire and smell their blood and the sight of his father's strange animal tableau had revived the memories, causing him to relive it again and again.

'I'll call the police in the morning . . . about Daisy. Dr Michaels says your mother's symptoms are consistent with arsenic poisoning. I blame myself for not seeing it before,' said Mallory as if his failure was preying on his mind.

Monty shut his eyes. At that moment he couldn't face the thought of Daisy. What he needed to do was more important than the sins of a ruthless and overambitious servant.

'Why don't you go, Father?' Monty mumbled. 'I want to sleep.'

After his father had crept from the room Monty waited a while before sliding out of bed and pulling back the curtains to let in the moonlight. Then he stumbled over to the huge mahogany wardrobe where his mother had preserved his neatly hung clothes like the precious relics of a saint and grabbed the most convenient trousers and shirt. On his insistence his tattered and malodorous greatcoat had been draped across a chair in the corner and he put it on again before sneaking down the stairs. After everything that had happened, Monty longed for peace and there was only one place he was guaranteed to find it.

The maid, Daisy, had been locked in her attic room by his father and the next morning she'd be turned over to the police. The Ghents would have to face the scandal just as Esme would have to come to terms with the revelation that she'd been duped by the most heartless man Monty had ever come across. It seemed as though, in his absence, Gramercy House had fallen under a curse and he regretted that he hadn't been there to prevent the disasters that had befallen his family.

During the war, cowards and deserters had been shot and when he deserted he'd gone to ground, assuming the authorities' desire for vengeance on those who had, in their eyes, shirked their duty, would continue into peace-time. But escaping unsympathetic justice wasn't the only reason he'd hidden from the world; his mind had needed time to heal and, strangely enough, the presence of little Peter Rudyard had helped that healing.

He stood in the hall and listened, hoping the household was asleep, and after sneaking out of the front door he made his way to the cemetery. It was peaceful there with the dead, and besides he wanted to visit his grandmother's grave again. He'd loved her when he was small; she'd been so much more loving than his mother who'd lived only for pleasure back then, barely noticing her children. He'd been paying his respects at the old lady's grave when he'd seen Mrs Pearce leaving the food that had sustained him since his arrival in Mabley Ridge, so it had felt as though his grandmother had still been watching over him from the hereafter, bringing him good fortune.

When he reached the cemetery he walked around for a while before stopping at the grave where Patience had been found, now eternal home to somebody else. He bowed his head for a few moments, trying to get things straight in his mind. Had Jimmy Rudyard's killer also been responsible for Patience's death — and that of Mrs Pearce? He remembered Charles Woodbead being there in Mabley Ridge at the time Jimmy Rudyard died, hanging around his mother, turning her head so she no longer had time for her own family. But would he really have killed an innocent child?

He had asked Peter what he remembered about the day his brother, Jimmy, died but the boy's answer had been confused. Brief flashes of memory came back to him every so often and he had dreams so real that when he awoke he was certain of the truth . . . before that certainty faded as the day went on. While Monty doubted whether Peter was able to tell fact from imagination, he suspected there was a grain of truth in his stories. In Monty's darkest hours he himself had had dreams and visions which had their roots in reality.

When they'd last met on the Ridge Peter told him how memories of his twin's killer were coming back to him in vivid fragments and Monty was afraid that, in his innocence, the boy might blurt this out in the wrong place — or to the wrong person.

Peter had never revealed the killer's name and Monty regretted that he hadn't asked. If he knew who Peter was likely to accuse, at least he would know who to fear.

He was seized by a sudden urge to return to the Ridge, to sit in his old refuge and seek solace among the rocks and trees. There was a full moon so the way was clearly lit. And there was always the chance that Peter might have gone up there too.

62

Dr Michaels made little attempt to hide his irritation when Gwen dragged him from the comfort of his armchair where he'd settled with a book and a glass of single malt, his reward for a hard day's work. However, as soon as she told him about Miss Fisher's injuries he scooped up his leather bag and hurried out, telling his wife he'd be back as soon as he could.

Once she'd let the doctor into her landlady's house Gwen headed straight for the cemetery lodge and knocked softly on the door. The last thing she wanted to do was wake the baby and incur Grace Rudyard's wrath.

She had one question to ask: was Peter there? When a subdued Grace Rudyard answered the door Gwen noticed that her eyes were red from crying. She waited on the doorstep while Grace checked upstairs and when the woman returned she appeared to be torn between worry and anger.

'The little monkey must have sneaked out. His dad'll take his belt to him when he gets back.'

'There's no need for that,' said Gwen quickly. 'I'll go and look for him.'

All of a sudden Grace's features softened. 'Thank you, Miss. He's a great worry to me, that lad.'

Their eyes met in understanding but Gwen had no time to waste. She half walked, half ran to the Station Hotel where she rushed to the reception desk and asked if Mr Lincoln was in. She needed to speak to him urgently.

She'd never seen the picture she'd found in Miss Fisher's hallway before in her life and guessed that Peter had been to the house looking for her. And the word 'boy' uttered by Miss Fisher suggested he'd had something to do with what had happened to her; or at least witnessed it. Perhaps Peter had been attacked too, she thought with mounting panic. Perhaps he was wandering about somewhere frightened and hurt.

Amongst all the crazy things Peter had said to her recently, one phrase stuck in her mind; an earnest statement she'd dismissed as yet another of his vivid fantasies.

'I saw a murderer, Miss. Honest, Miss, cross my heart and hope to die.'

★ ★ ★

Albert was in his pyjamas when he heard the knock on his bedroom door.

'There's a lady to see you in reception, sir. She says it's urgent.'

Albert could hear the disapproval in the manager's voice. As far as he was concerned a lady calling on a single man in his hotel at this time of night could only mean one thing.

Albert told him he'd be down presently before dressing in a hurry. As he donned his jacket he felt the unopened letter in his pocket, forgotten with everything that had happened that day. But there was no time to open it now so he dropped it on his bedside cabinet where it sat, tantalising. He hesitated, knowing that it would only take a second to slit it open, just to see if it contained anything that needed to be dealt with urgently. And there was always the possibility it was connected with the Mabley Ridge case.

He tore at the envelope and found a single sheet of paper inside covered with small, neat handwriting. At first he took it for a woman's hand but the signature at the end told him it was from a Reverend Jonathan Hegg, Chaplain, and the address above the date was Strangeways Prison, Manchester.

He scanned the contents of the letter and after a protracted explanation as to why Hegg was writing, he came to the point.

I am not sure whether you received the message I left with your colleagues at Scotland Yard but, as I am obliged to go away for a fortnight, I thought it would be best to write to you.

The fact is that in the contemplative hours before her execution, the prisoner Flora Winsmore begged me to let you know what became of her child and I agreed, somewhat reluctantly. The child, a boy I understand, was found a good home by the vicar of Winsmore's former parish, a Reverend Bell, and will, no doubt, be raised in blissful ignorance of his mother's heinous crimes. Having discharged my duty to the unfortunate prisoner I assure you that I am, sir, yours sincerely.

Albert stared at the letter. He remembered Bell as a sympathetic man and he wondered whether to approach him or leave well alone. Perhaps it should be enough for him to know the child would be well cared for. Besides, at that moment he needed to find out what his female visitor wanted. People didn't call on him at this hour unless the matter was urgent.

The chaplain's words echoed in his mind as he descended the grand staircase but he forced himself to drag his thoughts back to the present. He'd been told his visitor was a lady and he suspected that the lady in question would be Gwen Davies. She'd been there at every twist and turn of this investigation, hovering on the periphery just like Flora had done eighteen months before.

She was waiting for him, perched on the edge of a leather chesterfield sofa, looking small and vulnerable against the large furniture. She rose to her feet as soon as she saw him, clutching her bag in front of her like a shield. She looked frightened.

'I think Peter Rudyard's in trouble.'

Peter Rudyard again. He was beginning to think the teacher was obsessed with the boy. She had no children of her own so maybe she'd formed an attachment to a child whose vulnerability touched her heart.

'What sort of trouble?' he asked.

She explained about the events at her lodgings and her visit to the cemetery lodge before taking Peter's crumpled sketch from her bag. Her hands shook as she handed it to him and he felt like reassuring her that if Peter Rudyard was in danger, he'd do his best to find him. But he couldn't make promises like that. He'd failed before and it was possible he'd fail again.

'How's Miss Fisher?'

'Dr Michaels is with her but I don't know how badly hurt she is.' She paused. 'When I asked her what had happened she said, 'Boy,' and that he'd pay for what he's done.' She paused as though she was reluctant to continue.

'I'm frightened that Peter might have something to do with her injuries.'

'Why would he attack Miss Fisher?'

'It might have been an accident. Or if something scared him he might have lashed out.'

There was an uncertainty in her voice, as though she'd had reason in the past to suspect her landlady wasn't the harmless spinster she appeared to be. Perhaps she'd sensed something deeper in the woman. Something darker.

'The picture . . . what do you think it means?'

Gwen shook her head. 'It's not the usual thing he draws, and he told me. yesterday that he'd seen a murderer. But surely if he'd seen who killed Mrs Bailey he would have said something before now.'

'Have you any idea where he'd go?'

'There's only one other place I can think of and that's the Ridge. Are you going to call on Sergeant Stark — get some men up there looking for him?'

Albert thought for a few moments. 'No, I'll let Stark enjoy his evening off duty. If Peter's gone up to the Ridge it's best if just the two of us go.

346

If he's near Oak Tree Edge and he sees a lot of policemen he might take it into his head to run.'

He didn't need to say any more. Oak Tree Edge was reputed to be haunted by the souls of those who'd chosen to end their lives by jumping off the precipice on to the rocks below. A cornered boy might run there in the darkness only for his broken body to be found below the Edge at first light. The situation needed to be handled gently.

'I'll borrow torches from the hotel,' said Albert, looking round for the manager. 'We should get up there now.'

Before they could set off they were interrupted by the arrival of a breathless Constable Mitchell.

'Sir. Charles Woodbead's escaped. I went to check his cell an hour ago and he's vanished. The lock on that cell's always been faulty,' said Mitchell, red-faced.

'Who decided to put him in there?' Albert was trying his best to hide his anger. The small provincial station had failed and now a killer was out there somewhere in the night.

'The sergeant's been meaning to get it mended for ages but the cells are usually used for drunks sleeping it off or to provide the odd vagrant with a bed for the night so the job never seemed urgent.' The young man sounded distraught, as though he felt the failure personally.

'When was the cell last checked?'

'At six when I picked up his dinner dishes. I told the sergeant he should be transferred somewhere safer but he said there wasn't time and he'd get it done in the morning.'

'Has anyone organised a search for him?'

'I'm seeing to it, sir,' the constable said proudly. 'I sent someone round to the sergeant's but there was nobody in. He's off duty and I think he and his good lady go to a church meeting in Wilmslow on a Friday so . . .'

'Then there's nothing we can do till morning. Woodbead hasn't got transport so he won't get far. Thank you, Constable.'

'You didn't tell him about Peter,' Gwen said as Mitchell disappeared out of the front door.

'I've already told you I don't want the boy to see a lot of police in uniform and panic,' Albert answered.

'But if Woodbead's the killer and he's heading up to the Ridge too . . . '

Albert put a reassuring hand on her sleeve. 'We'll just have to get there before him, won't we?'

63

Monty Ghent trudged up the road, his hands thrust in the pockets of his greatcoat. His family had done their best to welcome him but they couldn't understand what he'd been through. They couldn't know the horrors that came to him each night when he tried to sleep and he didn't want his screams to disturb his mother because she'd been through enough already.

He knew that if he returned to his cave until he felt calmer, he might feel up to returning home. But he couldn't get rid of the fear that he might have harmed Patience Bailey without being aware of it; that for a brief, terrible moment his damaged mind had told him the open grave was a trench and Patience was the enemy who had to be destroyed.

If only he could remember. If only he could banish the awful possibility of his own guilt.

The police had Charles Woodbead in custody but if anyone could manage to wriggle out of trouble it would be him. Woodbead was resourceful and Monty knew his own testimony might not be taken seriously because of his mental confusion . . . and because he'd be classed as a deserter, the worst form of coward. Also he knew his mother would be reluctant to accuse Woodbead of blackmail because that would mean admitting her own wrongdoings which, if they were made public at a trial, would undoubtedly result in social disgrace. Charles Woodbead was the kind who'd land in shit and come up smelling of roses.

Monty stumbled on and as soon as he reached the Ridge he plunged into the shelter of the trees where he experienced an overwhelming feeling of peace. This wild place had sheltered him from the world and he made his way into its heart. That damp cave had been his refuge and he needed it now.

He'd be safe there; safe from the wickedness in the world. Unless the horrors of war had turned him into a monster without him realising it. Unless he had killed without being able to help himself.

★ ★ ★

Charles Woodbead needed to get as far away as possible from Mabley Ridge and to do that he needed money. Even though he'd left the Alvis at Ridgeside Lodge he couldn't risk going back because it would be the first place the police would look.

But there was one person who'd help him and that was Esme Ghent, who was bound to fall for any sob story he told her.

He'd never been on the run from the police before and he was surprised how exhilarated the new experience made him feel. He had always thrived on excitement and now he was running for his life it felt good — like the time he'd escaped the trenches.

As soon as he reached Gramercy House he ran

down the drive towards the lighted windows, adrenalin coursing through his body. A while ago Esme had pointed out her room to him and he could see a light there behind the closed curtains. He was confident that she'd be sitting there, brooding about why he hadn't been in touch, so as soon as he was near enough he scooped up a fistful of gravel from the ground and flung it upwards towards her window.

He heard the small stones hitting the glass and shot back into the cover of the bushes. When the front door opened slowly he'd expected to see Esme framed in the doorway but instead it was another familiar figure — one who would suit his purpose just as well.

He didn't show himself at once because he wanted to be certain her husband wouldn't suddenly appear behind her. When she came out on to the doorstep alone, hugging her loose cardigan around her thin frame to keep out the cold night air, he emerged from his hiding place.

'Jane. Just the lady I need to see.'

She stepped back, hugging the cardigan tighter as though she wanted to make herself look small and insignificant. This wasn't the Jane he once knew; the Jane who was up for all manner of adventures up on the Ridge while her husband was working hard at his mill. The woman in front of him was a new, timid, creature but he hoped this would make his task easier.

'I need a favour, Jane.'

'I don't owe you anything.'

He grasped the uncertainty in her voice. 'You can't have forgotten our afternoons at that little flat I had in Wilmslow before the war. And those times on the Ridge. I told you I'd kept all your letters, didn't I. I couldn't bear to throw them away. Not when they bring back so many happy memories every time I read them.'

He was close to her now and he saw she'd turned pale. 'What do you want?'

'I've had a spot of trouble with my motor car so I need to borrow your husband's. Is he here?'

For a second she looked as though she was weighing up whether to lie. Then she spoke. 'He's upstairs . . . in his room.'

'And the motor?'

'In the stables round the back.'

He could tell she was eager to get rid of him but he hadn't finished with her yet. 'I need money.'

'If I give you some will you destroy the letters?'

'If you like.' He was so desperate at that moment that he would have agreed to anything.

There was a moment of hesitation before she told him to wait and shut the front door in his face. He took a step back and looked up in time to see Esme's face at the window. As soon as she saw him she retreated and he wondered whether the spell he'd woven to trap her had finally been broken. However, if all went as planned, he'd soon escape to begin a new existence with a new identity and never return to Mabley Ridge again, so these two women would be out of his life forever.

After a few minutes the door opened again.

'This is all I have,' Jane said as she held out a

sheaf of white banknotes. 'Now go. I don't want to see you again and neither does Esme.' She hesitated. 'Promise me you'll destroy those letters,' she said as he took the notes.

'You have my word as an officer and a gentleman,' he said, counting the money. He stuffed it in his pocket and smiled. 'A kiss for old times' sake, Janey?'

She slammed the door in his face again but at that moment he was feeling invincible so it had been worth a try.

When he reached the stables, he looked back at the house and saw a face at one of the attic windows; a small, pale face which wore the desperate look of a condemned prisoner. Esme had often talked about an insolent maidservant called Daisy but if this was her, there was nothing insolent about her expression now.

Unlike himself, she was just another loser in life's lottery. He had the winning ticket. He knew who'd killed little Jimmy Rudyard back in 1914. The only problem was he doubted whether anybody would believe him.

64

Gwen was overcome with relief when she saw Peter Rudyard.

'I'll take him home,' she said to Albert as they both hurried to catch up with the boy who was marching along the road to the Ridge as though he had urgent business to attend to.

When they drew level with him Albert put his good hand on his shoulder and the boy stopped. In the moonlight Gwen saw terror on his face. Then after a split second his horror turned into relief when he realised the identity of his pursuers.

'What are you doing here, Peter?' said Gwen. 'Your mother's worried about you.'

Peter didn't answer.

'Were you at Miss Fisher's earlier? Did you go there looking for me?'

'I never did nothing. Honest.'

'We never said you did,' Albert said gently. 'I'd like you to come to the police station and tell me exactly what happened tonight. There's nothing to worry about.'

The look of panic reappeared on Peter's face. 'No, I can't.'

'Don't worry,' said Gwen. 'The inspector'll be with you.'

'That's right.' Albert turned to Gwen. 'Miss Davies, if you go and see the Rudyards and tell them what's happening, that'd be a great help.'

Suddenly Peter's shoulders dropped, as though he was resigned to some dreadful fate, and as the three of them walked down to the village the boy dragged his feet. Gwen wondered whether his reluctance stemmed from a guilty conscience, whether her worst fears were about to be realised and that he had indeed been responsible for Miss Fisher's injuries.

When they reached the police station door Albert took Gwen to one side and told her what he wanted her to do, but as she watched him walk into the building with Peter she was tempted to follow and insist on staying with them. At that moment Peter seemed so fragile that she feared if too much pressure was put on him he'd retreat once more into the world of his imagination. She hoped Albert Lincoln would treat him gently but as she was walking back to Miss Fisher's cottage after a brief visit to reassure the Rudyards that their son was safe, she began to have doubts.

Albert had asked her to do something for him, something her instincts cried against. She had secrets of her own, private things that were her business alone so she baulked at the idea of intruding into the privacy of others. However, according to Albert, Dr Michaels had given Miss Fisher enough laudanum to keep her unconscious until the morning so this would be her only chance.

She let herself into the silent house with her latch key and once she was in the hall, her eyes drawn to the dark stains of dried blood on the wall. She fought the temptation to turn on her heels and run from the house she'd always considered so oppressive. But she'd made a promise to Albert and, unlike some, she always kept her promises.

She climbed the stairs slowly and once on the landing she paused by Miss Fisher's bedroom door, wondering what she'd do if the laudanum hadn't taken effect. If her landlady woke up and started asking awkward questions she'd have to bluff it out so she took a deep breath and turned the doorknob.

Although the room was in darkness the curtains were thin enough to let in the filtered moonlight so she could make out the shape of her landlady beneath the bedclothes, making soft snuffling sounds like a sleeping infant.

She fetched the paraffin lamp that was still burning on the landing and re-entered the room, holding the lamp aloft. After watching Miss Fisher for a whole minute to make sure she didn't stir, she crossed to the dressing table and placed the lamp in front of the mirror. Then she began to pull out the drawers, starting at the bottom.

As she rifled through drawers filled with underwear, she was surprised to see that some of it was silk; the sort she'd imagined an actress like Dora Devereaux would wear. This was a side of Miss Fisher she had never imagined and as she continued her search she came across face powder, rouge and scent, although she had never seen her landlady wear it.

The contents of some of the drawers appeared to belong to a different woman — or a woman who led two separate lives — and after another glance at the bed she continued her search, feeling the backs of the drawers to make sure she hadn't missed anything.

When she'd finished she replaced everything as neatly as she could, closed the drawers and stood back, seeking inspiration. There was still the wardrobe — and the little carved box on the bedside table. She picked up the box carefully, only to find it was locked.

It was then she noticed the thin chain around Miss Fisher's neck, one she had never noticed before because her landlady was in the habit of wearing high collars. Gwen had to investigate. She folded the eiderdown back gently and when Miss Fisher showed no sign of moving she tugged at the chain because whatever was on it had worked its way round to the back of her neck so that the sleeping woman was now lying on it. The chain loosened and Gwen saw a small key; now it was a matter of feeling for the catch.

When she touched Miss Fisher's warm flesh, the woman stirred and Gwen froze, waiting for discovery. But when she showed no sign of waking she continued and eventually managed to release the catch.

With the key in her hand and another nervous glance at Miss Fisher, she picked up the box and unlocked it before carrying it over to the dressing table where the light was better.

Inside she found a pile of letters tied together with blue ribbon. Love letters Gwen had received similar ones herself from George Sedding when their affair was at its peak. She undid the ribbon and started to read, assuming she'd discover precious relics from her landlady's past, perhaps from some man who'd courted her then gone away to war never to return. But what she read shocked her.

There was nothing romantic about the descriptions of sexual violence and the fantasies of death and murder. This wasn't love, it was unhealthy obsession.

I often think of what we did and I dream about having that ower again. We held the ultimate power over life and death and if the nobodies in this village knew our true nature now they'd respect us. All those little people with their meaningless lives would say we should be sorry about what we did when the boy caught us together. But I can't be sorry and I can't help laughing when I think how we fooled all those idiots, rich and poor, into thinking we're docile cattle just like them. But we're more than that; we're the ones who decide who lives and who dies. Does that make us like gods, do you think? I can't wait to feel that power again. Is that so wrong?

Gwen read it with dawning horror. Whoever had written these letters had mentioned a boy and that could only mean Peter Rudyard's twin, Jimmy. Judging by the use of the word 'we' it looked as though Miss Fisher was party to the child's murder as well. She stood with her hand clasped to her mouth, tears stinging her eyes. If her suspicions were correct, the woman lying motionless in the bed a few feet away had, with another, killed an innocent child. She continued to read.

The old woman deserved to die for keeping us apart like that and I watched you when you pressed the pillow down on her face. She fought for her life but you showed no mercy even though she was your own mother. How I admire you. How I long to be with you again.

There was no signature on the letters, which meant she had no idea of the man's identity. But Miss Fisher's world was small so it had to be someone from the village. A monster in disguise. Peter Rudyard had often spoken of monsters but his were in his head. This one was real.

The letters were evidence and she didn't want to give Miss Fisher an opportunity to destroy them so she took them out of the box, locked it carefully and replaced it on the bedside table before refastening the chain around the woman's neck with trembling hands, praying that she wouldn't wake.

Once Gwen was satisfied she'd left no signs of disturbance, she picked up the lamp and crept into her own room, stashing the letters at the back of her wardrobe inside her best pair of winter boots, hoping it would be the last place Miss Fisher would think to look. Then she had second thoughts. She should keep them with her until she had the opportunity to show them to Inspector Lincoln. He'd know what to do with such explosive evidence. She placed them in her handbag and fastened the clasp.

She replaced the lamp on the landing and let herself out of the house quietly. Her legs felt heavy as she began to run down the road towards the police station and as she passed the Rose and Crown the windows glowed with welcome. For a split second she was tempted to burst in and tell John Rudyard, who was bound to be in there, that she knew the identity of his son's killer. But she fought the impulse. This needed to be dealt with by the authorities, even though every extra yard between her and the police station seemed fraught with danger -she knew the second killer was still out there somewhere.

She saw a Rolls-Royce parked at the side of the road, and slowed her pace. A man was leaning against the driver's door smoking a cigarette and something about him made her uneasy.

He spotted her and called out, 'What time is it?'

As she drew closer she recognised him as the good-looking man she'd seen driving through the village in an Alvis. She'd heard he was a war hero who'd arrived a few months ago and taken a house near the Ridge. Even so, she approached him with caution.

'Must be around half past ten.'

'Damn motor's run out of petrol.'

'Can't help you, I'm afraid.'

'You can if you've got a bicycle?'

'I haven't but my landlady has one.'

'It'd save my life if I could borrow it.'

He looked at her appealingly, his charm on full throttle.

'I'm sorry. I haven't time. I really have to go,' she said, preparing to hurry on. But she felt her arm being grabbed, so tightly that it made her wince. 'Let me go.'

'All I'm asking is to borrow it for a while. It won't take you a minute to get it.' She heard a threat behind the words.

'And if I don't?'

The man's grip tightened. 'Don't be a silly girl. Just get it. Where do you live?'

Gwen thought quickly. If he had to ask then he obviously didn't know. 'This way,' she said, setting off in the direction of the police station.

He walked by her side, still gripping her arm so that, to the casual passer-by, it would look as if they were a couple out for an evening stroll. She noticed he walked with a slight limp as though he'd been injured in some way. The police station's blue light came into sight, guiding her like a beacon. She could tell he'd seen it too because he slowed down.

'It's just past the police station,' she said, trying to sound confident.

He gripped her arm tighter and lowered his head, pulling his hat over his face with his free hand.

She timed it perfectly. As they drew level with the open door of the police station she let out a piercing scream and the man loosened his grasp.

'Bitch,' he hissed before pushing her to the ground with some violence and dashing into the darkness as a constable appeared at the door.

Gwen was on her knees but she pointed down the street, shouting instructions. A man had tried to abduct her and if the constable was quick, he'd catch him. It only took a couple of minutes for the young man to return in triumph with his captive in an armlock.

Gwen followed them through the station door in time to see Albert Lincoln emerge from a door behind the front desk.

'Mr Woodbead. Good of you to join us again,' he said. 'We've missed you.' He turned to the constable. 'Put him in a cell will you, Mitchell — and not the one with the useless lock this time. The charge is murder.'

As Woodbead was led away he shouted back to Albert, 'I'm not the only murderer in this village. Who do you think told me about the door?' before his words were muffled by the slamming of the cell door.

'Monty Ghent was in that cell before,' said Constable Mitchell who was watching the commotion from behind the desk. 'Must have been him who told him. Should I go and arrest him, sir?'

'I don't think that's necessary just at this moment.'

'Is Peter Rudyard still here?' Gwen asked.

'He's in the interview room. He hasn't finished making his statement yet.'

'He should be back home.' There was determination in Gwen's voice.

Albert hesitated. 'Very well. He can make his statement tomorrow after he's had a good night's sleep.'

'I'll take him,' said Constable Mitchell. 'He shouldn't be out on his own at this time of night.'

'That's all right, Constable. I'm sure Miss Davies will be happy to see him home.'

'Yes, of course,' Gwen said quickly, thinking of the letters in her bag. 'But first, may I have a word in private?'

'That'll be all, Constable, thank you.' Albert waited until Mitchell was out of earshot before ushering Gwen into his office. After a brief conversation, they emerged again — only to find that Peter Rudyard had already left.

65

Peter

The inspector from London left some paper on the desk and a pencil so I did another drawing of the Shadow Man only this time he's got a face. It's a nice face and I don't know why he wanted to hide it. I think he's sad and I wish he wasn't. I thought I heard his voice through the wall in the police station. It might not have been him but it sounded like him — all posh like.

I drew another picture too. I used to think the man who killed our Jimmy was one of the knights who lives on the Ridge but now I know who it really was. I didn't see him very well 'cause I was hiding but now I know he wasn't a knight. But if I tell I'll get called a liar again.

Me and our Jimmy were hiding behind the bushes when we saw him with Miss FishFace and they started making funny noises. I wanted to go but Jimmy wouldn't come with me 'cause he wanted to stay and play so I went away and left him. That means it's all my fault he died.

I've drawn the man who dragged our Jimmy into the middle of the stones and now I'm scared he'll come and kill me too if he finds out I saw him with Miss FishFace.

I've just finished my drawing when the door

opens and he's standing there smiling. He says I've got to go with him and Mam says I must always do what a policeman says.

66

Albert's leg felt stiff and he was angry with himself for not being able to run faster because Peter Rudyard was with his twin brother's killer and he was in grave danger.

Albert had recognised the handwriting on the letters Gwen showed him at once. He'd seen it enough times since his arrival in Mabley Ridge and, along with the statement Grace Rudyard had made about the night of Patience Bailey's death, everything was starting to make sense. He'd checked the duty rotas for the evening in question and there was no reason Grace would have seen him there in the cemetery at that particular time — and certainly no reason she'd lie.

'Where do you think he's gone?' Gwen was at his side and he was glad he wasn't alone out there in the dark.

'The Ridge?'

'Too far,' she said, on the verge of tears. 'He has to be somewhere nearer. Unless . . . '

She was thinking what Albert hardly liked to put into words. If the boy was unconscious he could be carried anywhere by a strong man. And the killer was strong.

'He knows the terrain,' said Albert. 'All the short cuts. Go back into the station, will you, and tell Mitchell what I'm doing.'

She obeyed at once, leaving him to limp on. It

366

was half a mile to the Ridge, then even further to Oak Tree Edge, but if Albert was in the killer's place this was where he'd be heading. He'd make it look like an accident and claim to be a hero who tried to save the child.

To his surprise Gwen soon joined him again, breathless from running fast. 'The constable said he'll catch us up. He can't believe it.'

'Neither could I until now. When I think back to the first investigation . . .'

'What about Mrs Bailey . . . and Mrs Pearce.'

'I think they witnessed something — probably an assignation between the pair. If that's the case they didn't stand a chance. Sometimes two people who are harmless individually egg each other on to act out their darkest fantasies and get a taste for murder. I had a similar case in London once; I'd just never associated it with Jimmy Rudyard's murder.'

Gwen heard the self-reproach in Albert's voice. 'You can't blame yourself for not seeing it back then.' She shuddered and Albert wasn't sure whether it was the cool night air or the thought of the killers' depravity. 'I'd always thought him completely trustworthy.'

'Perhaps he was until he met her. The ingredients for explosives can be harmless on their own but mixed together . . .'

So far the moon had provided enough light to guide their way but now they'd reached the path that led through the trees. Beyond that inscrutable barrier of waving greenery was the wild landscape Albert had come to fear. The epicentre of his worst nightmares.

He hardly liked to acknowledge that he was in pain. The wound in his leg that had bothered him on and off since the war was throbbing now but he couldn't stop.

When he stumbled and Gwen put out a hand to steady him he waved it aside because he didn't want her to think of him as an invalid. He didn't want anyone to think he wasn't fit enough to do his job. As soon as the canopy of trees cut out the silver moonlight he flicked on the torch he was carrying.

He was about to call Peter's name but he stopped himself. It might alert Peter but it would also alert his captor. For a few seconds he began to wonder whether he was jumping to the wrong conclusion because there was still the possibility that Peter was responsible for Miss Fisher's injuries and that he'd fled the interview room of his own accord, terrified that he'd be punished. Then he remembered the picture the boy had drawn — and the letters Gwen had found in Miss Fisher's room — and carried on.

The woodland was filled with strange sounds: rustlings, snapping twigs and the desperate cries of hidden birds and animals. Albert imagined he could feel the presence of the souls of the men who laboured here hundreds of years ago; and the spirits of the landscape watching and mocking. This place had got the better of so many over the years.

As they drew close to the stone circle Albert raised his hand, a signal to stop and listen. The breeze was hissing in the branches overhead but he could hear something else. A voice, deep and resonant, speaking softly with a hint of menace behind the mumbled words. He crept forward and a twig cracked beneath his feet like a gunshot.

The voice stopped and he flicked off the torch. In the last rays of light he had seen the fear on Gwen's face and he suddenly regretted involving her in a situation fraught with unknown dangers.

As if she'd read his thoughts she whispered in his ear. 'If Peter's there, you'll need me to look after him while you ... He's only a child, Inspector.'

'Albert. Call me Albert.' In the intimacy of the moment it seemed appropriate.

Then a high-pitched voice tore through the darkness. 'I won't tell on you, honest. Cross my heart and hope to die.'

Albert switched on his torch again and hurtled forward, ignoring the pain in his leg as he burst from the cover of the trees. To his surprise the first thing he saw, looming in the trees at the other side of the clearing, was a tall figure in an officer's greatcoat. Monty Ghent was moving towards the circle of stones as though he was in a trance.

Then a child began to scream in terror and Monty descended, his coat flapping out like the wings of a great bird.

67

Albert rushed to tackle the boy's attacker. But when he reached the edge of the stone circle he realised he'd misread the situation and Monty Ghent was wrestling with a dark figure while Peter Rudyard lay on the ground, half screaming, half sobbing; terrified for his life.

'Get Peter away,' he barked at Gwen before entering the circle and shielding her from the fighting men while she dragged the boy up. Peter struggled at first, flailing out with his thin arms and shouting 'No, no.' But once he realised who had hold of him he flung himself into her arms and held tight like a baby clinging to its mother. Then, murmuring words of reassurance, Gwen guided him off to safety, shielding his body with hers.

'Stop,' he shouted, grabbing Monty's coat. 'Leave him.'

Then he heard a familiar voice. 'He's under arrest.'

'What for?'

'Desertion. And kidnapping the lad.'

Peter was standing in the shelter of the trees with Gwen and before she could stop him he rushed forward. 'You're a liar,' he shouted, his voice broken with sobs. 'The Shadow Man didn't do nothing. It was you.'

Sergeant Stark turned to face Albert with a mirthless smile on his lips. 'Everyone knows the boy imagines things. You can't believe a word he says.' He looked straight at Gwen. 'His teacher'll tell you. Won't you, Miss?'

Gwen stared at him, lost for words.

'I thought you were off duty tonight, Sergeant.'

'I got a message when I arrived home. Mitchell told me you were on your way here so I thought you'd need a hand.'

Peter had returned to Gwen, edging behind her for protection.

Albert looked down at Monty, who had fallen to his knees, head bowed. 'Peter's telling the truth,' Monty said. 'He's remembered what happened when his brother was killed but he thought no one'd believe him.'

'Look at him,' Stark said. 'He's a desperate man and desperate men'll say anything. It's a well-known fact.'

'Shut up, Sergeant. Hear him out.'

Stark's fists clenched and Albert could sense his tension. 'We should be looking for Wood-bead. That's the man you want. I came across young Ghent here attacking the young 'un. I reckon between the two of them — Woodbead and this — '

'I said shut up.' Albert's voice cracked. He didn't have the whole story yet but it was coming to him in fragments like the shards of glass on Miss Fisher's carpet. In the meantime he needed to arrest the right man. He squatted down so his face was level with Monty's. 'Tell me what happened.'

'It was getting too much for me at home so I

came up here for some peace. I heard Peter crying out and I came to help.'

'Nonsense,' Stark butted in. 'I found you kneeling over him. You were going to kill him.' He paused. 'Come to think of it, you were around when his brother died, weren't you? You were just a lad back in 'fourteen but you were still capable of murdering a little kid. You and that 'friend' of yours. The Jew you used to go round with. What kind of friend was he? I often used to wonder about that. If that kiddie saw you together and . . . '

Monty struggled to his feet. 'You're a bloody liar.'

Albert placed a restraining hand on his shoulder. 'Let's go down to the station. I'm sure Mr Ghent has some questions to answer. He gave Monty's shoulder a reassuring squeeze and began to steer him out of the clearing as he turned his head and added, 'You too, Sergeant. You're needed.'

Peter suddenly shouted: 'He brought me here. He said I had to go with him. But he killed our Jimmy — him and Miss FishFace. I've remembered now. I drew a picture to show Miss Davies.'

Albert shone his torch straight in Stark's face and saw him put up his arm to shield his eyes.

'Surely you're not going to take what he says seriously,' said Stark, regaining his composure. 'He makes things up.'

'I've always thought there was a grain of truth in his fantasies,' said Gwen quietly. 'The knight he drew was wearing a helmet — policemen wear helmets. I think the two things got mixed up in his mind.'

'Everyone knows he's a liar. Now are we going to arrest Ghent?'

Albert didn't take his eyes off Stark, keeping the torch beam steady on his face. 'Mr Ghent. Will you escort Miss Davies and Peter back to the police station, please?'

He thought Monty was going to object but after a few moments he led Gwen and Peter away. Albert waited until they were out of sight before he spoke. 'By the way, if Mitchell had really called you as you claimed he'd have told you that Woodbead's back in custody. Your handcuffs, please, Sergeant.'

Stark drew himself up to his full height. 'What if I don't want to give them to you?'

'That's an order from a superior officer.'

Stark's lips curled up in a snarl. 'Look at you with your gammy leg and your useless hand. Now we're here man to man you're no match for me, admit it. It's dangerous up here. People have died falling off Oak Tree Edge.'

Stark clenched his fist and aimed a punch in Albert's direction, knocking the torch from his good right hand, but somehow Albert managed to dodge the blow and when the second punch came Stark was way off target.

Then Stark seemed to gather strength and rushed at him, knocking him to the ground. The sudden pain that shot through Albert's injured leg made him cry out and he realised he couldn't scramble to his feet quickly enough so he shielded his head from the blows he was sure were about to come. Stark had him pinned on the damp ground and he couldn't move. Albert knew he was facing death. He closed his eyes tightly, waiting for the inevitable. Then he heard Stark's voice.

'You should have left that boy well alone. Nobody believed him apart from that stupid teacher of his and she's a whore, no better than she ought to be.'

'Why did you kill Jimmy Rudyard?' Albert gasped. If he could keep the man talking . . .

'I couldn't risk him blabbing to his mother that he'd seen me and Ethel together. The whole village would have found out and I've got a position to keep up: I'm respected. I held my hand over his face until he stopped breathing so he didn't suffer. We thought it'd be taken for an accident. This Ridge is a dangerous place.'

'What about Patience Bailey?'

'What makes you think I had anything to do with that?'

'Mrs Rudyard saw your bicycle propped up on one of the gravestones when she looked out of the window.'

'I always check the cemetery when I'm on patrol. You get people up to no good in there and — '

'But you weren't on duty that night. I've checked the duty rotas.'

There was a long silence before Stark spoke again. 'Very well. The Bailey woman turned up on the Ridge walking her brat in its pram and she saw me and Ethel together in the woods. It's a handy place to meet on a fine evening now

Ethel's had to take in a lodger. She was staring at us as if she couldn't believe what she was seeing and I knew it'd soon be all round the village. Besides, she was in the habit of taking tea with my wife so . . . ' He gave a little laugh. 'We kept an eye on her, waiting for a chance, and followed her to the cemetery that night — although Lord knows what she was doing taking the kiddie to a place like that. Anyway, Ethel picked up the spade and finished her off. I said not to harm the baby though. We left it on one of the graves.'

'Good of you.'

'Yes.' It seemed Stark hadn't caught the irony in Albert's remark. 'Then the old biddy arrived — Mrs Pearce.'

'So you silenced her too.'

'We had no choice. She saw Ethel hit the Bailey woman and she let out a scream and ran off — she was fast for an old 'un, I'll give her that. Ethel said we had to shut her up before she talked so she paid her a call.'

'She cut her throat.'

'Ethel's always had a taste for the theatrical.' He dragged Albert up by his coat collar, took out his handcuffs and snapped them on the inspector's wrist.

Albert felt himself being frogmarched through the trees. He guessed where they were heading and he knew he didn't have much time.

'Miss Davies has evidence of your affair with Ethel Fisher.'

Stark suddenly stopped. 'You're bluffing. If she says anything against me do you really think anybody will believe her?'

'She took the letters you wrote from Miss Fisher's room. They were in a wooden box by the bed.'

This time Stark seemed worried. But after a momentary hesitation he carried on, more determined than ever, pushing Albert ahead of him. 'Even if she has letters, I never signed them so I'll just deny I wrote them.'

'You may not have signed them but they're in your handwriting. There are samples of it all over the station.'

'I'll say they're forgeries. There are a lot of people out there who'd like to embarrass a policeman who arrested them. Revenge is an occupational hazard as you should know — even in Scotland Yard.'

They'd reached the Edge and Albert could see lights twinkling in the far distance; the lights of Manchester. Between the city and the Edge there was nothing but darkness, like a void in the earth. He felt himself being shoved forward, his feet slipping on the bare rock.

'Monty Ghent and Miss Davies will testify against you if anything happens to me.'

'This is a dangerous place. Easy to lose your footing — especially with your old war wounds. Ghent is a coward and a deserter and Miss Davies is an impressionable young woman. She used to be the mistress of George Sedding, one of our most respected citizens, so her morals are highly questionable. And she's fallen for that child's fantasies so she's hardly a credible witness.'

Albert knew he had to act quickly if he was to

376

survive. He collapsed to the ground and rolled away from the edge, crying out in agony as his leg gave way and his knees hit the bare rock. Taken by surprise, Stark stumbled over his prone body in the darkness and Albert heard the scream as he tumbled off Oak Tree Edge.

68

Peter was home with his family. Gwen had thought it was for the best rather than making the child stay in the police station for half the night while statements were taken. The formalities could be dealt with in the morning.

Albert had managed to stumble back to the village, his hands still fastened together by Stark's handcuffs. Somehow he had found his way. Peter would undoubtedly have said the ghosts of Mabley Ridge had guided him to safety although Albert's explanation was less fanciful. He put his good fortune down to being familiar with the place after so many visits.

Too exhausted to go into detail, he lied to Constable Mitchell, telling him he'd seen Sergeant Stark up there and he'd gone missing. Explanations could wait.

One thing was certain, though. Miss Fisher wouldn't escape justice and there was no way Albert would allow Gwen to return to her cottage to be at her mercy when she awoke from her laudanum sleep.

Instead he took her to the Station Hotel and asked the man on the reception desk to provide her with a room for the night. It was a police emergency, he explained, hoping this would avoid any awkward questions.

Gwen's room was next door but one to his own and in the early hours of the morning he heard a light tap on his door. He pulled on his dressing gown before answering, thinking it might be Constable Mitchell come to report on a new development in the case. But when he opened the door a crack he saw Gwen Davies standing there, still fully dressed.

'I couldn't sleep,' she whispered. 'May I come in?'

For a few moments Albert said nothing. It was hardly proper to be entertaining a lady in his room at that time of night and Stark's accusation rang in his head. The village schoolmistress had once been the mistress of one of Mabley Ridge's wealthy residents. Her reputation was already tarnished so another scandal was hardly likely to make much difference. He opened the door wider and she slipped in quietly.

'Has somebody been to Miss Fisher's?' she said as she sat down in the chair by the dressing table.

'I sent Mitchell and told him to stay there until she wakes up then bring her in for questioning.'

Gwen opened the bag she had with her. 'You'd better take care of these. They're evidence.' She handed him the bundle of letters he'd asked her to keep safe because he hadn't wanted to leave them at the police station. 'Why did they do it?'

'I think it was a kind of madness,' said Albert. 'They developed a passion for each other but at the same time they both had to preserve their respectability, especially Stark. He was very conscious of his position in the community and, as far as Mabley Ridge was concerned, he led a blameless life with his job, his apparently perfect marriage and his role in the church.'

'According to the Bible the worst sin is hypocrisy and judging others — that's how I read it anyway, although I'm sure there are those who'd disagree.'

Albert smiled. 'Let he who is without sin cast the first stone.'

She lowered her eyes and took a deep breath. 'Some people in Mabley Ridge consider me a scarlet woman. While I was here in the war doing my bit on a farm just outside the village I met George Sedding. He was charming and funny and his marriage wasn't happy, or so he told me. We became lovers and I went back home to have his child — a boy. My married sister in Liverpool agreed to pretend he was hers.'

'Do you see your son?'

'I stayed with my parents during the school holidays but my brother-in-law didn't like me coming round because he thinks I'm a disruptive influence. He says I'll confuse the boy.'

'I'm sorry.'

'I'm leaving Mabley Ridge and going back to Liverpool so at least I'll be near him. They might not let me see him very often but it'll be something, won't it? I'm going back to live at my parents' house. My sister can't avoid me there.'

He could see the pain on her features. She'd lost a child just as he had. The night seemed made for confidences. He sat on the bed facing her and reached over to take her hand in his, hiding his injured hand because he was conscious of its ugliness.

'I lost a child too. My son, Frederick, died just as the war was coming to an end and . . . And I had another child too by a woman who wasn't my wife. A boy. But I don't know where he is.'

'You should try to find him,' she said, squeezing his hand. 'Do you know where his mother is?'

'She's dead.' He hardly liked to tell her that his mother was a murderess who'd faced the hangman.

'Don't give up hope,' she said, leaning forward and kissing the top of his head. He grasped her hand and pulled her towards him, his lips seeking hers. They kissed, her free hand travelling up to his scarred face, feeling the smoothness of his damaged flesh.

Then she pulled away. 'I'd better go,' she said softly, standing up. 'I'll see you in the morning.'

'There'll be a search for Stark as soon as it's light. You'll be needed as a witness.'

'I know.' She delved in her bag and brought out a small notebook. 'I'll give you my parents' address in Liverpool. Just in case you're ever up that way.'

She tore the page out and handed it to Albert, who folded it neatly and placed it on his bedside table.

Then he watched as she left the room, his heart heavy with regret.

69

The hunt for Abraham Stark was started at first light, shortly after Miss Fisher had regained consciousness and been placed under arrest. According to Stark she'd been the one who'd actually murdered Patience Bailey and Mrs Pearce, but Albert wondered whether he'd been trying to shift the blame. The pair had encouraged each other in their depravity and now she was likely to pay with her life, as Flora had paid for her actions all those months ago.

While the search was going on there was one visit Albert felt obliged to make. He walked to the cemetery lodge and when Grace Rudyard opened the door to him, she actually smiled.

'I know it's taken a long time, Mrs Rudyard, but we've finally got him. Thanks to your Peter.'

To his surprise she invited him inside and put the kettle on the range after telling him to take a seat. 'I'm keeping him off school today. He's had a rough time. Besides, I don't want him telling tales to all and sundry. You know what he's like.'

'I know, Mrs Rudyard. But he's a brave lad and I couldn't have caught your Jimmy's killer without him.'

'Why couldn't he just have said who it was when it happened?'

'If we see something terrible our minds can block it out.' He touched his face. 'I don't really know how I got this. All I remember is waking

382

up in agony. Sometimes the memories come back in flashes . . . or don't come back for years. With Peter they became mixed up with his fantasies. We all have our own ways of dealing with pain.' He stood up. 'I won't stay for that cup of tea if you don't mind. There's a lot to do before I leave.'

'You're going?'

'Back to London.' He took her hand. 'Take care, Grace. And look after Peter, won't you.' He heard a baby crying. 'I thought he'd be back with his real mother — the actress.'

A satisfied look appeared on Grace's face. 'She says she's got to work so she's asked me to look after him for her. I told her I didn't mind. She's even giving me a few bob.'

Albert walked to the police station with a feeling that all his unfinished business had been dealt with. He'd have to interview Ethel Fisher then, once charges had been made, he'd return to London until such time as he was needed to give evidence at her trial.

As soon as he walked into the station he was greeted by Constable Mitchell. Since the revelation about his sergeant, the young man seemed to have grown in stature. Albert hoped promotion would soon come his way.

'Charles Woodbead's made a statement, sir.'

'Has he confessed to the murder of his men?'

'No, sir, but he said he was on the Ridge when Jimmy Rudyard was murdered and he saw Stark with a woman answering Miss Fisher's description. He said they were . . . you know.'

'No need to be embarrassed, Constable.'

'Anyway, Woodbead was with a lady too, although he'd rather not give her name, and they saw the Rudyard twins running towards where he'd seen Stark a few minutes earlier, so it's likely the children saw him as well. Woodbead says he and his lady friend decided to leave because the Ridge was getting too crowded. He says that when they were walking away he heard a child scream in the distance.'

'I interviewed everyone in the village at the time.'

'Woodbead was living in Wilmslow back then, sir. He wouldn't have been questioned.'

'Even so, why didn't his lady friend say anything?'

'She was married, sir.'

There was a long silence. 'Thank you, Constable. I understand Daisy, the Ghents' maid, is to be brought in. Attempted poisoning.'

'Mr Ghent locked her in her room last night, sir. Someone's gone to fetch her.'

'Good work, Constable.' Albert had always believed in giving praise where it was due.

By lunchtime the faulty lock on the cell door had been mended and the cells were fully occupied. Miss Fisher and Daisy were tearful as they awaited transfer to a larger station for an appearance before the magistrates. Charles Woodbead, in contrast, seemed positively cheerful. Perhaps, Albert thought, he was finding it hard to believe his luck had finally run out.

Monty Ghent was back with his family and word had it that Mallory Ghent hadn't seen Connie Jones, alias Dora Devereaux, since his son's return. Albert had resisted all suggestions that Monty should be handed over to the authorities. As far as he was concerned, young Ghent had suffered enough and nothing would be gained by punishing him further. In Albert's opinion he'd proved himself a hero that night on the Ridge when he'd saved Peter's life.

Bloodstains had been found on the rocks beneath Oak Tree Edge but there was no sign of Stark himself. The locals reckoned he was unlikely to have escaped unscathed and that it was only a matter of time before he was picked up; however Albert wouldn't rest until the man was in custody. He toyed with the idea of visiting Mrs Stark who, he was sure, had been an innocent party in the whole affair, another victim of her husband's double life, but he couldn't bring himself to face the woman. Sometimes he thought he'd seen enough pain to last a lifetime.

Once he'd given orders for the search for Stark to be widened he was tempted to seek out Gwen Davies but then he thought better of it.

The prisoners had been charged and it was time to think about going home, so Albert returned to the hotel to sort out his things. He'd had enough of Mabley Ridge and, if he had his way, he'd leave and never return.

He opened his suitcase and took out the correspondence he'd placed inside. There was one letter in particular he wanted to reread; the one from the Reverend Jonathan Hegg telling him the child, his son and Flora's, had been found a home by the Reverend Bell in Wenfield.

The sight of the chaplain's words gave him new hope.

The thought of returning to Wenfield filled him with dread — but he needed to find out the truth.

70

Although the area was being searched and rein-
forcements had been called in from Wilmslow
and Macclesfield, there was still no trace of Abraham Stark.

Albert didn't go up to the Ridge himself. If
he'd been a superstitious man, he would have
agreed with Peter's claim that the place was
populated by ghosts and malevolent spirits.
Besides, it held too many bad memories.

He decided it would be more helpful to speak
to Monty Ghent, who'd lived there undetected
for a while and knew the hidden places a man
might use if he didn't want to be found. As the
maid, Daisy, was now languishing in a cell in
Macclesfield, it was Monty himself who
answered the door and it struck Albert that he
looked considerably better than he had when
they'd last met. The first thing he did was to
reassure Monty that he'd do all in his power to
ensure that the authorities would quietly forget
the case against him for deserting his post and
the relief on the young man's face told Albert
that this had been weighing on his mind.

Jane Ghent was also feeling better, though still
weak. According to Daisy's statement she'd
convinced herself that if she got rid of Jane then
Mallory Ghent would marry her. She'd been
unaware of his relationship with Dora Devereaux
and was still refusing to believe it. She'd thought

Mallory had been in love with her. People so often delude themselves, Albert thought.

Once he was sitting in the drawing room with Monty, who was now smartly dressed with his hair neatly trimmed, he asked the question that was on his mind.

'You know the Ridge well. Can you think of any way Stark could have escaped?'

Monty thought for a few moments. 'There are ledges beneath Oak Tree Edge in a few places so if he'd happened to land on one of them instead of plummeting the whole way down . . . And there are mazes of tunnels but it'd take weeks to search the place properly. That's how I managed to . . .'

'Are you all right?'

'Getting there, Inspector. I've arranged to see Barbara again, and David's coming up from London next week so . . .'

'Good,' said Albert, standing up.

'I'm still having the nightmares, you know. They won't go away.' He looked down at his hands and Albert noticed they were shaking slightly. 'I sometimes think I'd be too much for Barbara to take on. It wouldn't be fair on her.'

'Why don't you ask her? I've met her and I think I know what her answer would be.'

Monty smiled and stood up. 'I'll show you out.'

Once they were at the front door Monty glanced back at the hallstand. 'I should return your hat.'

'Keep it. Consider it a gift.'

As soon as he left Gramercy House Albert made for the railway station and caught a train to Manchester before taking the once-familiar line out to Wenfield.

His stomach churned as he alighted at the little stone station, blackened by the soot of decades, and walked through the cobbled streets into the heart of the village. As he passed the familiar stone houses and cottages the events of eighteen months before flashed vividly into his mind. The arrival; the investigation with its dead ends and frustrations; then that dreadful moment when he discovered the truth.

All around the village the Derbyshire hills glowered down, their bleak tops shrouded in thin grey cloud and the fields on their lower slopes filled with sheep. It was colder now than it had been on his first visit so he wrapped his overcoat tightly round him and pulled down his hat, praying nobody would recognise him.

When he passed the house where Flora had once lived he looked the other way. He'd heard her father, Dr Winsmore, had left the village after her arrest. The man had suffered too for his daughter's crimes. As he crossed the bridge over the rushing river he saw the square church tower peeping over the roofs and headed towards it. The vicarage, he remembered, stood at the edge of the churchyard and he felt the sting of nerves as he walked between the blackened gravestones.

He was surprised to see that the curtains of the vicarage were all drawn across the windows, giving it an unoccupied look, and the door was answered by a grey-haired maid who frowned as though she was trying to recall where she'd seen him before. He made no attempt to enlighten her but she remembered anyway.

'You're that inspector from London, aren't you?' she said accusingly. 'Surely all that dreadful business is over and done with.'

'Yes, of course. I'm here to speak to the Reverend Bell about another matter. Is he at home?'

Her hand went to her face and she looked as though she was about to burst into tears.

'Is something wrong?' he asked, wondering if he'd said something to upset her.

'Oh, sir, haven't you heard? The reverend passed away a week ago. Doctor said it was most likely his heart.' She didn't sound too sure. 'Anyway it were very sudden, like. Funeral was yesterday and Missus and her mother have gone to stay with her sister down south. If you want to speak to the curate . . . '

'Thank you . . . no.'

Albert stood on the doorstep for a while, stunned. He'd liked Bell — and his wife — and the news saddened him more than he would have expected. His hopes had been dashed. The one man who could have helped him find his son — the one man who might understand — was dead.

He thanked the woman and retraced his steps, telling himself there were others who might know. Mrs Bell perhaps. He remembered her as a woman who could feel the hurt of others, a silent holder of hands and a good listener, and

390

she'd been one of the few people in Wenfield who'd showed him any sympathy when Flora's crimes had been discovered. She was far away at that moment but one day she'd be back so he would never give up.

The ache in his leg was growing worse as he made his way wearily back to Wenfield station and waited for the Manchester train on the draughty platform. When he finally arrived back in Mabley Ridge he limped the short distance back to the hotel where he found a telegram waiting for him.

Telegrams, in his experience, usually heralded bad news and this one was no exception. It was from Vera and her words bore a stark simplicity, no doubt to save unnecessary expense. *Mary very ill, stop. Come home, stop.*

Albert made his way upstairs and locked himself in his room, trying to cry tears that wouldn't come. He knew he had to go back to London as soon as possible but he dreaded what he'd find there.

He opened his suitcase and when he saw the scrap of paper bearing Gwen Davies's Liverpool address lying on top of his folded clothes, a sliver of hope crept into his soul.

Things couldn't get worse. They could only get better.

Peter

I meet the Shadow Man a lot and we go up to the Ridge to watch the birds. He says there aren't no ghosts up there now. But I know there are.

They looked for Sergeant Stark but they never found him and the Shadow Man says we should be careful when we're up there, just in case he's hiding somewhere. When I said he might have stood on the Devil's Grave and got dragged down to hell the Shadow Man went all quiet. Then he said he'd seen hell and it wasn't on the Ridge. He said it was in France where he went to fight.

The policeman from London's gone now. I liked him even though he talked funny and he didn't find out who killed our Jimmy for years and years. Me mam used to say that he couldn't catch a cold but now she seems to like him.

They say Miss FishFace is going to be hanged for what she did and if they catch Sergeant Stark the same will happen to him.

I think I saw our Jimmy yesterday — and this time he was smiling.

71

Abraham Stark had become accustomed to sleeping rough amongst the discharged soldiers who waved their wounds at passers-by or sold matches from makeshift trays in the hope of a few coins. He'd made up a history for himself. He'd been injured at Passchendaele and when he'd returned to Blighty his wounds had prevented him finding work in a cotton mill even though he'd been a skilled man. Amongst his fellow down and outs he'd kept his rank of sergeant and he'd acquired a limp, modelling it on Inspector Lincoln's after careful observation.

So far he'd managed to fool everyone in London where nobody knew him. Unlike Mabley Ridge it was a big, anonymous place where he'd been able to transform himself into a new being. Al — short for Aloysius — Spring. He liked the name he'd chosen. Spring held the promise of new life, a fresh start. Ethel had a date with the hangman but he intended to carry on living, although he wasn't sure he wouldn't kill again because he'd enjoyed the feeling of power it had given him. There was nothing like killing for making you feel alive.

He sat beneath a railway arch dreaming of home. One day he might return up North, once enough time had passed for everyone to forget. But he was determined about one thing: nobody would ever catch him.